SAMSON

G

GALLERY BOOKS

NEW YORK   LONDON   TORONTO   SYDNEY

G

Gallery Books
A Division of Simon & Schuster, Inc.
1230 Avenue of the Americas
New York, NY 10020

Designed by Diane Hobbing

Manufactured in the United States of America

ISBN-13: 978-1-61664-406-2

SAMSON

CHAPTER 1

The first Sunday in June was a perfect day for the installation ceremony of a new pastor.

Samson Taylor admired his reflection in the mirror adorning a wall in his uncle's office. His suit, made just for this occasion, was tailored to complement his athletic build. He deliberately chose navy because it represented knowledge, power, and integrity.

Women loved his creamy, smooth peanut-colored complexion, his greenish gray eyes, and his neatly trimmed wavy hair. Samson's six-four height and muscular body had carried him through four years of college basketball at Duke University, from where he graduated at the top of his class, earning a bachelor degree in sociology, and on to the Duke Divinity School, where he earned a master's of divinity degree.

In a few minutes Samson would be preaching his first sermon after his installation as assistant pastor of Hillside Baptist Church in Raleigh, North Carolina.

There was a soft knock on the door. Before he could utter a word, a young woman stuck her head inside, gave him a quick once-over, and then said, "You look real handsome, Samson. I just wanted to be the first to congratulate you."

He broke into a grin. "Thank you, Pamela."

She met his gaze, then flashed a seductive smile. "I was thinking that maybe we can celebrate later."

"Maybe," he responded.

"I guess I'll see you in the sanctuary." She disappeared as quietly as she'd come.

He and Pamela had dated during their college days at Duke. She was attending law school now and had made it quite clear that she wanted to renew their relationship. Samson found her attractive, but he knew he had to watch himself now.

He returned his attention to his reflection in the mirror and checked his teeth. Samson had gone to the dentist on Friday to have them cleaned and whitened. His aunt had arranged to have a photographer take a formal picture of him, which would be placed in the lobby beside the one of his uncle Zachariah, the senior pastor of Hillside. Smaller photographs of his father, grandfather, and great-grandfather—the man who had founded the original church—graced another wall in the foyer.

Over the years, Hillside had grown from a small congregation of eight to a membership of nearly two thousand. Samson would be the fifth family member installed as a pastor there, following his father, who was now deceased.

The Spirit of the Lord stirred in him, and Samson sensed that something great was about to happen. As far back as he could remember, his father had always told him he was set apart for service to God. After his dad's death, his uncle Zachariah continued raising him in the knowledge of his calling.

"Your parents would be so proud of you," said a voice behind Samson.

He turned around to face his aunt. "I really wish they could be here to see me—hear me preach this morning."

"You are a lot like your father. Elijah was an eloquent speaker, and that man knew the Word," Hazel told him. Her voice changed as she added, "He had a weakness for beauty, you know. I know that you think I need to mind my own business, but I worry about you. I see the way those fast-tail girls are always up in your face. If you're not careful, Samson, a woman can ruin everything you've worked so hard to accomplish."

Samson realized she must have seen Pamela pop in before. He walked over to his aunt and gave her a hug. "Aunt Hazel, you don't have to worry about me. I'm not letting anyone distract me from what I've been called to do. I already tried to run from my calling while I was in college, but I couldn't escape." He held her by both shoulders. "Aunt Hazel, I give you my word. No one will come between me and God. I won't let that happen."

She glanced up at him. "I pray for you daily."

"Trust me. I have everything under control," he reaffirmed with a smile. "I admit that I love the attention, but I won't let that control me or take my focus off the Lord. You'll see."

"Famous last words. I don't know why I bother to tell you men anything. You think you know everything, but you don't. Mark my words . . ."

"Honey, what are you all afire over this morning?" Zachariah asked as he walked in on them talking in his office.

"Uncle, she was just warning me not to walk the same path as my father."

Zachariah slipped on his blazer. "Well, I have those same worries, Samson. Elijah was a good man, but he let those women ruin him. It bothered me greatly when he was forced out of the church, but there really wasn't much I could do."

Samson nodded, the memory putting a slight damper on his mood. "I don't think I ever saw my mother cry as much as she did that day. When we got home, she told him that we were leaving. My mom packed us up and we left for the train station." He became quieter, lost in the awful memory. "Dad followed us. I remember they were standing outside the train station talking. My mom was still upset and standing close to the street. That truck was coming so fast—I had a feeling something was about to happen. So did my dad, because he put his arms around my mom as if to protect her just as it jumped the curb. I heard him tell her that he loved her, and then he asked God to forgive him. Those were the last words I ever heard my dad say."

Hazel wrapped an arm around him. "It was a sad day."

Samson's parents were killed on impact by a PET Milk truck. After it was discovered that the driver had been drinking, Samson's aunt and uncle sued the company and were awarded over two million dollars, which they placed in a trust for Samson. The trust had come under Samson's control on his twenty-fifth birthday, and the only luxuries he allowed himself were a couple of nice suits, the down payment on a brand-new town house, and the purchase of a Lexus SUV.

"You really think my dad would be proud of me?" Samson asked.

Zachariah nodded. "My brother and Ruby would both be thrilled to see the man you've become, son. And you know that Hazel and I couldn't be any more pleased than we are right now."

One of the ushers passing by the office paused briefly to remind them that the service was about to start. Samson and his aunt followed Zachariah out of the office and quickly made their way to the sanctuary.

After the praise and worship services, the moment had come for Samson to deliver his sermon. Confident, he walked up to the podium, carrying the Bible that had once belonged to his father in his hands. He flashed his aunt a bright smile, then said, "Good morning, Church."

"Good morning," the congregation responded in unison.

"The scripture references today will come from Hebrews chapter ten, verses thirty through thirty-one. The King James Version reads like this: 'I will recompense, saith the Lord. And again, The Lord shall judge his people. It is a fearful thing to fall into the hands of the living God.'"

He paused to let them consider these words. "There was a man sitting at his dying wife's bedside. 'Honey,' she breathed, her voice little more than a whisper, 'I've got a confession to make before I go. I'm the one who took the ten thousand dollars from your safe and spent it on a fling with your best friend. And I was the one who forced your mistress to leave the city. Also, I'm the one who reported your income tax evasion to the government.'

"This was his response: 'That's all right; don't give it a second thought. I'm the one who poisoned you.'"

Laughter rang out around the sanctuary.

Samson's uncle gave a slight nod of approval.

"My message this morning is about what happens when you sin. The first thing you should know is that there is a price to pay. Now here are two interesting facts: Our sinful nature is inherited. Ephesians chapter two, verse three, tells us, 'Among whom also we all had our conversation in times past in the lusts of our flesh, fulfilling the desires of the flesh and of the mind; and were by nature the children of wrath, even as others.'

"The other fact is that sin is the result of a human choice. Now, make sure you catch this in the spirit. Romans chapter one, verses eighteen through twenty, says, 'For the wrath of God is revealed from heaven against all ungodliness and unrighteousness of men, who hold the truth in unrighteousness; Because that which may be known of God is manifest in them; for God hath showed it unto them. For the invisible things of him from the creation of the world are clearly seen, being understood by the things that are made, even his eternal power and Godhead; so that they are without excuse.'"

Samson's eyes darted around the sanctuary, noting the

expressions on the members' faces. Pleased that they appeared engaged, he gave a brief overview of what sin does before moving on to the consequences.

"Man becomes a slave to sin, and sin places a barrier between God and man," Samson explained. "Sin ruins relationships. Sin brings guilt, it brings death, and more importantly, it is eternal separation from God."

He finished his speech to a rousing standing ovation. Several members approached him afterward, offering congratulations and words of support and encouragement.

"Man, you even had me interested today," his best friend Trey said, joining him. Trey and Samson had been friends since third grade. They were similar in features, only Trey's complexion was the color of a new penny and he had shaved his head bald. Trey's muscular build served him well as a physical therapist. "You did an awesome job. Congrats."

Trey's words meant a lot to Samson, especially since Trey was virtually a stranger to church. "Thanks for coming to support me. I really wasn't expecting to see you here."

"That's what friends are for. Right, Pastor?"

Samson laughed. *"Pastor.* Trey, can you believe it?"

"I'm still working my head around it," he admitted. "I always thought you were doing all this to please your aunt and uncle. To be honest, I never really thought you'd go all the way. Not Mr. Oh-so-smooth Samson Taylor."

"I'll always be smooth. That will never change," Samson responded with a chuckle. "It's just who I am." Trey was referring to his love for women. He and Trey shared a lot of the same interests, even when it came to women. They were both drawn to the same type of woman. Only, Samson always seemed to get to them first.

"I hear you, bro," Trey said. He lowered his voice to a whisper and added, "You know you have to change your ways now. You are a man of the cloth."

"I am still a man, Trey," Samson countered. "There's no denying that I love women, and that won't ever end, but

I'm not going to do anything that will taint my ministry or stain my uncle's sterling reputation." For a second, Samson thought about his father.

A couple of women strolled by, smiling like the sun was shining down on them.

Samson and Trey both smiled back.

"Lord, deliver me from temptation," Samson muttered.

Trey laughed. "Look at you . . ."

Samson held his hands up in innocence. "Hey, I never said it was going to be easy, Trey, but I will overcome. I don't want to stand up in the pulpit and be a hypocrite." *I have no intention of being like my father.*

"You're making it hard for yourself by becoming a pastor," Trey responded. "You could have just stayed a regular old sinner like me."

Surprised, Samson burst into laughter. "I wish it were that simple, Trey. The truth is, this isn't about my family or what they want for me. This is the call that God placed in my heart and there's no running from it. I already tried that, remember?"

Trey scanned his friend's face, noting the subtle lift of Samson's chin. "You're really serious about this, aren't you?"

"Yeah, I am. This is what I was born to do. By the way, I'm hoping to see more of you in church from now on."

Trey shook his head. "Samson, you know me," he said seriously. "I'm still searching for something, but when I find it, I'll know."

"The only thing missing from your life is God," Samson told him.

"We've had these discussions before, bro. I'm not knocking what God means to you, but I'm just not where you are. I might get there one day, but for right now, I'll just keep searching."

"I'll keep you lifted in prayer, Trey."

"Hey, we should be celebrating," he told Samson, changing the subject. "Let me take you to lunch."

"Sounds like a plan." He knew that Pamela was expecting to spend time with him, but Samson wasn't in the mood for her whining. She was clingy at times, a quality that Samson found unattractive. That and her constant whining.

Hazel walked up, stopping the two men before they could make their escape. "Oh, no you don't," she said, wagging a finger. "We have all this food prepared in Samson's honor. You and Trey just march yourself over to the banquet hall. You're eating here."

"Yes, ma'am." Trey towered over her, and he wrapped an arm around her tiny frame. "It was your nephew's idea. You know that, right?"

She glared sharply at Samson, who said, "Why do you always believe everything Trey tells you? Aunt Hazel, he's the real culprit."

She looked from one to the other. "See, that's why I used to punish you both."

"Man, I remember those days," Trey said. "And then when I went home, I was punished again."

"When you went home," Hazel echoed. "Boy, you practically lived at our house. You went home on the weekends."

"That's because my mom worked nights at the hospital and she didn't want to leave me home by myself."

"Honey, I know," Hazel said as she gave his hand a little squeeze. "Trey, you know that we loved having you around. In fact, I wish you'd start coming around more—seems like the only time we see you these days is when you're picking up my nephew."

Trey pretended to be solemn. "I'll be better about that from now on, Miss Hazel."

"See that you are," she responded.

"Some things never change, huh?" Samson muttered when his aunt went off to find her husband.

A young woman sashayed past them, swinging her hips. She glanced over her shoulder to make sure they were watching her.

"Bro, you sho' right about that—some things never change," Trey said. "You just stepped out of the pulpit and look at you. I saw the way you were looking at that girl."

"I'm human, Trey. Not blind."

They laughed as they made their way toward the church cafeteria.

"Mr. Preacher Man, the ladies sure are checking you out," Trey said in a low voice. "You better make sure the only thing you're doing up in this place is preaching, Samson. I hope you can stay focused with all this attention." He took another glance around. "Bro, I don't envy you one bit. I don't know if I could handle all this temptation."

Samson shrugged nonchalantly. "Trey, I got this. Don't worry, I'm the one in control."

CHAPTER 2

The next day, Samson was still flying high from his installation ceremony. The first thing he did when he got up that morning was settle down on the patio. It was his favorite place to spend time with the Lord. Samson loved breathing in the fresh air and admiring God's handiwork while he read from the Bible, prayed, or just kept quiet as God spoke to his heart.

Then Samson strolled into the backyard, where he performed a series of kicks and punches and performed karate movements and techniques called kata. Samson was a black belt and had won four tournaments. He even taught classes from time to time.

After Samson completed his workout, he sat out on the patio for almost an hour, before going inside to make scrambled eggs, bacon, and toast. While he cooked, his gaze traveled to the photo of his parents, sitting on the counter.

"I wish you two could be here to see me," he said. "To see the man I've become. I think you'd be proud."

Samson ate his breakfast, and then went upstairs to

shower and get dressed. He was scheduled to meet his uncle at the church at ten.

He spent most of the morning with his uncle and in meetings with members of his advisory board. Samson had enough money in trust to support his lifestyle, so he decided to work full-time in the ministry alongside Zachariah without taking a salary. He was excited about being able to do the Lord's work.

Samson left Hillside Baptist Church shortly after noon. He was having lunch with his uncle and Aunt Hazel, but needed to make a quick stop along the way, so he drove separately.

Twenty minutes later, he got out of his car and headed into Captain Marc's Seafood Restaurant, located in the heart of downtown Raleigh. He glanced around, his eyes searching his surroundings.

"Hello, handsome," a feminine voice cooed from behind him.

He turned around, a smile tugging at his lips. "Teà, how are you?"

"Much better, now that I see you," she murmured seductively. "Samson, I hope you didn't just come here to have lunch. Hopefully, you're here because you couldn't bear to go another minute without seeing me."

He broke into a grin. "Actually, I am here just to see you, but I won't be staying for lunch. I'm meeting my aunt and uncle at another restaurant."

Teà flipped her hair over her shoulder. "So, what can I do for you?"

Samson lowered his voice to a whisper. "Are you busy later on tonight?"

She shook her head. "I don't have anything on my calendar. What's up?"

"Will you have dinner with me? I haven't seen you in a while and I thought we could catch up."

Teà edged a little closer to him. "What time should I be ready?"

"I'll pick you up around seven."

Samson did not linger. He was running behind and needed to be on his way.

The other restaurant was on the corner of the next block. He parked his car and went inside.

"I'm sorry I'm late," Samson said as soon as he sat down across from his uncle. "I got caught in some traffic."

"There was a car accident on Interstate 540," Hazel announced as she scanned her menu. "They were talking about it on the radio as we drove into the parking lot. Samson, I ordered you a sweet tea."

"Thanks for ordering the tea for me. I'm thirsty," Samson said. "I saw the police cars, but nothing else." He picked up a menu. "Uncle, I'm coming by the house next Saturday to mow the lawn. I want to have it done by eleven."

"Samson, we can get one of the boys from church to cut it," Zachariah said.

"I don't think you want to hear Aunt Hazel's mouth if he cuts down her flowers."

"I know that's right," she muttered. She studied her menu a while longer and then put it down. "Honey, how are things going with you and Cynthia? I haven't seen her in a couple of weeks and she wasn't at church on Sunday. She usually comes by the office to have lunch with me."

His aunt worked at the Social Security office three days a week.

"Auntie, I think she's a little upset with me right now," Samson replied. "She's ready to settle down and I'm nowhere near there yet." The truth was they'd had a nasty fight a week ago and he hadn't spoken to her since.

He caught the way his aunt looked over at Zachariah. "Auntie, I know that you think I should get married, but I'm not going to even consider it until I find the right girl."

She nodded. "I certainly do understand that, but I think more members would take you seriously if you had a wife."

He knew that some of the older members were opposed to him becoming the assistant pastor not only because they thought him too young and inexperienced, but also because he was single.

Samson shrugged nonchalantly. "Auntie, I'm not worried about those folks. I'm not going to marry the first person I date. Cynthia is a nice girl but she's very needy. She already has a problem with me being in the ministry. For me that's a big red flag."

His uncle agreed.

Hazel laid down her menu. "Why would she have a problem with that? It's an honorable job."

"Cynthia believes that most pastors are married to their churches. I tried to explain to her that I'm an assistant pastor, but she didn't want any part of it. She also said she didn't want to be a first lady."

"Okay, she's a little nuts, then," Hazel replied offended. "I had high hopes for her, but you did the right thing, hon. You needed to let her go. So, Samson, it's not that you don't want to get married—you're just waiting on the right girl. I want to be clear."

Samson laughed. "Yes, ma'am. Oh, and, Auntie, I don't need any help finding her."

Zachariah leaned forward and said in a dry tone, "Now, you know that your aunt gonna go carry that back to the ladies in the church. She's the ringleader behind the plot to get you married."

The waiter came to take their orders. When he left, Hazel asked, "How in the world are you going to reach the married couples when you're a single man? I know that I wouldn't listen to a man who's never been married. What can he tell me?"

Samson knew better than to debate this issue with her.

Hazel wasn't a fan of single pastors. She felt they were more vulnerable to worldly temptations.

Despite his earlier plea, Hazel said, "There's a nice young lady that just joined the church. Her grandmother died last week, so she's in California, but she'll be back at the end of the week. I'll have to introduce you two."

"Are you talking about Tina?"

Hazel grinned. "Oh, you've met her, then?"

He nodded. "She's nice looking, but she dresses like she's as old as you."

Hazel's lips turned downward. "Humph, I would've thought you'd appreciate the fact that she's not trying to reveal her mysteries to the entire world."

Samson and his uncle chuckled. Hazel had never been one to hold her tongue, and he didn't expect her to be any different now.

Just then their meals arrived.

Samson blessed the food, then said, "While you're over there trying to find a wife for me, I hope you have time to enjoy your salmon."

"All right, fresh mouth," Hazel said. "I have my bat in the car. You ain't too big for me to whup you up some."

The smile on her face gave away that she was only teasing with him, but Samson didn't doubt she had a bat. Hazel kept one near her at all times for protection.

As they ate, a couple of women sitting nearby kept eyeing Samson and whispering.

He smiled and gave a slight nod in greeting.

"All these fast-tail girls running around." Hazel was clearly disgusted by the women's behavior. "Samson, they don't mean you any good. You should be the one doing the chasing." She glanced over her shoulder in their direction, then turned back to face him. "If a girl is running behind you—you need to run away as fast as you can. Run for the hills, as my mama would say."

The waiter checked on them. When he left, they resumed their conversation.

"Times have changed, Aunt Hazel," Samson said. He wiped his mouth on the edge of his napkin. "There's nothing wrong with a woman letting a man know she's interested. It doesn't turn me off."

"Hazel's right," his uncle put in. "Women today are too aggressive."

"You two are just old-fashioned. I admit that there are women who will practically stalk you, but I try to stay away from those types. To be honest, I like a woman who plays a little hard-to-catch."

Hazel nodded in approval, then took a sip of her iced tea.

"Why don't you come by the house tonight and have dinner with us?" Zachariah suggested. "I'm sure you're tired of eating your own cooking, if you can call it that."

Samson chuckled. "My cooking skills have greatly improved, just so you know. Thanks for the invitation, but I'm going out to dinner with Teà. You remember her, don't you?"

Hazel's mouth tightened, but she did not comment.

Samson laughed. "You might as well say whatever you're holding on to, Aunt Hazel."

Samson's aunt didn't care for Teà. She thought Teà dressed much too provocatively and was too aggressive. Teà was one of Samson's former lovers, but they were friends as well. They always had a great time together and she didn't make demands on him.

"You're a grown man, Samson. You already know the kind of woman Teà is—I don't need to say a word."

Samson waited for her to continue. He'd be surprised if she stopped at this point.

Hazel wagged her finger at him. "But I will say this to you: If you aren't careful, women will be the ruin of you. Find yourself a nice girl and settle down."

"I'm trying, Auntie."

"You're too picky," she responded, laying her fork down. "You're trying to find a woman with all this"—she pointed to her chest—"out so far that you see them before you see her face. And junk in her trunk. All that don't make a good wife. I know you want someone you're physically attracted to, but she should be have more than that if you're looking to build a relationship."

"Auntie, I agree with you. We're on the same page."

"I certainly hope so. Some of the girls I've seen you with really make me wonder."

He laughed. "Auntie, tell the truth. No woman on earth is good enough for me as far as you're concerned, and you know it."

She allowed him a smile. "Maybe if you'd let me pick—"

Samson cut her off by saying, "I don't think so. Auntie, you know I love you, but I don't want you picking out a woman for me. That's just wrong on so many levels."

"I don't see anything wrong with it," she said. "You're focusing on the outside too much. Hon, you have to look at the heart."

"Do you really think I just look at physical attributes?"

Hazel didn't miss a beat. "Yes, I do. Practically every girl I've seen you with possesses D cups, hair down their back, a small waist, and wide hips. Looks like a trend to me."

Samson glanced over at Zachariah. "Do you agree with Aunt Hazel?"

His uncle calmly finished off his chicken before answering, "I don't look at other women, so I won't be any help to you."

"C'mon, Uncle. You're supposed to have my back."

Zachariah smiled. "Son, I do. But you know your aunt, and she's got some pretty strong opinions. Usually she's right, too."

"Teà is a nice girl, Auntie, and we're just friends. She

knows it and she doesn't press for more," Samson said, ending the discussion.

He signaled for the waiter to bring their check. "This is on me."

Zachariah opened his mouth to refuse, but Samson shook his head. "It's already settled. I'm taking care of this bill. It doesn't come close to repaying all you and Auntie have done for me, so just let me show some appreciation. Okay?"

• • •

Back at the church Samson sat in his office, behind the huge mahogany desk that once belonged to his father. He was enjoying the feel of the soft leather chair and looking out his window at the manicured landscape when his aunt stopped by.

"You look good in here," she told Samson. "And one day you'll occupy the office down the hall. Zachariah is grooming you to take his place, you know."

"I used to play in there while my dad was working," he said, before another memory darkened his brow. "It was never the same for me after he was gone."

"You will lead this church one day," Hazel said.

Samson smiled. "I believe that's what I was born to do, Auntie."

They talked for a few minutes more, and then Hazel said, "I'll see you later. I need to get back to the office."

Shortly after four, Samson left Hillside and drove to the gym, where he worked out for an hour before going home to prepare for his date.

At home, Samson showered, then sat down to read the Bible. He enjoyed studying early in the morning, and then again in the evening.

After forty-five minutes of Bible study, he left to pick up Teà for their date.

Teà lived a short fifteen minutes away, and when she

opened the door to Samson, he admired her strapless black dress, which fit as if it were made just for her body. "Teà, you look beautiful."

"So do you," she said with a giggle.

He escorted her to the car, and then opened the door to the passenger side.

She climbed inside the SUV. "I love this car, Samson. I'm still waiting on my insurance check so I can get me another one. I'm going to buy an SUV, but it won't be a Lexus." Teà had had a car accident a few weeks earlier that totaled her automobile.

He walked around to the driver side and got in. "I've been wanting one for a while, but figured I'd wait until I finished school and everything."

They were eating at a nice Italian place that specialized in grilled entrees. Once they were seated, Teà ordered an apple martini while he decided on a glass of iced tea.

When she finished that one, she ordered another.

"We haven't even had dinner yet," Samson said. "Maybe you should slow it down a bit."

She smirked at him like he was crazy. "Honey, I'm fine."

He wasn't so sure. Teà liked to drink. There were many nights he'd had to drive her home because she'd had too many drinks for her to drive herself.

When their food arrived, Teà ordered another apple martini. Samson opened his mouth to say something, but she gave him a cross look. "Don't . . . I just want to enjoy the evening. I want to have a good time."

She sampled her grilled chicken, ignoring his frown. "This is delicious."

Samson sliced off a piece of his steak and stuck it in his mouth.

"How is it?" she asked.

"Good." Samson took a sip of his iced tea while Teà downed her third drink.

After dinner, Teà ordered another martini. Samson, who

had remained sober, noticed how she laughed at every stupid thing.

"I think you had a little too much to drink at dinner," Samson said to her in the car.

She dismissed his words with a wave of her hand. "I'm not drunk, but I do have a buzz going on." Teà flashed him a lopsided grin. "I feel so good right now. Let's go to your place. I want to see your new town house."

"I still have some decorating to do," Samson warned her when they arrived. "I've only been in it for almost a month so there's really not a lot to see."

"You showed me the floor plan," Teà said. "It looks huge."

Samson acknowledged it was big. "It gives me all the room I need and some to grow if necessary."

He started to give her a tour of the town house. Upstairs, Teà asked, "So what are you going to do with four bedrooms?"

"I'm thinking about turning one of them into a gym. The others are going to be guest rooms." Samson had all sorts of ideas, which he told her about.

"Aren't you going to have an office at home?"

Samson nodded. "Instead of a formal living room, I opted for a home office."

"Oh yeah," she muttered. "I did see a desk in that room downstairs."

When they entered the master bedroom, Teà turned around to face Samson. She drew him in for a kiss, her curves molding to the contours of his body. He savored the warmth of her lips, leaving him burning with fire.

Yet when she began to slip out of her dress, Samson stopped her. "Teà, wait. I'm a preacher now. We can't do this."

"Why not?" she asked, looking puzzled. "God created sex, so why shouldn't we enjoy it? Besides, it's not like we haven't done this before. We used to do it a lot."

"That was before I made this commitment to the Lord,"
he tried to explain. "Things have to change now, Teà."

"They don't have to change at all, handsome."

She kissed him hungrily.

"Teà . . ." His resolve was weakening and she knew it.

Samson wasn't strong enough to keep pushing her voluptuous body away. Giving into temptation, he picked her up
and carried her over to the bed.

CHAPTER 3

The next morning, Samson was filled with remorse. This was not the way a pastor should be acting. Silently, he cursed himself for being so weak.

Samson glanced over at the sleeping body next to him. "Teà," he said gently. "Wake up."

She moaned softly, her eyelids fluttered, and she turned on her side, but she didn't open her eyes.

Getting impatient, Samson called her name once more.

Teà opened one eye, then the other. Smiling, she said, "Morning, baby."

"Good morning," he responded tersely. "C'mon, it's time to get up."

She reached for him. "Not yet . . ."

Samson pushed her hands away. "Teà, last night was wonderful, but it shouldn't have happened. When I was installed as a pastor, I vowed to make some changes in my life and that includes no more of this."

She sat up in bed, not bothering to hide her naked body. "Are you serious? *No sex?*"

Samson nodded. "I should practice what I'm preaching, don't you think?"

"I don't think you need to worry about that. Samson, I'm not going to tell anyone what we do—it's nobody's business."

He was trying hard to keep his frustration under control. "Teà, you need to get dressed. I have to leave in an hour."

"Come back to bed, Grumpy," she pleaded. "I'll make you feel all better."

Samson refused. "I'm serious. Now, I need you to get out of bed and get dressed."

When she realized how serious he was, her smile disappeared. "You don't have to be rude about it, Samson." She swung her legs out of the bed.

"I'm sorry. I don't mean to be rude to you, but, Teà, you don't seem to be listening to me. Last night was a mistake— one I can't make again."

"Well, that's certainly a first," she huffed. "I've never been called a mistake."

"What we did was a mistake, Teà," he clarified. "You know what I mean. Look, don't make this difficult. I told you that my life has a calling, and I answered that call. I have to take this seriously."

She gave him a scornful look. "So, now since you've officially become a pastor you're going to be celibate? That's what you're telling me, right?"

He nodded.

Teà burst into laughter. "*You?* Samson, you won't make it past a week. Baby, I know you."

"I can do all things through Christ, who strengthens me," he responded, but deep down, he worried that she was right. He loved sex, and it had been one of the reasons he hadn't wanted to become a pastor. He couldn't be a pastor and succumb to worldly desires. In answering his call to the pulpit, Samson had vowed to lead by example. But inside of a week he had already broken that promise.

"Last night, I had you in bed as soon as we got here,"

Teà bragged. "If I did it then, I can do it again. I *know* you, honey. You love getting it on."

Samson tried to curb his frustration. "It won't happen again."

She strutted in front of him, giving him an up-close view of her naked body. "Are you sure?"

He vowed not to let the sight of her gorgeous body get to him, and closed his eyes. "Positive," he said with a gulp. Feeling overwhelmed, he quickly got out of bed and walked to the door. "I'll be downstairs in my office."

"Whatever," she muttered.

Samson was furious with himself. He did not want to start off his ministry in this manner. *How could I have been so weak?*

When she finally made her way downstairs, Samson told her, "Teà, I don't think we should see each other anymore."

She raised her eyes to meet his gaze. "Excuse me? What did you just say?"

Samson leaned back in his chair. "You heard me."

Anger flashed in her eyes. "What? I'm not good enough to be your girlfriend now that you're a preacher?"

"Girlfriend? You were never my girlfriend. Teà, I've always been honest with you about our relationship. Besides, you're not exactly looking to be tied down to one man."

"That's beside the point," she muttered. "I'm a good woman, and if you can't appreciate me, then it's your loss, Samson."

"God bless you too."

Teà rolled her eyes. "Before this month is out, you'll be calling my number."

"I don't think so. C'mon, I need to drop you off before I head to my meeting."

They walked to the door. The whole way Samson kept a safe distance away.

"Seriously, Samson . . . are you really telling me that you don't want to see me anymore?"

He turned to her. "Teà, you know that I like you a lot, but I can't do this and call myself a man of God. I hope you'll respect that."

She shook her head in disbelief and said, "Wow. I can't believe I've been dumped by my nonboyfriend."

"It's not like that."

"Yes it is," she interjected. "Samson, if this is what you want, I'm not going to beg. I'm fine and I can get another man."

She sashayed out of the house. Samson followed her.

Teà didn't say a word in the car.

When he pulled into her driveway, Samson opened his mouth to speak, but she held up a hand to stop him.

"Don't bother. You've already said too much." She opened the door. "Lose my number, you hear?"

Samson couldn't expect her to be happy about being rejected. It was probably better this way, he decided.

As he neared the church, guilt came over him.

"Lord, I know what I did last night was wrong, I wasn't strong enough to refuse Teà. I'm not trying to lay blame on her," he whispered. "I was wrong, but I want to do better. I am committed to serving You, Father God. Please give me the strength to fight temptation. I do not want to be a hypocrite or become the man that my father was. I really need Your help."

Samson's voice died as he eyed the woman in the car next to his. She was beautiful, with huge bedroom eyes and sexy full lips. She grinned and winked at him, prompting Samson to mutter, "Lord, I *really* need You."

CHAPTER 4

On the following Saturday, Samson and Trey entered the Midnight Ballroom at the downtown Radisson Hotel, where a charity event was being held to raise awareness for domestic violence.

"I don't know why we always come to these things," Samson muttered, pulling at his bowtie.

"We come because of the women," Trey responded with a chuckle. "And to do our part for charity, of course."

"Of course," Samson repeated, a big grin plastered on his face. Being in a room surrounded by a bevy of beautiful women challenged him, and for a second he regretted his decision to become a pastor.

Trey accepted a glass of wine from a passing waiter. "There is a sea of gorgeous women here tonight," he said. "I don't know if I've ever seen so many in one place before. There weren't this many people here last year."

Samson agreed, reminding himself of what he was.

They stopped to chat with a couple of friends attending the charity ball. Samson smiled at the daughter of the couple he was conversing with. She smiled back and gave a little wave, but he knew that she was being polite, not flirtatious. He knew what her parents did not—her interest was strictly other women.

When her mother hinted at what a cute couple she thought they would make, Samson decided it was time to politely excuse himself. He and Trey made his way over to the nearest wet bar, where he ordered a soda.

Trey finished up his wine and ordered a glass of sparkling water.

On the way to their table, Samson stopped to speak to another pastor, a close friend of his uncle's, while Trey had a conversation with a former patient.

When they finally made it to their table, Trey sat down on Samson's left, leaving him full view of the dance floor.

"She's shaking everything she's got," Samson muttered as he eyed a woman dancing vigorously to the music.

"Yeah . . ." Trey gave Samson a nudge, and then pointed and said, "Oh, man, this is the woman I've been telling you about. We met at the fund-raiser for sickle cell anemia last year. Then I saw her again a couple of months ago."

Samson's greenish gray eyes traveled the room. Then he saw her and his heart quickened. Her curvaceous figure was covered in a gown with a Bohemian flair. Samson admired the healthy glow of her butternut complexion. He didn't care for women who wore loads of makeup, and the woman standing a few yards away from them didn't look as if she wore any. Hers was a natural beauty.

"Her name is Savannah," Trey said. "Hey, do you believe in love at first sight?"

Samson laughed. "C'mon, man . . . Trey, she's way out of your league. She has that 'you can look all you want but you'd better not touch' persona."

Trey tapped him on the arm. "Trust me, she's interested. We've gone out a few times and we have a lot in common." He pushed away from the table, saying, "I'll be right back."

"Let me know if you need backup."

Trey laughed. "Sorry, bro. I got this under control."

"Hey, aren't you going to introduce me, man? I'm supposed to be your best friend."

Trey gave him a funny look, then gave in. "Sure. I'll bring her over."

Samson nodded and smiled at a passing woman. He watched his friend weave his way through the crowded room to where the object of Trey's desire was standing. Samson felt a stirring in his loins. He loved long hair and her dark curls reached past the middle of her back and looked like it was growing out of her scalp. Her almond-shaped eyes drew him in like a magnet.

His attraction was wrong on so many levels, he told himself. The woman was interested in Trey. Samson stared at her, trying to decipher what she was saying to his friend. Samson felt a thread of jealousy when she flashed Trey a winning smile.

Trey took her by the hand, escorted her across the room to their table, and introduced her to Samson.

"It's nice to meet you, Savannah."

Her perfect lips turned upward, the smile reaching her sparkling brown eyes. "It's very nice to meet you as well, Samson."

"I invited Savannah to join us at our table," Trey announced.

"Great," Samson responded.

Savannah's eyes met his, and for a brief moment, Samson thought he glimpsed possible interest.

"I'm going to get drinks for us," Trey said. "You two play nice while I'm gone."

Samson chuckled.

"He talks about you all the time," Savannah said. "I feel as if I already know you, Samson."

"Don't believe a word of it," he responded with a grin.

"It was all very nice. Trey thinks of you as part of his family."

The feeling was mutual, Samson thought. "How long have you two been dating?"

"We've gone out a few times, but I wouldn't really say we're dating. Just two friends getting together."

"I'm pretty sure Trey wants more than friendship from you, Savannah."

Her eyes met his gaze straight on. "For now, friendship is all that I have to offer him."

Samson gave an understanding nod. Savannah clearly wasn't interested in a relationship with Trey—at least not one beyond friendship.

"Trey's very sweet," she said. "But I have other interests."

He had a sudden desire to be one of those interests. An invisible thread pulled them together. He looked deep into her dark brown eyes, and when he looked downward to her perfectly shaped lips, he felt the urge to taste them.

"Samson, I have a confession to make," Savannah blurted out. "The truth is that I've wanted to meet you for a long time. I saw you last year at this very same event."

Samson didn't recall ever seeing her before now, but then, his attention had been focused on his date at the time. "So what exactly are you trying to tell me?" he asked.

Before she could respond, Trey showed up with glasses of wine for himself and Savannah. "Sorry it took so long. There's a line at the bar." He sat down in the empty seat beside Savannah.

Why couldn't Trey have been gone for just one minute more? Samson silently railed.

"You never told me what you do for a living," he said to Savannah.

"She's an attorney," Trey responded before she could answer for herself.

Samson stared at her, willing her to look up. When she did, he smiled. She smiled back, and then turned her attention back to his friend. "I need to return to my table, but I'll give you a call tomorrow."

Trey gave a slight nod. "I'll walk you over there."

Savannah shook her head. "You don't have to do that. Samson, it was very nice meeting you, by the way."

When Savannah disappeared in the crowd, Trey turned to Samson. "She's gorgeous and smart."

Samson smiled. "Tread carefully with this one. I have a feeling that Savannah loves to play games. If you don't know the rules, then you can't play to win. You know?"

"I'm not in the mood for games," Trey said. "I've had enough of that already with my last girlfriend. I don't think Savannah is like that, though."

"Just be careful."

"I think I'll ask her to dance with me," Trey announced.

Samson didn't respond. His best friend wasn't listening to anything he had to say. Trey was too consumed with thoughts of Savannah.

Samson didn't want Trey getting hurt, but he couldn't help it if his friend refused to listen. Samson kept trying to convince himself that his concern was solely for Trey. It had nothing to do with the fact that he desired Savannah for himself.

• • •

Savannah was still weighing on Samson's mind by the time he went home. So was Trey. He put forth a valiant effort to put her out of his thoughts, but it proved harder than he expected.

"Savannah told me herself that they were just friends," he said softly.

What about the code? his conscience queried. Samson and Trey had the same tastes when it came to women, which once had caused a huge hole to form in their friendship. When they were in high school, they were both interested in the same cheerleader. Trey pursued her, but she chose Samson in the end. Hurt, Trey didn't speak to him for almost a year.

"I can't do this to my best friend," he whispered. When he and Trey had renewed their friendship, they'd included a code: neither of them would date any girls the other had been involved with. This meant that Savannah was hands-off.

But apparently she had other ideas.

A voice mail message from her was waiting for him when he arrived at the church the next morning. Samson warred with himself on whether to call her back. Finally, he gave in and picked up the phone.

"Hello, Samson," Savannah greeted him when the call was transferred to her office. "I wasn't sure I'd hear from you."

"I was surprised you'd called me," Samson confessed.

"You appear to be a very interesting man, Samson. I would like the chance to get to know you better. How about dinner?"

Samson groaned inside. "I'm not sure that's a good idea, Savannah."

"Why not?"

"I can't do that to Trey."

"You're not doing anything to him. Trey and I are just friends," she insisted. "We went out a couple of times."

"Somehow, I don't believe that's how Trey sees it."

"It's just dinner. I thought that maybe we could become friends."

"Are you sure that's what you're after?" Samson was not about to play games with her. He knew that she was interested in him.

His question threw her for a moment. "Samson, I saw the way you were looking at me and I recognized that look in your eyes. I believe that we have a real connection."

Samson couldn't deny that Savannah was right.

"If you don't want to have dinner with me, just say so," she prompted.

"It's not that."

"What is it? Are you worried about Trey? We don't have to say anything to him. Only if something comes of this—then we have to be honest with him."

Sure, that was all right. He didn't know her yet.

"What time should I pick you up?" Samson asked.

"Seven o'clock."

"I'm looking forward to seeing you," he said. Samson could hardly wait for the work day to end. He thought about his best friend and whispered, "What am I doing?"

CHAPTER 5

$\mathcal{S}$amson couldn't take his eyes off the clock. He was counting down the minutes till he and Savannah would be together. Trey phoned his office, but he didn't take the call. He didn't know what to say to his best friend at the moment.

He left the church shortly after five and stopped at the gym before going home to shower and prepare for his date. He kept telling himself that there wasn't anything wrong with building a friendship with Savannah.

Two hours later, he and Savannah were seated in one of his favorite restaurants.

"See, this isn't so bad," she murmured.

"Savannah, if you're not interested in Trey, then I think you should be honest with him."

She met Samson's gaze and smiled. "I have been very forthcoming with him. Look, I just thought we should explore whatever this attraction is between us. It may turn out to be nothing."

He chuckled. "You don't really believe that, do you?"

Savannah shook her head. "No, I don't."

The waiter arrived to take their drink orders. When he walked away, Samson asked, "Why didn't you say something the night you first saw me last year?"

"You were with a date and I didn't know whether you were in a committed relationship. I wouldn't have said anything this time, but Trey mentioned in passing that you weren't seeing anyone."

"Did you know that he and I were friends?"

She nodded. "I saw you two talking that night. It wasn't hard to tell."

The waiter returned with two glasses of iced tea. He wrote down their entrées, then disappeared into the crowded restaurant.

"Samson, you have no reason to feel guilty about anything. Trey and I are good friends, but you're the man I want."

• • •

Since their first dinner together, Samson had seen Savannah every night that week, and they talked two or three times a day. On Sunday he spent fifteen minutes talking with her and they set up their date for that night.

"Great. I'll see you then, Savannah." He hung up the phone, but before he could celebrate, he saw Trey standing in his doorway. Samson hadn't seen his best friend enter his office because he'd had his back to the door.

"Did I just hear you correctly?" Trey asked. "You were talking to Savannah Ramsey? The same Savannah I've been going out with?"

"What's up, man?" he said lamely.

"*What's up?*" Trey clearly was not happy about this turn of events. "I can't believe you went behind my back like this—you knew that I was interested in Savannah. What happened to the code, brotha?"

Samson settled back in his leather chair, his eyes never

leaving his friend's face. "I didn't want you to find out like this, but you might as well know the truth. She's into me, Trey, and the truth is I'm attracted to her as well."

"*Really?*" Trey said sarcastically. "So is that why you've been doing all the pursuing? Don't bother to deny it, because I know exactly how you operate. I thought we put an end to this silly competition years ago."

"Trey, this isn't about competition. She told me that the two of you are only friends. All I can say is that she's the woman for me," Samson stated flatly. "We had an instant connection."

"I know you're not trying to tell me that you're in love with her," Trey said in disbelief. "How long have you two been seeing each other? Every night since the benefit?"

"Every night this week," Samson answered. He wasn't going to lie to his friend. "I don't know what I'm feeling, in all honesty, but I want to explore it with her. I hope you don't have a problem with it."

"Would it matter if I did?" Trey snapped.

Samson met his best friend's angry gaze. "Is this going to be a problem?"

After a moment, Trey shook his head. "If she wants to be with you, there's nothing I can do about it," he admitted. "Look, I need to get out of here. I have some stuff to do before I go into work. We have two therapists out on vacation this week and I'm working late."

"Hey, I thought we were having lunch together," Samson said. "That is why you came all the way over here, Trey."

"That's when I thought you were my friend."

"Trey . . . we're not going to let a woman come between us, right?"

"This ain't about her, Samson. *It's about you.* You had no regard for my feelings. This isn't the first time you've done this to me, remember?"

Samson tried to reason with him. "Trey, you have to face it: You are not the man she wants. This is Savannah's decision. Not mine."

"You and Savannah can both go straight to hell."

"C'mon, Trey. We can get past this."

Trey dismissed Samson's words with a wave of his hand. He stormed out the office, walking away from a friendship that had spanned more than thirty years.

Samson didn't mean for this to happen. Trey would get over it, he told himself. This interest in Savannah was different. This was the real thing.

• • •

Samson showed up at Savannah's house promptly at seven and she invited him in. It was the first time he'd been in her home. He glanced around at Savannah's sparse furnishings and asked, "Did you just recently move in?"

She smiled and shook her head. "I like open space. Having a lot of furniture can clutter a place, in my opinion."

He sat down on the sofa and Savannah sat down beside him.

"What's wrong?" she asked. "You look like something's bothering you."

He wasn't going to hold back. "Trey knows about us."

She ran her fingers through her curls. "He called me right before I left work, but I was in a meeting. I guess that's what he wanted to talk about. I didn't call him back because I wanted to rush home to get ready for our dinner. I'll give him a call tomorrow."

"He's upset. More angry with me, I think."

"I'll tell him that I went after you," she said reasonably.

"You don't have to do that. I can handle Trey."

"I'm actually glad that it's out in the open."

Samson nodded in agreement. He just wished Trey hadn't reacted so badly.

"I need to check on dinner," Savannah announced as she rose to her feet. She walked into the kitchen and pulled a casserole from the oven. "Everything's ready. I hope you brought your appetite."

"I sure did." Samson stood up.

Savannah carried the food to the dining room and Samson followed her in. They sat across from each other. Samson blessed the food before they dived in.

"This lasagna is delicious," Samson told her.

"It's spinach lasagna, because I'm a vegetarian," she responded.

"I'm a steak-and-potatoes kind of man, but this is really good."

Savannah grinned with pride. "I'm glad you're enjoying it." She took a sip of wine, then asked, "I notice that you haven't touched your wine. I gather you don't drink."

"I enjoy a nice glass of wine every now and then."

She paused as though weighing whether she should say something. "Samson, there's something I think you should know."

He wiped his mouth on the edge of the cloth napkin. "What's wrong?"

"There's nothing wrong," Savannah responded quickly. "I just think you need to know that I'm a Buddhist."

Samson couldn't hide his surprise. An image of a fat smiling face jumped into his mind. "Really? Are you serious?"

"I am. I was in a relationship that lasted eight years, and even though we weren't married, I feel like I've been through a divorce." She added, "My being Buddhist is a big part of the reason my last relationship didn't work out—"

Samson didn't see the problem. "Buddhism isn't strange to me because I've spent years studying karate and eastern philosophy. But I'm curious: Why did you become a Buddhist?"

"I didn't set out to do it," Savannah said. "I felt like something was missing from my life and I began this quest for God. I read Christian, Hindu, and new age books. Then, unexpectedly, I met this woman, a Buddhist nun. She ran meditation classes. I was very impressed with her as a person and with the Buddhist philosophy. Soon after, I went to a retreat with Lama Yeshe, and his presence made a deep impact on me. I feel like I've found my spiritual niche in Buddhism. I grew up Catholic and I've tried various faiths during my life, but I know now that this is the path I should travel."

An image of Savannah sitting cross-legged on the floor with her eyes closed and chanting formed in Samson's mind. He had always thought sitting that way must be uncomfortable.

"Samson, what do you know about Buddhism?"

"Not a whole lot," he admitted. "I know there's a lot of meditation and chanting."

"Buddhism is more than just a daily practice of meditation. It's an entire lifestyle lived by a philosophy based on compassion and empathy, forgiveness and peace."

"I subscribe to the same philosophy," he told her. "I do know that Buddhism is more of a lifestyle than a religion. Savannah, honestly, I don't have a problem with you being a Buddhist."

"You're a pastor, Samson. What do you think your church members will say?"

He was not about to let this gorgeous woman sitting across from him get away. "I'm a Christian, but our system of beliefs is really not that different. Even though I haven't known you very long, I know there's something special about you. A few weeks ago, I wasn't interested in settling down, but then I met you."

She responded in the same vein. "I think you should know that I'm not interested in dating casually. I want something more permanent in my life, which is why I'm very careful about the type of man I want in my life." Savannah smiled and reached for his hand. "I don't know what it is about you, but I like you, Samson."

They finished dinner and Samson helped her clean the kitchen.

"Are you always like this?" Savannah asked him. "So willing to compromise? Or is this just an attempt to impress me?"

"I'll let you be the judge."

He didn't overstay his welcome, although Samson would have liked to have spent more time with her. Before he left, they made plans for the following evening.

Samson thought about Savannah during his drive home.

There was something really special about her, he decided. He found her to be well-informed on a number of subjects, she was funny, and they shared similar interests when it came to books, sports, and the arts.

She was an okay cook, but despite her lack of skill in the kitchen, Savannah had a lot of potential.

• • •

Savannah seemed to be all Samson thought about these days.

Samson had enjoyed spending time with Savannah over the past week. The more he was with her, the more he believed that Savannah was perfect for him. He loved her personality and positive outlook on life in general. She was becoming very special to him. Tonight they were going out again.

Samson had tickets to a play and invited Savannah to join him. Afterward they'd have a late dinner.

When he arrived to pick her up that evening, Samson found she had gotten flowers for him.

"I thought I'd surprise you," she told him with a grin.

He pulled her into his arms spontaneously, kissing her. "I can truly say that no woman has ever done that for me. I'm touched."

She softened in his arms. "I've been waiting all week for you to kiss me."

"I've wanted to, but didn't want to rush things between us," Samson confessed.

Savannah reached up and stroked his cheek. "I really enjoy your company. I want you to know that I like you a lot."

"That's good to hear. Because I like you a whole lot."

Yet she wasn't about to get carried away. "Samson, what are we really—?" Savannah asked.

Samson stopped Savannah from talking anymore by covering her mouth with his own.

They came apart reluctantly.

"I want you to know that you can trust me with all your heart," he told her. Samson could tell by her expression that she desperately wanted to believe him. All he had to do was keep trying. It was only a matter of time before he owned her heart.

CHAPTER 6

$\mathscr{S}$amson had reached out to Trey a few times over the next week, but his phone calls went unanswered. Samson and Trey had had disagreements before, but they never stayed angry long. He had hoped his best friend would understand his feelings for Savannah.

Samson finally forced thoughts of his former friend out of his mind, choosing instead to focus on the woman sitting beside him on the couch in his family room.

"You make me feel so safe," Savannah whispered as she snuggled against him. "I haven't felt like this in a long time."

He kissed her. "That's because we belong together."

"I've been thinking about that, Samson, and I want you to know that I'm open to going on this journey with you." He could tell she had made a decision. "I can no longer live in the past."

Samson opened his mouth to respond, but Savannah stopped him. "But it's important that you understand I'm a Buddhist and I have no intention of converting to Christianity. I want to be clear on that before we go any further.

If you have a problem with that, then it's best that we just remain friends."

"I can live with that," he told her.

"Are you sure?"

"I'm positive, sweetheart." Deep down, Samson truly believed that one day, Savannah would convert, but for now he wouldn't press her. In time she would do it because of her love for him and respect for his calling. He was positive this was simply a phase she was going through.

In fact, he wasn't worried as much about Savannah as he was his aunt and uncle. They would have a problem with him dating a Buddhist.

His plan was to have them meet Savannah and get to know her first before they found out about the Buddhism. Once they had a chance to see how genuine and sincere she was, they would be more accepting.

Aunt Hazel and Uncle will be happy for me, he thought. *Everything is going to work out perfectly.*

Having his aunt and uncle meet Savannah seemed like a great idea, but Samson kept finding reasons for putting it off. He was glad that Savannah didn't pressure him. He hadn't met her parents yet, although she mentioned that they planned to invite him to dinner, something Samson was looking forward to. From everything Savannah had told him about her parents, they seemed fine with the news that she was dating a Baptist preacher. But then again, they were practicing Catholics with a Buddhist daughter. They were more open-minded than his aunt and uncle.

He pushed his thoughts away and focused on the beautiful woman in his arms. They had opted to stay home instead of going out.

"I'm going to Chicago next weekend," Savannah announced. "I'm going to spend some quality time with one of my sorors. We are going to pamper ourselves."

"I'll miss you," Samson said.

"I'll miss you too. Alicia and I haven't seen each other in

a couple of months, so I thought I'd fly up Thursday night and we'll have the entire weekend together. I won't be back home until after six on Sunday."

"Do you need me to take you to the airport?"

She shook her head. "You're sweet, but you don't have to do that. I can drive and just park my car. That's what I usually do whenever I travel."

He wasn't giving up so easily. "I don't mind dropping you off or picking you up, sweetheart."

"I know, but I don't want you going through all the trouble. I'm perfectly capable of driving myself to the airport."

"You're my lady now, and I want to make sure you're safe. Especially since you're coming back so late." He touched her on the tip of her nose. "I would feel much better if you let me take you to the airport and pick you up."

Savannah smiled. "Okay, baby. That's fine."

He wrapped his arms around her, pulling her closer to him, and kissed her deeply, desire flooding through his body.

"That was nice," he murmured once they pulled apart.

She nodded. "But as nice as it was, we should stop now before we get carried away. We're both celibate, remember?"

He had learned that Savannah had been celibate for almost eight months. He was just beginning and finding it harder every day.

She tried to pull away from him. "I'd better get out of here."

Samson trapped her in his arms. "I don't want you to leave."

"To be honest, I don't want to go, but I have to get out of here before we do something we're going to regret."

"I don't think I'd regret it." Never had truer words been spoken.

Savannah smiled. "You're so bad."

Finally admitting defeat, he got up and walked her outside to her car. "I guess it'll be a cold shower for me tonight."

"It will do you good," she responded with a chuckle. "I'll see you tomorrow night."

"Looking forward to it."

When she left, Samson walked back into the house, groaning softly. It was going to be a long, lonely night.

• • •

"I won." Samson shouted.

Savannah fell back against the sofa, laughing. "No, you didn't. I don't think that's even a word."

They were playing Scrabble at his house the next night.

"It's a word," he insisted. "Get the dictionary and look it up."

Savannah met his gaze fondly. "You're the first man I've met who enjoys playing Scrabble as much as I do."

"Trey and I used to play all the time," Samson said with a slight wince. He actually missed playing Scrabble with Trey. "So say it: I've won."

"No, you haven't," she countered. "Samson, that is not a word. It's not even in the dictionary."

"Are you sure?" Samson asked, skeptical. "H-A-L-A-H-K-A . . . ha-lah-ka. It's Hebrew."

She gave him a mischievous grin. "You spelled it wrong. It's H-A-L-A-K-A-H."

He studied the board. "You're right." Samson groaned.

Savannah readjusted the cushions behind her. "You didn't win, baby."

"The game's not over yet."

"It is now," she said decisively, arranging all of her letters on the board. "I win."

A-N-G-E-L. Samson broke into a grin. "So you did."

He helped her clean up before calling it a night. "I hate leaving you," he whispered. "I want you to know that I didn't get to sleep until almost two last night. I kept thinking about you."

As they headed over to the sofa, Savannah announced, "Oh, my parents want to meet you, Samson. They want to have dinner with us this weekend. I don't know if you have any plans, but I'd really like for you to meet them."

He made a face of mock horror. "I guess this is getting pretty serious, huh?"

Savannah tossed her dark curls across her shoulder. "No, you're just meeting my mom and dad."

"You want to show me off," he persisted.

"Something like that. Are you okay with that?"

Samson kissed her. "I'd love to meet your parents."

She wrapped her arms around him and laid her head on his chest. "Thanks, honey."

He held her close in his arms. "Savannah, I really don't want to let you go. I don't want to leave . . ."

Samson was tempted to convince Savannah to let him stay, but he didn't want to make the same mistake he'd made with Teà. "You owe me another round of Scrabble."

She was agreeable to that idea. "I have to warn you. I am the Scrabble champ in my family."

"You're going to lose that title," Samson said. He didn't beat her though. He got creamed on a triple word play. He kissed her once more before walking out of her house.

"Lord, I don't know how much more I can take," he whispered. "I have never wanted anyone as much as I want Savannah. I'm going to have to marry her, before I go nuts."

• • •

Savannah's parents were surprised to find out that she was dating a Baptist pastor, although they tried to mask it.

Like their daughter, Robert and Lucy Ramsey were vegetarians. Samson enjoyed the meal, but since he was a meat lover, he found it lacking. He was glad that he had some leftover roast in his refrigerator at home. He would be making a sandwich as soon as he got back.

"So how did you two meet?" Savannah's mother asked.

"It was at the Black and White Charity Ball," Savannah answered.

Savannah's father didn't seem impressed, Samson noted. The man had been studying him since he arrived. Samson chalked it up to his being an overprotective father.

"So you are a Baptist minister and you're dating my Buddhist daughter," he commented. "I find that interesting, to say the least."

"Daddy," Savannah said. "Be nice."

"I care a great deal for her, Robert."

"She's a nice girl and she's gorgeous," her father pointed out wryly. "I can certainly understand why you'd feel the way you do. I'm just not sure how far you two will go. I don't see how it can work."

Samson held his tongue, despite his irritation. He wasn't seeking her father's permission. After all, Savannah was a grown woman. From the tense expression on her face, Samson could tell that she was angry too.

"Daddy, this is not your concern."

"Savannah, you are my daughter, and I don't care how old you get—I will always be concerned for you. I'm only speaking the truth."

"I'm not trying to get on your bad side," Samson interjected, "but Savannah and I will work out our relationship."

Robert gave him a sharp look, but Samson wasn't fazed.

"Samson's right," Savannah said. "We'll do whatever we have to do to make our relationship work because we care deeply for each other." She reached over and took Samson by the hand as if to make a point.

Her mother smiled. "I think they'll be fine," she told her husband. Robert didn't seem convinced.

The ominous silence was brought to an end when a young woman came downstairs. She was almost as beautiful as Savannah, and they looked a lot alike.

"Honey, I want you to meet my sister," Savannah said. "This is Kenya. She's home this weekend from college."

The woman scrutinized Samson from head to toe, and then nodded in approval and broke into a grin, eyeing him almost hungrily. "It's nice to meet you." Samson glanced over at Savannah to see if she noticed the way Kenya was looking at him, but she was so excited about him finally meeting her baby sister, she hadn't noticed a thing.

Kenya couldn't seem to take her eyes off Samson during dinner. She was just as bold as her sister, Samson thought in amusement.

"So do you think I passed?" he asked Savannah when they were driving home.

"Of course," she responded. "They loved you."

Samson, however, hadn't gotten good vibes from her parents; he didn't think they approved of him at all.

Before Samson dropped Savannah off at her place, he invited Savannah to church the next day. He was preaching. She gently turned him down, saying that she had some work to catch up on. She planned to go into the office.

He was disappointed, but hid his true feelings from Savannah.

I'm not giving up on you, he silently vowed. *I love you, and once I make you completely mine, you'll have to give up Buddhism.*

CHAPTER 7

"So who is this young woman you've been seeing?" Hazel inquired when Samson stopped by the house on the Fourth of July. "A couple of people from church told me they've seen you out and about with a pretty girl on your arm. How come you didn't bring her to the barbeque?"

"Her name is Savannah. She's smart, beautiful, and a fantastic real estate attorney." Samson broke into a big grin. "Aunt Hazel, I think I'm in love. No, I'm pretty sure that I'm in love with her."

"If she's as great as you seem to think, then when do we get to meet her? And how come you haven't brought her to church? Does she have a face that only her mother could love?"

Laughing, Samson took a sip of lemonade. "The reason I haven't brought her by the house is because I don't want to scare her off, Auntie. If I make her meet the family, she might start thinking I'm trying to rush her to the altar."

"She doesn't want to get married?"

"That's not it, Auntie," Samson said quickly. "Savannah and I are supposed to be taking it slow."

"Really?" Hazel asked. "Well, how come some jewelry store manager called here talking about a ring being ready?"

He was busted, but Samson wasn't going to confirm or deny. Instead he said, "Aunt Hazel, the ring could be for me, you know."

She shook her head. "Hon, I know you too well. You don't wear rings. You've never cared much for jewelry."

He gave her a warm smile. "You and Uncle will meet Savannah real soon. I promise."

"Well, I hope it happens before the wedding," Hazel muttered. "We'd like a chance to get to know this woman."

Samson laughed as though she was being funny.

"I'm serious. I don't know why, but I have a feeling you're keeping her away from us for a reason. What are you trying to hide, Samson?"

"Nothing, Auntie," he responded with deceptive calm.

Still his aunt wasn't about to let this go. "Then we would like to meet this young lady, and soon."

Samson glanced over at his uncle. "I suppose you agree with Aunt Hazel."

He nodded. "Son, if she means this much to you, then of course we'd like to meet her. We've heard a lot about her from other people. It's strange we've never met her ourselves."

"How about I bring Savannah over on Saturday? We can all have dinner together."

Hazel nodded in approval. "I'll cook all of your favorites."

Samson gave her a tight smile before saying, "Auntie, you and Savannah have something in common. She loves vegetables."

"We can't wait to meet her," Hazel replied.

• • •

"I have a confession to make," Savannah said when they pulled into his uncle's driveway on Saturday.

"What is it, sweetheart?"

"I don't know why, but I'm very nervous about meeting your family."

"You don't have to be," he assured her. "My aunt and uncle are cool."

Savannah turned in her seat to face him. "Samson, I feel like our relationship is changing."

"What's wrong with that?"

She cocked her head to one side, studying him. "Nothing at all, I guess. I don't know why, but I just feel closer to you."

"I feel the same way." Samson glanced up at the house. "Look, I bet my aunt is peeking out at us. Savannah, she's been dying to meet you."

"They mean the world to you, don't they?"

Samson nodded. "I love them dearly. Aunt Hazel can be a true pain in the butt at times, but she always has my back. She and my uncle were wonderful parents to me. I never once felt as if I was a burden to them. They have always treated me like a son."

"Your aunt sounds a bit high-strung from all that you've told me about her."

"She is," Samson confirmed. "My uncle is a lot more laid-back. They really complement each other." He opened the door, got out of the car, and walked around it to open the passenger side for her. Samson took Savannah's hand in his and led her around front, where he found his aunt standing on the porch waiting for them.

He made the introductions.

"Dear, it's so wonderful to meet you," Hazel said, her quick eyes doing a once-over. "Let's get inside, shall we?"

Samson caught her eye and she gave a nod of approval.

Inside the house, he greeted his uncle and introduced Savannah a second time. They gathered in the family room while Hazel worked in the kitchen, finalizing the meal. Samson and Savannah sat together on the love seat while Zachariah made himself comfortable on the sofa.

Hazel joined them a few minutes later and sat down beside her husband. At the shift of the couch cushion, Zachariah winced in pain.

"Hon, are you feeling okay?" Hazel asked, instantly concerned. "You've been having pains too often in your back. I keep telling you it's time to see a doctor."

"Uncle, what's going on?" Samson inquired.

Zachariah had recovered by now. "Just your aunt worrying too much."

Hazel stood up and excused herself. She returned a few minutes later with a bottle of Tylenol and a glass of water. Samson watched him as they continued to talk, but he didn't notice anything wrong.

"Dinner's ready," Hazel announced when the timer started to beep. She rushed off to the kitchen. They all got up and gathered in the formal dining room.

"Hon, are you feeling any better?" Hazel asked her husband after they'd all sat down.

He kissed her on the forehead. "I'm fine."

"It's obvious that your aunt and uncle are totally devoted to each other," Savannah whispered to Samson, who nodded in agreement.

Zachariah blessed the food, and then Savannah, as a guest of honor, fixed her plate first. Hazel followed, and then the men served themselves.

Hazel passed a plate of rolls to Savannah. "Where do you worship, dear?"

Samson abruptly stopped chewing and turned his gaze to Savannah.

"The Temple of Mindful Living," she responded.

"Say what?" Hazel asked, dropping her fork on her plate. She glanced over at her husband in concern.

Savannah kept her expression blank as she wiped her

mouth with the edge of her napkin. "I'm a Buddhist, Mrs. Taylor. I thought Samson would've mentioned this to you."

Samson could feel his uncle's eyes on him, but he concentrated on his meal. He'd wanted to tell them at the right time, and this especially was not that moment. Samson had wanted his family to get to know Savannah before finding out she wasn't a Christian.

"What in the world do you do when you go to this temple?" Hazel wanted to know.

"We use dharmic instruments to provide rhythm for chanting and singing," Savannah explained. "Then there's usually the reading of a sutra—that's a Buddhist scripture. Reading of different sutras reminds us of the teachings of Buddha. After that, we chant Buddha's name, which helps to purify our minds and reminds us of their special virtues. You can't imagine how many people have found solace from chanting."

"I see."

"Then we have teaching," Savannah added.

Hazel took a long sip of her iced tea, wiped her mouth, and then said, "Samson has always been one for surprises."

Zachariah cleared his throat before changing the subject. "Honey, dinner is delicious, especially the honey mustard chicken."

She glanced over at the untouched breast on Savannah's plate. "I guess you don't eat chicken."

"No, ma'am, I don't," she responded. "I'm a vegetarian."

Hazel sent a sharp glare in her nephew's direction. "I'm so sorry, dear. Had I known ahead of time, I would have prepared another menu for dinner."

Savannah gave her a reassuring smile. "It's fine. I've enjoyed everything I ate, and believe it or not, I'm stuffed."

She offered to help Hazel clean the kitchen, but the offer was politely turned down.

Samson and Savannah didn't stay much longer after that.

The air seemed electrified with tension, so he decided to take her home.

"Well, that was awkward," Savannah said when they got into his car. "Why didn't you tell your aunt and uncle about me?"

"I wanted them to get to know you first. Honey, this isn't going to be a big deal. They were in shock, that's all." He was trying to convince himself as much as her. "Trust me; they are going to be more understanding once they get to know you."

Samson knew that his aunt and uncle needed some time to deal with the news. He was relieved that they finally knew everything, but he worried that they were disappointed in him. He adored them and didn't want his relationship with Savannah to become an issue.

He stole a peek at the beautiful woman beside him. *There's no way I can give her up,* he thought. He had to make them understand that Savannah's beliefs wouldn't be a problem for him. Besides, if they decided to spend their life together as man and wife, Savannah would merge her beliefs with his.

"You're not coming in?" she inquired when he pulled up in front of her house.

"Not tonight. I think I should speak with my aunt and uncle. I want to talk this out."

Savannah nodded in understanding. "Call me tomorrow."

"I'll come by your office and take you to lunch," Samson offered.

Samson knew his aunt and uncle would still be up and probably were waiting for him to get home so they could call. Instead of having the conversation over the telephone, Samson decided to do it face-to-face; he wanted them to know how much Savannah meant to him.

His uncle was pacing across the kitchen floor when Samson strode into the house. When Zachariah spotted his nephew, he said, "Boy, what in the world are you thinking?

That young woman sat here at our table and said she is a Buddhist. She doesn't believe in God, Samson. You mean to tell me that doesn't bother you in the least?"

"Buddhism is more a lifestyle than a religion," Samson stated in a tone that brooked no argument. "Uncle, I really care about this woman. I'm even thinking about marriage. I'm sorry, but I don't think there's anything wrong with my being with Savannah."

Zachariah relented slightly. "Certainly, no scripture prohibits this, Samson. But I'm not sure it's the wisest and best course of action. Remember what Paul said—"

Samson cut him off by blurting out, "Uncle, I know all about the 'do not be unequally yoked with unbelievers' verse, but if you really want to know the truth, Savannah is probably more upright, morally and ethical, than most Christians I've run into."

"Buddhism is not Christianity," Hazel interjected, entering the kitchen. "As far as I'm concerned, even the most morally upright and ethical Buddhists belong to darkness since they do not trust in Jesus Christ as Savior."

Samson tried to explain his way of thinking. "Although Savannah doesn't accept what we believe, she is willing to consider our beliefs. She told me that Buddha never asked his disciples to believe something just because he said it. He said that one needed to prove it true for oneself. Well, we know that the Bible proves itself, and soon Savannah will gain understanding. Maybe that's why God brought me into her life."

"You sure it was God and not—" Hazel stopped short when her husband sent her a sharp look. Lifting her chin in defiance, she said, "Well, you get the gist of what I was about to say."

"Samson, I know that you love this girl, but you are a man of God," his uncle said. "What do you think the members will say when they find out you're married to an unbeliever?"

"Most of them will be able to relate," he responded weakly.

"She does not believe in the resurrection of the dead and that we will have eternal life as believers. That should be a problem for you," Zachariah warned.

"It's not," Samson stated with his head down.

"Then maybe you should step down as assistant pastor," his aunt suggested.

His uncle disagreed. "I don't think Samson should do that." He sighed loudly, wrestling with this problem. "Maybe he's right. Maybe Savannah will convert to Christianity."

"What has gotten into you two?" Hazel demanded, her hands on her hips. "Dear Lord in Heaven! I need to run into my prayer closet right this minute."

"Savannah is a good woman, Aunt Hazel," Samson pleaded. "She gives no thought to material things. She believes in empowering herself."

"I'm certainly thrilled for her on a personal level, but her spiritual level—that's another thing entirely," Hazel said sharply. "Instead of marrying you, Savannah needs to be worrying about her eternal marriage with Christ. If you insist on doing this, offer her the gift of salvation. Let that be your wedding gift to her."

"Believe it or not, Buddhism addresses many areas of Jesus's ministry," Samson stated. "I've been doing some research."

Hazel planted a hand to her chest and looked upward. "Lord, the next thing we know, my nephew is going to come here and tell us he's a Buddhist."

Samson laughed. "You don't have to worry about that, Aunt Hazel. I'm trying to convert Savannah—it's not the other way around."

"You say that now."

"Auntie . . ." Samson embraced his aunt. "I love you for caring so much, but you don't have to worry. You and Uncle raised me well. I know what I'm doing."

She looked up at him, finally giving in. "I know you think you do. Samson, you're a grown man. Just know that I'm not Christian enough to come back and say I told you so."

Samson knew that she was teasing him and chuckled. "I love you both."

Hazel sighed. "We love you too. Now I've got to get your uncle off his feet. He's still having some pain, even though he's trying hard not to show it."

All of Samson's former concern returned. "I think Auntie's right. You should make an appointment to see a doctor."

Zachariah grunted. "She worries too much. I'm fine."

Samson arrived home shortly after eleven. He considered calling Savannah, but knew she often went to bed early because she was an early riser. Instead he headed straight up to the shower, glad that everything was out in the open. Despite the initial awkwardness, Samson felt like he and Savannah could now move on with their life together.

CHAPTER 8

"I don't think your aunt and uncle cared too much for me," Savannah told him as soon as they sat down in a restaurant the following day for lunch. "I do understand why you didn't say anything to them about my being a Buddhist, but I really wish you had. Then they could have had some time to get used to the idea before meeting me."

Samson reached over and took her by the hand. "Honey, I didn't see the need to. I want them to get to know you—the person." He spoke with cool authority. "Look, you being a Buddhist doesn't bother me, and that's what's important. And how we feel about each other."

"Baby, you keep saying that, but what about your church members?" Savannah asked softly, her eyes narrowing. "You have to consider how they are going to feel about us."

Samson didn't agree. "They don't control my life, Savannah. Hillside Baptist is my uncle's church. Yeah, I'm one of the pastors, but if the members have that big of a problem with it, then I don't mind leaving and going somewhere else. You are more important to me than they are."

As romantic as that sounded, she was still worried. "Look,

I really don't want you to turn your back on what you have been called to do because of me."

After the waiter took their orders, Samson said, "I'm not turning my back on my calling. I'm just not going to let a bunch of church folk bully me. Savannah, I've never felt about a woman the way I feel about you. I'm sorry, but I'm not going to give you up." She wasn't convinced and he decided to change the subject. "I have to preach next weekend in Asheville. How would you like to come along? We can go up there a day early."

"Sure," she responded. "Separate rooms, though, right?"

"Yeah."

"Have you ever taken a tour of the Biltmore Estate?" Savannah asked.

Samson had heard of it. "No, but I'd like to."

"Great," she murmured, and started ticking off her fingers. "We'll do that and also check out the Thomas Wolfe Memorial and the Smith-McDowell House Museum."

"I see you've already got our little getaway planned."

She laughed briefly. "I love to travel and I love learning about the history of the city or state I'm visiting."

"I'm game for whatever."

Savannah stroked his cheek. "Samson, one of the things I love about you is that you allow me to be a free spirit. You're open-minded and always willing to compromise. I really love that."

"I enjoy making you happy. I really do."

• • •

Early Friday morning Samson and Savannah drove over to Asheville and checked into separate rooms at the Royal Inn.

"My room is on the fourth floor," Savannah said. "Where are you?"

"One floor up." Lowering his voice, he added, "That's probably a good thing too."

She chuckled.

"So what do you want to do now?" Samson inquired. "Are you tired, or would you like to do some sightseeing?" Samson was fine with just staying in, but he had a strong feeling that Savannah wanted to go out.

He was right. "Let me freshen up and we can check out the museum," Savannah answered.

"Meet you at your room in about ten minutes."

"Give me fifteen."

Savannah got off the elevator and headed to her room while Samson went to his. He hung up his suit, washed his face, and brushed his teeth. Samson made a quick phone call to his uncle before heading down to meet Savannah.

As they got on the elevator, Savannah said, "I can't wait until you see the Biltmore Estate. It's gorgeous. We'll see it after we leave the Smith-McDowell House."

"I heard it's something. What are we going to do for lunch, Miss Planner?"

"Well, there's this great restaurant not too far from here. I thought you might really like it because I hear they serve the best baby-back ribs in town. I know those are your favorite." Samson smiled at this choice. Yes, Savannah was perfect for him, he decided. Throughout their relationship, she had shown a willingness to compromise, which he appreciated.

Their first stop was to the Smith-McDowell House, a four-story mansion built twenty years before the Civil War. Hearing it was the oldest house in Asheville, Samson said wryly, "Slave labor was probably used to build this home."

Savannah agreed. "Don't look back at the past with anger. Instead, you should look toward the future with joy."

After a tour of the Smith-McDowell House, Savannah took him to Ed Boudreaux's Bayou Bar-B-Que in downtown Asheville so that Samson could enjoy a plate of ribs. She settled on a salad for lunch.

"I'm glad you came to Asheville with me," he told her.

"I'm glad I came too. I love spending time with you, Samson." Savannah took a sip of her water, and then asked, "Have you spoken to Trey at all?"

Samson shook his head. Deep down, he was still bothered by the fact that Trey hadn't returned any of his calls. He'd never ever considered that a woman would come between them again.

"I'm sorry. I never meant for this to happen," Savannah told him.

Samson pretended to be nonchalant. "Things work out the way their supposed to work out. There's nothing we can do but move on with our own lives."

Savannah reached across and placed a hand over his. "Trey's angry and hurt right now, but I really believe he'll come around."

He hoped she was right, because he missed his best friend. Samson met Savannah's gaze and pointed a finger at her. "I hope he'll come to realize that when people are soul mates, you can't keep them apart."

• • •

Samson's gaze traveled over to where Savannah sat beside the hosting pastor's wife, both dressed in stunning summer dresses. Savannah's lilac-colored silk sheath complemented her shapely curves. Seeing how beautiful she looked made him proud to have her on his arm, and before the weekend was over, he vowed that she would be his fiancée.

He was planning to propose to her later on this evening. He had considered proposing last night while they were strolling along the river, but had changed his mind.

She was watching him now and he gave her a quick smile as the hosting pastor, Calvin Davis, stood up and introduced Samson to the congregation.

Smiling, Samson strode confidently up to the podium.

After a brief introduction, he said a prayer, and then dove into his topic. "I'm going to talk about knowing when to hold on and when to let go. We would be in a far better place if we held on to God's presence in our lives and let go of worldly illusions."

Savannah smiled at him as she nodded in agreement.

"We all hold on to things we should let go of—past regrets, grudges, fear, ego, or pleasures. Learning to let go is crucial to our spiritual growth. Often it's the things we *should* hold on to that are the most difficult. The love of truth and our sense of compassion—we need to keep those things."

The people in the audience seemed to be hanging on to his every word, and Samson was secretly thrilled because he really wanted to impress Savannah.

"But truth is of a different order that involves growth, movement, and openness. Truth that is not grounded in motives of love and service is not truth at all. Truth is more than having the right answers; it's having a good reason for having the right answer. Church, holding on to God's truth is what makes us wiser than our enemies. Holding on to God's truth makes us wiser than the elderly, because it raises us above the level of mere experience and external authority. Holding on to God's truth makes us wiser than our teachers, because it leads us from speculation to certainty, from mere knowledge to actual truth. Holding on to God's truth does all this and more, because it reveals us to ourselves and shows us a way out—by way of letting go . . ."

When he finished his sermon, Samson glanced at Savannah and she was beaming with happiness.

"Honey, you really are a good preacher," Savannah told him afterward. "Your words really moved me and gave me a lot to think about."

"Hopefully, you'll come to church with me every now and then—especially when I'm giving the sermon. I liked seeing your face in the congregation."

"I was happy to be here with you today," she said.

"I'm glad to hear that. It meant a lot to me to see you sitting down in front."

As the congregation filed out, she asked, "So what are we getting ready to do now?"

"Pastor Davis and his wife want to take us to lunch. Savannah, do me a favor and don't mention being a Buddhist."

Her smile disappeared. "I'm not ashamed of who I am, Samson," she told him, looking offended. "Why should I hide my faith? How would you like me ask you to keep the fact that you're a Christian a secret?"

"Please, Savannah, I just need you to do this one favor."

She released a long sigh. "Whatever will make you happy, Samson."

"Thank you," he whispered just as the pastor and his wife joined them.

"What are you two interested in eating?" Pastor Davis asked.

"Savannah is a vegetarian, so a restaurant that caters to vegetarians and nonvegetarians would be perfect."

His wife grinned and said, "I know just the place. We can go to the Laughing Seed Café."

Samson glanced over at Savannah. "Have you ever eaten there?"

She nodded. "Once. I enjoyed the food."

Samson wasn't sure if he would but he was willing to give it a shot. Savannah had unselfishly chosen to have dinner at Ed's, so he wasn't about to be outdone. They would have lunch at the Laughing Seed.

He was mildly surprised by the soothing atmosphere of the restaurant. A mural of a rain forest and a babbling fountain immediately put the diners in a relaxing mood, temporarily melting away the tensions of everyday life. Anything from fresh fruit smoothies to wine, martinis, and beers could all be found at the bar.

The warm weather and picturesque mountains prompted them to dine outside on the sheltered patio.

Savannah chose the Indian Thali Plate, which included basmati rice, a vegetable dish, and a salad. Samson decided he couldn't go wrong with the Caribbean Empanada served over a bed of mixed greens.

When the food arrived, Savannah waited for him to sample his meal. "So what do you think?" she asked.

"It's not bad," Samson answered. He sliced off another piece of his empanada and stuck a forkful into his mouth.

During lunch Savannah did as Samson had requested and held her tongue about her Buddhism. Samson made it clear to the Davises that he and Savannah were in separate hotel rooms because he didn't want anything to put a stain on his reputation. He had already confided to the pastor and his wife that he planned to propose to Savannah on this trip.

Samson and Savannah spent the rest of the afternoon shopping.

When Savannah was in a dressing room trying on a couple of outfits, Samson selected a dress and paid for it, leaving specific instructions for it to be delivered to his room at the hotel. He then arranged for a romantic dinner in one of the hotel's private dining rooms.

"What do you think of this dress?" Savannah questioned.

Samson surveyed the black and white stripes and shook his head.

She looked disappointed. "You really don't like it?"

"It's not you, baby," he told her. "Try the other one on."

Savannah did as he requested. "What about this one?"

He gave her a long look. Samson knew that she really loved the black-and-white one—it was the one he'd purchased for her in secret after seeing her in it when she tried it on earlier.

"I'm not crazy about that one either."

She changed back into her clothes, then walked out of the dressing room.

"We'll look in one of the other stores," Samson offered.

Savannah shook her head. "It's not that serious, honey. It's only a dress, and it's not like I really need it."

He bit back a smile. Samson couldn't wait to see her face when she opened her gift later tonight.

When they returned to the hotel, Savannah went to her room to take a nap before dinner. He noted that she enjoyed napping on the weekends.

In his suite, Samson admired the ring he had chosen for her. Savannah wasn't a woman who loved diamonds. She was more into precious gems, so he'd chosen a white sapphire engagement ring for her.

Samson went downstairs to the dining room early to make sure everything was set up as planned and to bring the gift and the roses down.

Savannah arrived on time. "What's all this?" she asked, looking around. "Are we the only ones eating in here?"

He nodded. "I didn't want to share you with the world— not tonight."

She kissed him on the lips a little harder than usual. "You're such a sweetie."

He led her over to their table. Everything looked just right.

Savannah picked up the bouquet of roses. "I love roses," she murmured.

"I know," Samson said. "I know how much you love the yellow ones, but tonight I wanted you to have red because you own my heart." He took the flowers from her and nodded casually at what was on the table. "I have something else for you."

"What is that?" Savannah asked, staring down at the gift-wrapped box.

"Open it."

She ripped off the wrapping and ribbon. Savannah couldn't

contain her joy when she opened the box and saw the dress. "You bought it for me. I thought you didn't like it."

"I wanted to buy it for you," he said.

"This dress is so gorgeous," Savannah murmured.

"When I saw it on you earlier, I knew that it was perfect for you, sweetheart."

A waiter entered the room carrying a tray of food.

"We have homemade cheese cubes with spinach and ground spices," Samson said. "Roasted eggplant, mashed, seasoned, and sautéed with onions and tomatoes and prawns, cooked in a sauce made with onions, ginger, garlic, coconut, and a bunch of spices I can't remember."

Savannah smiled. "Everything sounds delicious."

"I hope it tastes good. I made my choices based on recommendations by the chef."

She glanced around the room. "I can't believe you went through all this trouble for me. Samson, this room is beautiful."

The staff had done a wonderful job decorating the room. The candles and floral arrangements all added to the romantic ambiance of the dining experience. Their table was draped in a rich royal purple with gold trim and matched the multicolored curtains and carpet throughout.

Samson pulled out a chair for Savannah, and then sat down across from her.

"You look nice in your tux," she told him.

"Not as nice as you."

Samson's heart was racing. He kept reminding himself to stick to the plan. He'd worked hard to plan every step of the evening and didn't want to rush. He was excited at the thought of marrying Savannah.

Then an inner voice asked him: What if she said no?

He forced the thought away and focused his attention on the vision of beauty sitting in front of him.

Savannah tasted the eggplant. "Honey, this is delicious," she exclaimed.

It wasn't bad, he decided. But it wasn't anything to rave about. Samson was definitely a meat eater. He'd starve to death if he had to become a vegetarian.

After dinner, they returned to his suite. Samson took Savannah by the hand and led her over to the sofa.

"I get to pick the movie we watch tonight," she said with a chuckle. "I've had my fill of adventure movies for a while. I'm in the mood for a romantic comedy or something like that."

"I'm in the mood for romance myself," Samson responded, gulping deeply. Here we go, he told himself. "Savannah, I'm sure by now you know that I'm crazy about you."

She broke into a grin. "I feel the same way about you too."

"What I'm trying to tell you is that I'm in love with you."

She met his gaze straight on. "Baby, I love you too."

"Do you love me enough to spend the rest of your life with me?"

"Excuse me?"

He flashed a big grin. "Savannah, I'm asking you to marry me. I love you and I want to wake up beside you every single morning."

"You want me to be your wife?" she asked, sounding surprised. "Samson, I'm of a different faith and you're a Baptist preacher."

"We've been through all that, and I don't see a need to go back over it again. I don't see it being a problem. Savannah, I love you and I want you to be my wife."

She studied him for several long moments. "I love you too, so if you're serious, I'll marry you, Samson."

He pulled a tiny box out of a drawer in the table next to the sofa. Opening it, Samson said, "I'm glad you said yes. I really didn't want to have to return this ring."

Savannah eyed the engagement ring. "Is this a diamond?"

"It's a two-carat white sapphire. I know that you're not into diamonds."

She hugged Samson. "I love it."

He was glad Savannah liked the gemstone engagement ring since he'd had it custom designed for her.

"This ring is gorgeous," she whispered. "Samson, I absolutely love it." Savannah wrapped her arms around him again. "You've made me the happiest woman alive."

The feel of her body against his ignited flames of desire within him, prompting Samson to say roughly, "I don't think I can handle a long engagement, sweetheart. I want you so badly, I can taste it."

She grinned. "How about eight months? Do you think you can wait that long for me?"

Samson groaned. "Months? Why don't we just get married tomorrow? We can always renew our vows later in a formal ceremony."

"It's only eight months, sweetheart."

"You really want a wedding?" he asked.

Savannah nodded. "I do. I want to start our lives together with a special ceremony. It's important to me."

"Eight months, huh? Are you sure you can't do it in four?"

She shook her head. "You'll be surprised how fast the months will fly by."

"We'll see," he grumbled, not at all happy about having to wait another eight months before Savannah would be his completely.

CHAPTER 9

*M*onday afternoon, after he dropped Savannah off at her place, Samson drove to his aunt and uncle's house.

He sat in his car for almost ten minutes before summoning up the courage to walk up the steps and into the house.

"I might as well get this over with," Samson whispered to the empty car. "They're not going to like what I have to tell them, but, oh well . . ."

He knocked on the front door before using his key to enter.

"Auntie, where is Uncle?" Samson asked when he entered the house. He had decided not to delay telling them about his engagement. He hadn't handled introductions properly and wasn't about to make the same mistake twice. Besides, Savannah refused to have it any other way. She made him promise to tell his aunt and uncle as soon as they returned home.

"Hey, when did you get back in town?" Aunt Hazel inquired. "How was Asheville?"

He followed the sound of her voice to the kitchen. "Not

too long ago. I just dropped Savannah off at her place, and then drove over here." Samson walked over to where his aunt was standing and planted a kiss on her forehead. Hazel dried her hands on a towel. "You just missed him. Zachariah went across the street to see Deacon Stevens, but he should be back shortly."

"Good." Samson sat down at the breakfast table. "I need to talk to you both."

"Does this concern Savannah?" Hazel questioned, studying Samson's face.

"Yes, it does." He grinned.

"I thought so, because you sure look mighty happy about something."

"I am."

Hazel maintained a tight expression on her face. While stirring whatever she was cooking in that tall stockpot, she appeared to be praying.

Samson heard the front door open and shut.

"Son, I didn't know you were coming by," his uncle said, entering the kitchen. "I was planning on coming over to your place to see you."

Samson took a deep breath. "I have something I want to tell you both, and I didn't want to wait." He paused, gathering himself before announcing, "Last night, I asked Savannah to be my wife, and she said yes. We're getting married."

The room was drenched in a loud thunder of silence.

"Congratulations," his uncle said after a moment.

Hazel glanced over at Samson, her eyes filled with unshed tears. She released a soft groan. "Samson, honey, you are supposed to offer salvation to nonbelievers, not marry them."

This wasn't going well at all. A wave of disappointment washed over him. "I actually thought you of all people would be a little more ecstatic about me getting married. I guess I was wrong."

She finally walked over to him and hugged him. "Samson, I want you to be happy," she said. "I really do, and if

Savannah makes you happy, then we will welcome her into our family with open arms. But I have to be honest. If you expect me to be delighted over this turn of events, then I think you're being unfair. I do not agree with this arrangement, but this is not my life—it's yours." She held him at arm's length. "Samson, you know that I love you like my own son, and I will be here to support you no matter what happens. However, I won't be a hypocrite."

He couldn't ask for any better. "I can respect that."

She stroked his cheek, soothing the sting. "I think I just need some time to get used to the idea."

"We're getting married in March, so you have eight months."

Hazel stepped away from him. "Eight months? Why can't you two stay engaged for a year? You haven't been together that long."

"I love her so much. Auntie, I can't wait to make her my wife. I would marry her tomorrow if Savannah would agree."

"I can't help wondering what the church members will say," Hazel murmured as she sat down in the empty chair beside Samson.

"When Savannah was in Asheville with me this weekend," he told them, "she supported me and heard me preach."

Zachariah raised his brows in surprise. "Really? Well, I think that's a step in the right direction."

Samson nodded. "She's going to come around. You'll see."

"I certainly hope you two had separate hotel rooms," Hazel stated firmly.

"Of course. If it makes you feel better, you should know that Savannah and I have not been intimate. We're waiting until we get married."

"Thank you, Jesus," she intoned.

Samson broke into a grin. "I knew that would make you happy."

Hazel smiled in return. "I hope you made sure that Pastor

Davis knows you're ingrained in Hillside Baptist Church. I
don't want him trying to steal you away from us."

"Auntie, you don't have to worry about that. I'm not
going anywhere. I know I belong at Hillside." With his mission accomplished, Samson rose to his feet. "I have to go.
I'm meeting Savannah at her house so we can discuss our
wedding plans." Samson's gaze landed on his aunt's face.
"I really need you to be on board with this. I can't put into
words how much I love this woman."

Hazel gave him a tender look. "Hon, I can see how much
you love her. I just don't want to see you get your heart broken."

He ignored that comment. "I have to get going, but I'll
talk to you later."

"Why don't you meet me for lunch tomorrow?" Zachariah told him. "I'd like to talk to you man-to-man."

Samson was fine with that. "Yeah, that would be great. I'll
see you tomorrow." He knew that his uncle wasn't thrilled
about his engagement to Savannah, but he also knew Zachariah would be open-minded.

"How did it go?" Savannah asked when Samson returned.
"Are they really upset about our engagement?"

"I wouldn't say they were upset. They were more surprised than anything, I think. Listen, my aunt and uncle just
want me to be happy."

She folded her arms across her chest. "Samson, I'm pretty
sure they're not happy with you marrying a Buddhist."

Samson wasn't hearing it. "They are willing to accept
you as my wife, but even if they weren't, it doesn't matter,
because this is about you and me, sweetheart."

She still looked doubtful but she moved on. "Do you
know who you want to be your best man?" she inquired.
"Kenya is going to be my maid of honor."

"Yeah, I know who I want." Samson couldn't see himself
getting married without Trey by his side. In order to make
that happen, he would go by Trey's office tomorrow. Samson

didn't hold out much hope that Trey would forgive him, if he learned Samson was going all the way this time.

• • •

Samson drove to Rex Hospital, where Trey worked.

He had just had lunch with his uncle, who wanted to make sure Samson was ready for marriage. Samson had assured Zachariah that he was and they'd enjoyed their time together. Samson had noted one strange thing during lunch—his uncle seemed to be in pain but valiantly tried to hide it. Each time Samson mentioned seeing a doctor, Zachariah would change the subject.

Samson decided to let it go. He had other problems on his mind. He had not spoken to Trey in a few weeks. It was long past time he made things right between them.

"Hey, man," Samson greeted cheerfully, walking into Trey's office.

He was met by an angry frown. "What are you doing here?"

"Trey, you're like a brother to me," Samson said, closing the door so they could talk without being overheard. "I don't like this gulf that's between us."

"I'm not the one who put it there. Samson, it's not like you haven't done stuff like this to me before, but I really thought this time would be different, especially since we're adults and no longer those immature boys always in competition for the prettiest girls."

"Trey, be honest. You weren't too into Savannah. If you were, it wouldn't have mattered what I said. You would have still gone after her. I'll admit that I went after Savannah in an underhanded way. All I can say is that I love her with my heart and soul. I love her so much that I've asked her to marry me."

That caught Trey's attention. "You and Savannah . . . you're getting married? *You?*"

Samson chuckled. "Yeah, me . . . can you believe it?"

Trey was flabbergasted. "Man, I never thought I'd see the day that you settled down. Wow."

"I know you're angry with me, but I'm hoping you can put aside your feelings and stand with me as my best man."

Trey pulled up short. "I don't know if I can do that, Samson."

"We're family, Trey. I know you're angry and hurt, but I hope we can get past it," Samson pleaded. "I never would have gone after Savannah if she'd shown any interest in being with you. As much as you don't want to believe it, she and I were meant to be."

His best friend wasn't impressed.

"Be honest with me, Samson. Does Savannah love you just as much?"

"Yeah, she does. We fell in love from the moment we met."

"So I never really stood a chance with her," Trey said, almost to himself. "She was never interested in me."

Samson tried to soften the blow. "Despite how all this went down, I want you to know I can't get married without you."

Trey met his gaze. "I still can't believe you're getting married. Not the playa of all time." He chuckled. "I guess I have to be a witness to this miracle."

"Does this mean I have a best man?" Samson said hopefully.

Trey nodded. "Congratulations, Samson. I'm happy for you. I really mean it." He tried to look happy but was failing miserably.

Samson almost felt sorry for his friend. One day Trey would realize that this had all turned out for the best. Besides, Trey wouldn't know what to do with a woman like Savannah.

CHAPTER 10

Chiang Mai, Thailand

*S*amson had waited eight long months before their wedding day arrived.

Savannah wanted to get married in Thailand; and the spring months provided the best time for wedding ceremonies. Samson tried to get her to change her mind about a destination wedding, but she refused. At last he gave in. He was intrigued by the idea. As long as they had to go somewhere, why not the other side of the world?

Once they arrived in Chiang Mai, Samson could understand why Savannah chose this location for their wedding. The town was surrounded by picturesque mountains and featured a pretty moat that protected the hundred temples found in the historic city.

Two days after they arrived Samson went alone to Hazel and Zachariah's hotel room. "Aunt Hazel, I need you to spend some time with Savannah, please. We're getting married tomorrow, and she's worried that you don't like her."

"I have nothing against Savannah. You know that."

He should have known she'd be difficult. "I've told her that over and over, but I think it'll help if you tell her yourself."

Shaking her head at the exotic surroundings, Hazel said, "She couldn't just have a church wedding or just go down to the courthouse like normal people do?"

"Aunt Hazel . . ." Samson said with a tiny smile. "Chiang Mai is a beautiful place to get married. I want you and Uncle to enjoy yourselves. You've been here for two days and you've hardly left the hotel."

"Traveling clear around the world put a toll on my body," Hazel complained. "Besides, your uncle and I walked around earlier and took in some of the sights before we had lunch. I have to admit it is beautiful here in Chiang Mai. I didn't expect it to be so warm here in March."

Samson agreed. Chiang Mai was surrounded by a ring of mountains and filled with over seven hundred years' worth of history. "The wedding planner told us that February and March were the best months to get married because it's usually warm around this time."

"Are you really sure about this?" his aunt queried. "You're getting married in a Buddhist ceremony."

"It's Buddhist and Christian, Auntie," Samson corrected. "Lanna weddings are the most romantic and spiritual weddings in Thailand. They combine our beliefs so that this wedding will be about me and Savannah. Our ceremony is going to be an expression of our love."

"Uh-huh . . ." Hazel muttered.

He chuckled. "C'mon, Auntie. You know what it's like to be in love. You told me yourself that your parents didn't want you marrying a minister. You and Uncle eloped."

She glanced at him severely. "That's different."

"How?"

Unable to come up with a good answer, Hazel responded, "I'll get back to you on that."

Samson hugged her. "I really love you for caring about

me. But you don't have to worry about me anymore. That's going to be Savannah's job starting tomorrow."

"I will always worry about you, Samson. As for Savannah . . ."

"What is it?" he asked, his jaw tightening. "Just say it."

His aunt hesitated, clearly unsure about whether to go on. "Son, there are times she seems a bit detached. I don't know why I feel this way, but I sense that she doesn't love you as much as you love her."

Samson didn't want to hear this. "Savannah loves me, Auntie. She wouldn't be marrying me if she didn't."

Hazel's voice softened as she said, "I pray that she does, because I know how much you love her."

They embraced and Samson said, "She loves me, Auntie. I know without a doubt that I have her heart."

Zachariah came up at that moment and wrapped an arm around his wife. "We wish you and Savannah much happiness, son."

Samson smiled. "I know that." He checked his watch. "I need to go find Savannah. We're going to take care of some last-minute shopping. I'll see you at dinner."

As he left the suite, he ran into Trey in the hallway. "Hey, what are you doing?" Samson asked.

"I was thinking about going to the pool. I'm in the mood for a swim."

"Have you seen Savannah?"

"I haven't seen her, but I heard her dad say that she and her mother were at the spa."

Samson smiled. "I shouldn't be surprised."

He and Trey walked to the pool, where they found Savannah and her sister seated in the lounge chairs.

"Honey, I didn't know you were out here," Samson said.

"My mother wanted to go to the spa, but Kenya and I decided to come out here for a little while. It's too beautiful to be inside."

Samson glanced over at her sister, who was eyeing him

hungrily, then he gave his fiancée his full attention. "Do you still want to go shopping?"

"I thought you were going to go swimming with me," Kenya interjected as she jumped up and removed her cover-up. Her gaze traveled to Samson, who pretended not to notice her gorgeous body, barely covered by a tiny bikini.

Savannah grinned. "I haven't spent much time with my sister, so why don't you and Trey join us?"

"I need to go upstairs and change," Samson said.

She planted a kiss on his cheek. "Why don't you do that? We'll wait down here for you."

Samson glanced over at Trey, who seemed to be okay with it. Since arriving here in Chiang Mai, Trey and Savannah had spent time discussing Buddhism. Samson was glad his friend was showing an interest. He really wanted everything to be okay again.

• • •

That night Savannah's parents hosted a prewedding dinner for the couple at the hotel.

Samson and Savannah strolled hand in hand into the banquet room. The hair on the back of Samson's neck stood up, prompting him to look around. He found Kenya watching him intently from across the room. He smiled and she smiled back.

Savannah's parents had smiles plastered on their faces, but Samson knew that deep down, they weren't thrilled with the idea of having him for a son-in-law. He had no idea why they didn't care for him, but it didn't matter. Tomorrow Savannah would be his wife.

His aunt and uncle came over to chat with Savannah's parents, while he and his bride-to-be made the rounds, greeting their guests.

"I can hardly believe we're here," Savannah told him. "We're actually here in Thailand and we're getting married."

He gave her a loving look. "It's exciting, isn't it?"

"I can't wait to be your wife," she whispered. "Plus I'm ready for all that comes with it."

Samson knew what she was really saying. He felt the same way. Their wedding night could not come fast enough for him.

They sat down for dinner. The waiters began bringing out the meals while Savannah's parents gave a short congratulatory speech. His aunt and uncle stood up and did the same.

Throughout the evening, Kenya continued to watch him. Samson was used to having that effect on women, but this was his fiancée's sister. After the way she'd been flirting with him at the pool earlier, he was sure that, given the chance, she would jump into bed with him. However, he loved Savannah with his entire heart and did not intend to do anything to hurt her.

Kenya was as beautiful as her sister, but her body was more voluptuous. Samson reveled in her beauty for a moment before returning his attention back to his bride-to-be.

"Pastor Taylor, you *do* know that you're marrying a Buddhist, don't you?" Kenya asked when she walked over to where he was standing.

"I love your sister, Kenya," Samson responded. "None of that matters to me."

She gave him a puzzled look. "But don't you think it should matter? After all, you two have very different belief systems. I could see it working if you weren't a minister and were just a regular Christian man. But you're not. How do your church members feel about your marriage?"

"It's none of their business," he replied. "Or yours, Kenya, for that matter. I take it you're not a fan of our getting married either."

"It's not that at all, Samson. Please don't misunderstand me. I love my sister and I'm happy for Savannah and for you, but I just don't want to see her get hurt."

He dismissed those fears. "That's something you don't

have to worry about. Savannah and I have talked all this out and we're really okay."

Kenya smiled. "Great! I guess I'll be seeing you at the wedding, then."

"Most definitely."

"What are you two over here talking about?" Savannah inquired when she walked up behind her sister.

"I was just making sure Samson is the right man for you," Kenya informed her.

"So is he?" Savannah asked, eyeing the man she would be marrying the next day.

Kenya broke into a smile. "I think so. I still can't believe you're marrying a Baptist minister. That's just too funny to me."

"We love each other and that's what matters most," Savannah told her sister. The two women embraced.

"Then I'm happy for you both," Kenya stated. "Congratulations and welcome to the family, Samson. It's going to be nice having a big brother around."

"Thank you. I think it's cool to have a little sister, too."

Kenya gave Savannah another hug before leaving to talk to some of the other family members in attendance.

"Kenya and I used to do everything together until she left for college. Before then, she went everywhere with me."

Samson was relieved knowing that after the wedding, Kenya would be back in Washington, D.C. He didn't want her around him because he worried the temptation would be too great. He couldn't even allow himself to think about Kenya for fear of becoming aroused.

Samson didn't need temptation in his life just as he and Savannah were about to be married. He intended to honor his marriage vows, despite his greatest fear: that he would become the type of man his father had been.

CHAPTER 11

Samson and Savannah's wedding day started off with a morning offering to the monks. The couple was escorted to the market to select foods and flowers.

"Why are we doing this again?" he asked in a low voice.

"To encourage good luck in our marriage," Savannah whispered back.

He knew his aunt was back at the hotel speaking in tongues and holding a prayer vigil. None of this sat right with her, and Samson couldn't blame her, but he had agreed to a Buddhist-Christian ceremony.

"What are you thinking about?" Savannah asked, cutting into his thoughts. "You haven't heard a word I've said to you."

Samson smothered her in an embrace. "I was thinking about how much I love you and can't wait to be your husband."

She kissed him, delighted at his passion. "We don't have to wait much longer. In a few hours, I'll be your wife, and then we'll have our wedding night."

They took their offering to the temple and received a formal blessing.

Savannah seemed relieved afterward. "Now that's over, we can get back to our guests." He and Savannah had arranged to have a wedding brunch before the ceremony.

"Just out of curiosity, what if the monks hadn't given us their blessing?" Samson questioned. "Would you have canceled the wedding?"

"We don't have to worry about that."

Not for the first time, he wondered how much she really knew about this bizarre religion. "I'd like to know the answer."

Savannah met his gaze. "The truth is that I really don't know what I would've done. The monks gave us their blessing, so we don't have to look back."

Samson was bothered by her response. It seemed so superstitious. He didn't want to argue on their wedding day, though, so he let the matter drop for now.

Later Samson went to his aunt and uncle's hotel room to check on them. "Aunt Hazel, why on earth are you wearing that huge cross around your neck?" He tried to joke. "That's something I expect to see on some hip-hop performer's neck. Who have you been hanging out with lately?"

"I'm representing Jesus Christ," she responded crisply. "And I'm not afraid to let everybody know. I won't be bowing down to Buddha or any other idol."

Samson laughed. He thought he was just getting married. "Are you really planning to wear that necklace? It doesn't look right with your dress, Aunt Hazel."

"You're not the fashion police, so I don't care what you think." She tossed her hair across her shoulders in a gesture of defiance. "I'm wearing my necklace and that's the end of the discussion. I bought one for your uncle, but he doesn't want to wear it."

"I'm wearing the same cross I've been wearing," Zachariah responded from across the room. "Hazel, you know I don't go for all that bling."

Samson cracked up. *"Bling?* Aunt Hazel walking around here looking like Missy Elliott. You two are funny." He made his way to the door. "I'll be back shortly. Be ready."

"You're the one who needs to get dressed," Zachariah said. "We're already dressed."

• • •

Hazel managed to make it through brunch without speaking in tongues and casting out demons. Afterward, everyone retired to their suites to rest before the wedding.

Two hours later Samson knocked on his aunt and uncle's door to make sure they were up.

"Shouldn't you be getting ready for your wedding?" his uncle inquired when he opened the door.

"Now, hold on, Zachariah. Maybe he's come to tell us that he's running for the hills." Hazel pointed to her suitcase. "Tell me that you've changed your mind and I can be packed in five minutes flat."

"What am I going to do with you?" Samson asked her with a chuckle. "I have everything laid out and I've already taken my shower. I just came to check on you two." He saw that she was still wearing that hideous piece of jewelry around her neck. "Please take off that necklace," Samson pleaded.

"Call off this foolishness and get married in a church," she countered.

"All right," he said with a sigh. "When you see the wedding pictures, you'll regret wearing it."

Hazel stood with her arms folded, looking up at Samson. "My Lord in Heaven will be pleased to see how I stood up for Him. That's all I care about."

Samson could forgive anyone on this day. "Well, at least you don't have one of those rings with 'Jesus' spelled out."

"I didn't think about that, but I do have the earrings," Hazel said, brushing back her shoulder-length hair so that

Samson could see her ears, embellished with gaudy JESUS studs.

At least they were hidden. "I don't know what I'm going to do with you."

"If you insist on going through with this ceremony, then you need to get dressed. The photographer is already here and waiting," Hazel said. "He called our room a few minutes ago. He was calling for you, but got us instead."

"I'll see you in a few minutes," Samson told them. Before he left, though, he stopped short. "I want you both to know that this means a lot to me, having you here."

Tears slid down Hazel's cheeks. "We love you, son."

Samson smiled and left the room. In less than two hours, he was marrying the woman of his dreams.

In a Thai marriage ceremony, the couple literally tied the knot in a deeply spiritual ceremony, which Samson thought was perfect for Buddhists and non-Buddhists. Samson and Savannah sat close together on a small stage with their hands bound together with a flower chain. Her grandfather, being the most senior person present, was instructed to soak the couple's hands in the water contained in a conch shell bowl, and wish them good luck. He was followed by her parents, Hazel, and Zachariah. He and Savannah wanted to enjoy the romance and spiritual experience of a Thai wedding and considered this a wonderful, unique way to start off their new life together.

Savannah had insisted on wearing Thai wedding attire, while Samson opted to wear a traditional tuxedo. She looked exquisite in the blue gown with elaborate gold trim, made of blended Thai silk in the traditional wedding style of northern Thailand. Savannah wore a golden headdress depicting leaves and flowers, which was often worn by Thai brides.

They were to say their vows enclosed in a tropical garden setting with a royal forest backdrop. Lama Yeshe greeted the guests, saying, "Samson and Savannah are happy today not only because they can share the joy of their love for each other with friends and family but also because they have the opportunity to express their aspirations for the future.

"Samson and Savannah, do you pledge to help each other to develop your hearts and minds, cultivating compassion, generosity, patience, enthusiasm, concentration, and wisdom as you age and undergo the various ups and downs of life and to transform them into the path of love, compassion, joy, and self-control?" Lama Yeshe asked.

"We do," they responded in unison.

"You must recognize that the external conditions in life will not always be smooth and that internally your own minds and emotions will sometimes get stuck in negativity. Do you pledge to see all these circumstances as a challenge to help you grow, to open your hearts, to accept yourselves and each other, and to generate compassion for others who are suffering? Do you pledge to avoid becoming narrow-minded or opinionated, and to help each other to see various sides of situations?"

"We do."

"Do you pledge to seek to understand yourselves, each other, and all living beings, to examine your own minds continually and to regard all the mysteries of life with curiosity and joy?"

Samson couldn't take his eyes off his beautiful bride. "We do."

"Do you pledge to take the loving feelings you have for each other and your vision of each other's potential and inner beauty as an example, and rather than spiraling inward and becoming self absorbed, to radiate this love outward to all beings?"

"We do."

"When it comes time to part, do you pledge to look back at your time together with joy—joy that you met and shared what you have—and acceptance that we cannot hold on to anything forever?"

"We do."

"Do you pledge to remember the kindness of all other beings and your connection to them?"

"We do."

It was time for the exchanging of rings. Samson turned around to take the ring from Trey. He caught a fleeting glimpse of sadness in his friend's eyes and realized Trey wasn't over Savannah.

"The wedding ring is the outward and visible sign of an inward and spiritual bond which unites two loyal hearts in partnership," Lama Yeshe explained.

Samson placed the platinum wedding band on Savannah's left ring finger. She did the same with his ring.

"By the power vested in me through the wishes of Samson and Savannah, as well as the blessing of the lineage of their spiritual friends, I now pronounce you husband and wife."

Samson didn't hear anything else over the loud thumping of his beating heart.

• • •

"Welcome to the family, Savannah," Hazel said after the ceremony, prompting Samson to send a warm smile her way.

The two women embraced.

"Your cross is interesting," Savannah commented.

Samson cleared his throat noisily while Hazel broke into a smile. "I guess you can say I'm a Jesus freak."

Savannah chuckled. "I see you have Jesus earrings, too."

"I love myself some Jesus," Hazel told her. "When you know Him like I do, you can't help but love Him."

Savannah gave her a tight smile. "I see."

Samson decided it was time to intervene. He didn't want his aunt offending his new wife. "Aunt Hazel, have you met Savannah's grandparents and her aunt Sophie? They arrived late last night. C'mon, I want to introduce you." He glanced over his shoulder at Savannah and mouthed, "Sorry . . ."

She blew him a kiss.

Once they were out of earshot Hazel said, "I didn't make your bride uncomfortable, did I?"

"No, I'm afraid your plan failed, Auntie."

She looked disappointed for a brief moment, then said, "Nothing beats a fail but a try."

"And you call yourself a Christian woman," he whispered in her ear. "Here you are wearing that big old cross around your neck and Jesus earrings . . . you going around here trying to break up a marriage."

"Samson, don't let me break you off at the knees," she warned. "I'm not the one married to a nonbeliever. I can't help it if the truth hurts you."

Samson had endured enough sniping. "Savannah and I are married. She's part of this family, remember?"

Seeing he was serious, Hazel hugged him. "You're right, dear. Okay, no more potshots at her, but the rest of these people . . . humph!" She stopped at one table and said, "Hello, I'm Hazel Taylor. This is my nephew. As I was walking by, my spirit man told me to stop and ask you if you knew Jesus."

"Uncle," Samson called out wearily. "Come get your wife."

"What's going on?" Zachariah said as he hurried over.

"This is my wedding day. Can you please ask Aunt Hazel to stop trying to win souls to Christ for one day?"

His uncle laughed. "I don't know if I can do that, son. Jesus could come back at any moment."

Samson shrugged in resignation. "Well, I can't argue with that."

"I'll see if I can get her to just relax and enjoy the reception, Samson."

"Thanks, Uncle."

Samson's smile disappeared when he saw his bride engaged in an animated conversation with Trey. The two were huddled together in a corner, talking and laughing. A thread of jealousy snaked down his spine.

"Excuse me," he said to his uncle. "I'm going to check on my wife."

He walked with purpose across the floor to join them. "What's so funny?" he asked.

"Trey was just telling me about the time you tried to impress a girl by doing tricks on your bike."

Samson winced at the memory. "I ended up with a broken arm and I never saw that girl again."

"From what Trey tells me, you were quite the ladies' man."

Samson sent Trey an arch look. "That's all over now that I have you."

"I see someone I need to speak to," Trey said suddenly. "I'll catch up with you later, Samson."

When it was just the two of them Savannah said, "I think everything is back to normal. Trey seems like his old self. I feel like he and I can be friends again."

Samson nodded. "That's great. Trey is family."

Savannah glanced up at him. "I love you."

"I love you more," he responded. "You have made me the happiest man alive."

"The wedding was beautiful, don't you think?"

"Yeah," he agreed. "Combining our Christian and Buddhist traditions gave us the best of both worlds."

She glanced around at the gathering. "I'm glad we got married over here. Since we've been in Thailand, I've felt so peaceful," Savannah said. "This was the perfect place for us to say our vows." She released a long sigh of contentment.

Samson wasn't so sure. He'd been running interference since he arrived. Still, in the end he didn't care where they married as long as she became his wife in the end.

CHAPTER 12

$\mathscr{E}$arly Sunday morning, Samson started his workout in the backyard with Tabata squats, then a round of push-ups, sit-ups, and finally kicks. He loved martial arts training, pushing himself to be better, and he thanked God continuously for the ability to do so.

Afterward, Samson came inside and headed to the bedroom to take a shower. Savannah was still sleeping.

Since their wedding a month ago, she had yet to come to Hillside to hear him preach. She had been to Hillside only once, right before their wedding. Samson suspected that the only reason she went was because he wanted to announce his upcoming marriage and introduce her to the members.

She stirred in bed, and then opened her eyes. "Good morning, honey. Why are you up so early?"

"It's Sunday," he responded. "Savannah, I'd really like for you to attend church with me this morning."

The members had been whispering about his MIA bride, and Samson didn't like it. Several of their friends had spouses who attended different churches, so he couldn't understand why they were making such a big deal about it. However,

Samson wanted his wife to support him in the same way that he supported her.

"I'd rather not," she responded, sounding tired. "I think I'm just going to sleep in." Her eyes smoldered with fire. "You kept me up most of the night, remember?"

Samson was all business, though. "You're my wife and I want to see your beautiful face in the congregation this morning."

"I'll go next week," she promised.

That was as good as he was going to get. "I'm going to hold you to it," Samson said. "I'll see you after service."

Savannah blew him a kiss. "I love you."

Samson didn't respond. He was annoyed with the way she kept putting him off. He had really hoped she would come around, but she was still holding on to her Buddhist beliefs.

When he arrived at the church thirty minutes later, he went out of his way to avoid his aunt. He was already frustrated, and certainly not in the mood to listen to her comments concerning his wife's absence.

Samson couldn't understand why Savannah was being so difficult. He had been nothing less than a good husband to her. He had allowed her to spend thousands of dollars redecorating, he had eaten her vegetarian dishes without complaint, and he was understanding when she refused to attend church with him. She was even taking a reflexology course two nights a week.

His aunt caught up with him just as he was leaving his uncle's office. "I was hoping to see Savannah with you," she said, embracing him.

"She'll be coming next Sunday," Samson told her.

Hazel was pleased by this news. "That's wonderful to hear."

Samson spotted one of the deacons and quickly excused himself. He rushed off before she could utter a response.

Two hours later when Samson arrived at home. Savannah was dressed and looked like she was getting ready to leave.

"Where are you going?" he asked.

"I thought I'd go shopping for some new drapes for the living room."

Samson frowned. "What's wrong with what's already in there? Baby, I paid a lot of money for those curtains."

"I don't like them," she responded. "I want something that will reflect more of my personality."

"Savannah, I live here too, remember?"

She wrapped her arms around him, pressing her body close to his. "Honey . . . don't be that way. You told me to make this house my home. Well, that's what I'm doing."

Samson felt his resolve weaken. He kissed her hungrily. "It's so hard for me to say no to you," he murmured softly.

"You're so good to me," Savannah told him. "When I get back, I promise to make it up to you."

"You can make it up to me next Sunday when you attend church with me."

"Honey, please don't forget that I'm a Buddhist," she said with a short sigh. "I thought we agreed to worship in our own way. I said I'll go with you next week, but I really don't want you pressuring me to go to church with you all the time."

Samson was so tired of hearing those words. "How many times are you going to throw that in my face? You can't compromise and come to church with me at least two Sundays a month? Is that too much to ask, Savannah?"

"How about one Sunday a month," she countered. "On the Sunday that you preach."

"I preach two Sundays a month," Samson stated. *"Just two Sundays.* Baby, I'm not asking you to travel with me or come to the other churches, but this is my home church. The members ought to see you at least twice a month minimum. Sometimes more if we're having something big."

Savannah chewed on her bottom lip for a moment before saying, "Samson, I love you and I really don't want to start off our day arguing. Look, I'm willing to commit to once a month for now. Maybe I'll do two, but I just want to commit to this and see how it goes."

"Fine," he said with a sigh of resignation.

"I don't want to leave while you're upset."

"I'm fine," he responded.

Savannah studied his face. "Honey, please don't be angry with me."

He hugged her. "I'm not angry. Go shopping. When you get back, we'll go out to dinner."

She broke into a big grin. "Wonderful."

Samson watched his wife leave, then settled down in the family room to watch television. He did love Savannah. He only hoped that she would keep her word.

• • •

The following Sunday, Savannah came down with a sudden headache. Samson wasn't buying her excuse and let her know it. "I'm tired of getting the same questions every Sunday—people asking me where you are."

She rubbed her temple with her right hand. "Well, if you would just tell them the truth, you wouldn't get the questions, Samson. Just be honest with everyone."

"I'm not being dishonest," he replied quickly. "Hillside is my uncle's church and the last thing I want to do is bring scandal to it."

"Before we got married, you went on and on about how you didn't care what anyone else thought about our relationship." She folded her arms across her chest. "I guess you were just blowing smoke, huh."

"I meant everything I said. But I thought you would be in church whenever I had to preach." He checked the clock on the nightstand and said, "We'll have to finish this discussion after I get back from church. I need to leave."

"I love you, honey."

Furious, Samson walked out of the bedroom without

responding. His anger had abated by the time he turned into the church parking lot. Samson saw his aunt and waved.

When he got out of the car, the two embraced. "Where is Savannah?" Hazel asked. "I thought she was coming this Sunday."

"She didn't feel well so she decided to stay home."

"Uh-huh," she muttered. "You say that almost every Sunday. Hon, I guess you just need to face the truth. Your wife has no intentions of sitting in a Baptist church."

"Auntie, she'll change her mind," Samson told her. He didn't want to admit to himself that she might be right.

Hazel shook her head. "I don't think she will. You're just going to have to accept that. You knew what she was when you married her."

"And she knew that I was a pastor," he countered. "Savannah's my wife and she should want to come to church with me sometimes. She went with me when I preached at the church in Asheville, and then again right before we got married, so it shouldn't be a problem now."

"Don't let this be a problem in your marriage, hon," Hazel advised. "Just give it over to God, because you can't make Savannah change—only the good Lord can do that."

He nodded sullenly in agreement.

Samson's mood hadn't gotten any better by the time he stood up to preach. Closing his eyes, he sent up a silent prayer. *Lord, please take me out of this sermon and put all of You in it. Please give me what You want Your people to hear. Amen.*

He opened his Bible.

"Our text today comes from Hebrews eleven. This book is probably one of the more popular chapters in the entire Bible. Hebrews chapter eleven, verse six, is the scripture we hear quite often. 'And without faith it is impossible to please God, because anyone who comes to him must believe that he exists and that he rewards those who earnestly seek him.'

To fully understand this scripture, you must connect it to the last verses of the preceding chapter . . ." He paused for a moment.

"Let's look at Hebrews chapter ten, verses thirty-eight through thirty-nine. 'But my righteous one will live by faith. And if he shrinks back, I will not be pleased with him. But we are not of those who shrink back and are destroyed, but of those who believe and are saved.' They are reminded that it is impossible to overcome without faith. Faith is impossible without assurance. Faith is the ability to look beyond the visible into the invisible."

"Say it," his aunt Hazel shouted. "Amen."

"Take note in Genesis that the universe was formed at God's command. What is seen was not made out of what was visible. Therefore, we are always confident and we know that we live by faith, not by sight. Try to imagine Moses enduring the hardships with the children of God because he was able to see Him who is invisible. He was able to look beyond the riches of Egypt."

Samson had worked on this sermon all week, and as his eyes traveled the congregation, he could tell he had his audience engaged. If only Savannah were sitting in the second row beside his aunt. Then this would be perfect.

He forced his attention back to his sermon, which was coming to an end. Samson concluded, and then invited anyone needing prayer or seeking salvation to come down front.

When church ended, he spent a few minutes with his aunt and uncle before leaving. Samson wanted to get home to Savannah.

She was seated cross-legged in the middle of the family room floor with her eyes closed. Meditation, he decided. Samson eased out of the room and headed to their bedroom to change out of his suit.

His wife joined him a few minutes later. "How was service?" she asked.

"Like you care," he answered.

Savannah flipped her hair across her shoulders. "Samson, there's no need for the attitude. I didn't feel well this morning, but after taking some Tylenol and resting, I'm feeling much better now."

"How convenient," he muttered.

She glared at him. "Excuse me?"

Samson met her gaze with his own. "All I know is that if you loved me as much as you say you do, then you wouldn't have a problem coming to church with me. Hey, if you want me to go with you to a temple, I'll do it. I'm willing to compromise."

Savannah gasped in surprise. "You would do that for me?"

He nodded. "Honey, I love you. I want us to support each other."

"You know what? You're absolutely right. If you're willing to go to a temple for me, then I will do the same for you. *I mean it.*"

Samson pulled his wife into his arms. "All I want to do is make you happy, baby. You are the love of my life."

She didn't respond, which bothered him, but Samson forced it out of his mind.

• • •

Samson kept his word and attended a Buddhist temple with Savannah. The statues guarding the entrance displayed scowling faces and he said, "What's up with the statues outside? They didn't look all that peaceful and happy to me."

Savannah chuckled. "They represent two mythological kings and ward off evil."

"Why are they covered with paper?" he asked.

"Worshipers write their petitions on bits of paper, and after chewing them, they throw them on the statues. If the paper sticks, we believe the prayer will be answered."

Samson glanced around at the people around him, thinking how misguided they were—his wife included.

The main sanctuary of the temple had a long, sloping roof, prominent support columns, and an array of decorative carvings along its façade. Plainly furnished, the interior light came from candles surrounding the altar. Around the altar were images of the Buddha and other, lesser deities. Little bells placed on cushions and lacquer boxes containing the scrolls surrounded the altar. The sticks of incense were supposed to add an aura of holiness, Samson assumed. He liked the exotic fragrance.

He noticed that worshipers placed their palms together with fingers and thumbs aligned, elbows close to their body upon entering. They bowed toward the shrine before taking their seats and waiting for the service to begin.

He listened quietly as Savannah and the others sang. Samson found the service interesting, but after observing the worshipers bowing and praying to the Buddha, he became more convinced than ever that his wife needed to convert to Christianity.

Afterward when they were driving home, Savannah asked, "So what did you think?"

"It was interesting."

"That's all you have to say about it?"

Samson gave a slight shrug. "It's interesting. The ringing of the bell, the chanting—it's all interesting."

"I know it's not something you're used to seeing, but I hope you enjoyed it."

"I liked the teaching by the reverend—"

"He's called a sensei," Savannah interjected. "We call it a dharma talk." She reached over and squeezed his hand. "Thanks so much for allowing me to share this with you."

"I told you that I'd do anything for you, sweetheart." Samson leaned over and planted a kiss on her lips. "Besides, I know that next Sunday, you'll be in the congregation when I give my sermon."

CHAPTER 13

"I made zucchini bread and sweet potato enchiladas for dinner," Savannah announced the next night.

Samson didn't respond. He was tired of eating vegetarian dishes. Initially, he was willing to give it a try, but it wasn't working for him. Several times during the week, he stopped by his aunt and uncle's house to eat before coming home. His aunt had started putting aside a plate for him.

The first time he brought one home, Savannah was offended and they argued most of the evening about her cooking. Samson wanted her to cook some of his favorites from time to time, but she flatly refused.

"Oh, I almost forgot. Trey called while you were outside talking to the guy across the street," Savannah announced now. "He wants to meet for dinner on Friday. He said that it'll be a double date."

Samson was surprised. "Really? He's bringing a date?"

"That's why it's called a double date," Savannah teased. "I think it'll be fun to go out with Trey. It's time for you and Trey to rebuild that close friendship you once shared."

"What did you tell him?" He leaned against the counter with his arms folded across his chest.

"Nothing," she answered. "Except that you'd give him a call later when you got home."

"I'll give him a call later on tonight. Right now I think I'll take a nap," Samson said. He kissed her. "I'll see you in about an hour."

He went into the bedroom and called his aunt to let her know that he would be stopping by the house to get something to eat. Thankfully, she didn't make any negative comments about Savannah.

Samson removed his shoes, lay down on the bed, and fell asleep almost immediately.

After he woke up an hour and a half later, he called his best friend. The nap proved refreshing and Samson felt energized. "Hey, Trey, what's up?"

"We haven't spent much time together in the past month, so I thought maybe we could go out on Friday."

"Savannah told me you're bringing a date. Sounds fine to me. I could use a night on the town."

"Great," Trey said.

"So who is this girl?"

"I'm bringing Fiona Williams. We've been seeing each other for the past month."

Samson remembered her from their high school days. She and Trey dated in their junior year. "Wow. I didn't know she was still in town. Is it serious?"

"She's been back for almost a year," Trey replied. "We ran into each other a couple of months ago and things kind of clicked, so we decided to try again. I'm not in love with her, but we have a good time together."

"How does she feel about that?"

"I've been real honest with her. She knows I care about her, but that's it. I don't want her thinking we're headed for marriage."

"If you're not looking for a committed relationship with Fiona, then why are you going out with her?"

"Like I told you, we have a good time together," Trey explained. "But I just don't feel that way about her. She's a good friend. Hey, enough about me. How are you enjoying married life?"

"I'm loving it," Samson said. "Savannah and I couldn't be happier." He was not about to tell Trey that they were having a conflict about religion. He didn't want Trey knowing that they had any marital problems whatsoever.

"Marriage is wonderful, Trey. I highly recommend it." Samson heard Savannah walking past their bedroom and his voice died.

After a long pause Trey asked, "Samson . . . you still there?"

"Yeah. I'm sorry. I guess I'm still tired."

"You okay? You don't sound like yourself. I know you, Samson. Something's not right."

"It's nothing."

"Hey, if you need to talk, I'm here," Trey told him.

"I know. But don't worry. Everything's cool."

Trey wisely changed the subject to sports. They talked for another ten minutes, then got off the phone.

Samson picked up his keys and headed down to the kitchen. "I'm going to my aunt and uncle's house," he told his wife.

"I see," Savannah muttered. "How long will you be gone?"

"I'll be back in an hour."

She stepped in his path, blocking his exit. "Samson, I know you've been eating over there. You don't have to hide it from me."

"I'm not hiding anything. I just didn't want to hurt your feelings."

"I'm a vegetarian and so those are the types of meals I prepare."

"You were raised on ham, bacon, chicken, and everything else," Samson said. "I can see if you weren't, then I'd understand your aversion to cooking meat. I do respect your decision to be a vegetarian, but, baby, don't expect me to stop eating meat. I love meat. I've lost almost fifteen pounds since we've been married."

She didn't respond right away. When she did, Savannah said, "I know you must be starving, so go on to your aunt's house. I'll see you when you get back. Tell them I said hello, please."

"You want to go with me?" Samson asked. "You can tell them yourself. I'm sure they'd love to see you."

Savannah smiled. "Sure. Just give me a minute to freshen up."

He was secretly thrilled that she would be joining him. Maybe they needed to spend more time with his aunt and uncle. Maybe then his aunt Hazel could teach Savannah what it means to be a pastor's wife.

• • •

Savannah and Hazel sat in the family room talking while Samson and his uncle sat in the dining room eating.

"You weren't waiting on me, were you?" Samson asked, gesturing toward Zachariah's plate.

"No," he responded. "I ate something earlier with Hazel. This is my second round."

His aunt had cooked baked chicken, turnip greens, sweet potatoes, and homemade yeast rolls. Samson savored the tender chicken that practically fell off the bone when his fork sliced into it.

He went into the kitchen for seconds. He hadn't eaten anything since breakfast and was starving. Samson caught Savannah watching him and smiled. She flashed him one back. He loved her so much, but they were going to have to talk through this vegetarian issue.

Later at home, they sat down and picked up the conversation they'd been having before they left.

"Savannah, I understand that you're a vegetarian and I respect your decision to be one. I'll prepare my own meat," he stated. "I have no intentions of becoming a vegetarian. Honey, I have to have some type of meat with every meal."

She nodded in understanding. "I love you, Samson, and I'm really trying to be a good wife to you, but there are some things I just can't do."

Samson smiled, pleased that she was finally coming around. "Thank you, baby. That's all I'm asking you to do."

"I'm glad we were able to talk all this out."

Samson agreed.

"I'm going upstairs to take a shower," Savannah announced.

Samson's mood lightened fifteen minutes later when he saw his wife stroll out of the bedroom wearing a sexy negligee.

"You look stunning," Samson said, his voice husky. He couldn't remember the last time he'd seen her dressed in something so provocative. He reached for her.

Savannah fell into his arms. "I love being with you like this," she told him. "There's been so much tension between us lately. We fight, and then make love, but nothing's resolved."

Samson pulled her body closer to his. "I love you so much, baby."

She simply smiled in response.

It bothered him whenever she didn't echo the sentiment, but Samson wasn't about to act all insecure, so he didn't complain. Besides, she wouldn't have married him if she didn't love him.

CHAPTER 14

$\mathcal{S}$amson admired his wife as she dressed for their dinner date with Trey and Fiona. Things were going pretty well between them now, although he didn't like having to come home every day and cook. Cooking his own meals had been his idea, but he didn't enjoy it as much as he did before they married.

"Did Trey tell you anything about his date?" Savannah asked.

Shaking his head, Samson slipped on his pants. "Just that she was a girl we knew in high school. They dated during their junior year."

"Does it sound serious?"

Samson shrugged. He glanced over at his wife, enjoying the way she looked in her black dress.

Savannah caught him staring at her and asked, "What is it?"

"I was just thinking how beautiful you look."

She awarded him a smile. "Thanks, honey." Savannah walked over to where he was standing. "Are you sure Trey is ready for something like this?"

"It was his idea," Samson reminded her as he slipped on a black shirt that she had given him as a gift. "He seemed fine at our wedding, don't you think?"

"Yeah, but I just get the feeling that he's trying to make a point with this dinner."

Samson looked at his wife. "What point would that be?"

She shrugged. "I don't know. It just seems strange that now he wants to double date all of a sudden. We barely ever hear from him."

"Do you want to cancel?"

"No," she murmured. "I'm almost ready."

He stole a peek at Savannah. Samson thought she looked a little disturbed, but when he inquired, she denied it, citing a headache.

"We can stay home," he offered. "I'll call Trey and let him know that you're not feeling well."

"I know how much you want to see Trey. I'll just take some Tylenol and I'll be fine."

They left the house fifteen minutes later.

Trey and his date were already at the restaurant by the time they arrived, and it turned out that Savannah and Fiona knew each other.

"It's so good to see you again," she told Savannah. "I'd heard that you had gotten married but I had no idea that it was to Samson. We went to high school together."

"I didn't know that you two knew each other," Trey said.

"Fiona and I went to college together," Savannah announced. "She was a year ahead of me, but her sister was my roommate."

"Small world," Samson murmured to Trey, who nodded in agreement.

They were seated five minutes later, and their waitress immediately greeted them. "What would you like to drink?" she asked.

"Iced tea for me and my wife," Samson said.

"We'll have iced tea as well," Trey told the waitress.

"So, Fiona, what are you doing now?" Samson inquired. He didn't really care but thought it was a good idea to spark up a conversation.

"I'm a pharmacist."

"Are you at one of the local drug stores?"

"Yes. I work for Kerr Drug. Been with the company for three years and transferred back here a year ago."

Samson noted that Savannah seemed to be discreetly studying Fiona. She pretended to be looking elsewhere whenever the woman glanced her way. *What's going on between those two?* he wondered.

The waitress returned with their drinks. She pulled out a pad to write down their meal selections.

"Savannah, are you still practicing Buddhism?" Trey asked after they placed their orders with the waitress.

"Trey, I know you're not thinking about becoming one?" Samson asked with a chuckle. He recalled how interested in the religion Trey had seemed when they were in Chiang Mai.

"Possibly," he replied. "I've been searching for something for a long time. I'm not sure what I'm looking for, but I know that it's not in a church. Church just doesn't do it for me, Samson, as much as you don't want to hear that."

"How would you know, Trey?" Samson asked with a short laugh. "It's not like you go on a regular basis. Once a year wouldn't do it for me either."

Savannah glanced over at her husband before saying, "Trey, the fact is, most people are unable to accept this ultimate truth, and they believe that as long as they have faith in a deity, attend regular assemblies with a congregation, and pretend to follow certain values, that somehow everything will be fine."

"I can't believe I'm hearing this," Samson muttered.

Fiona rose to her feet, saying to Trey, "I think I'll make a visit to the ladies' room while you seek enlightenment."

Samson chuckled, but Savannah didn't seem to find any humor at all in her statement. "Church is not for everyone," she told Trey. "I would think that even Samson will agree."

Samson nodded.

"So, if I wanted to become a Buddhist, what do I have to do?" asked Trey. "Ever since we left Thailand, I've been giving Buddhism some serious thought."

"Read about the life of Siddhartha Gautama," Savannah suggested. "He's the father of Buddhism. Learn about the Buddha's teachings, which include the four noble truths and the eightfold path. Practice meditation in order to free your mind from worry, and focus on the present to achieve inner peace."

"Yeah, Trey, this sounds just perfect for you," Samson teased.

"Samson, stop it," Savannah snapped. "Trey, if you're seriously considering this, then you need to research and understand the concepts of rebirth and karma. Practice the Buddha's teachings in your everyday life. You must learn to accept change, because all things are transient, so we must not get too attached to anything. Humility is essential." Savannah gave her husband a long look before adding, "And you can't be self-important. You are no different from any other living thing."

Samson's mood veered to anger. What was she trying to insinuate? "So why did you look at me when you were talking about being self-important?"

"Samson, it's obvious that you have a very high opinion of yourself," Savannah said.

He shrugged. "I don't think there's anything wrong with having confidence."

Savannah chuckled. "Honey, you're arrogant and you know it. Let's just tell it like it is."

"I just know who I am, Savannah and I don't apologize for it."

"You shouldn't be sorry," she agreed. "But on the other hand, you shouldn't think so much about self."

"Don't go quoting Buddha to me. I answer only to God."

Savannah chewed on her bottom lip and didn't say much after that.

"Are you okay?" Fiona asked when she returned to the table.

Savannah nodded stiffly. "I'm fine."

Samson reached over and took her hand. "Baby, I'm sorry if I offended you. I didn't mean to hurt you."

"We're okay," Savannah responded tersely.

Samson looked up to find Trey watching him. The last thing he wanted was to let his best friend see that things weren't quite right between him and Savannah.

• • •

"How dare you sit there and try to embarrass me like that," Savannah said as soon as they were in the car and on their way home. "I know that you have little respect for my faith, but the least you can do is shut up about it when someone asks me questions. I don't do that to you."

"What's your problem?" he demanded.

"Your snide little comments are my problem," Savannah responded curtly. "I'm tired of you acting like you're one of the good guys and that what I believe in is foolish. I have to be honest with you. I don't know what Trey sees in her. She is clearly not the woman for him."

"I think they look good together. Savannah, you shouldn't be so sensitive."

"And you don't have to be so rude."

"I spoke the truth. I can't help it if the truth hurts."

Savannah glared at him. They didn't talk to each other during the rest of the drive home, and as soon as they arrived, she went straight to the bedroom and slammed the door behind her.

"Whatever," he muttered. "I don't have time for this."

Samson turned on the television in the den and settled down on the sofa. He knew Savannah was upstairs pouting and didn't want to get into another argument with her, so he was just going to stay downstairs while she cooled down.

Tired, he closed his eyes.

He didn't open them again until the next morning. It took a few seconds for him to register that he'd slept on the sofa. Samson stood up and, after a good yawn, went upstairs.

Savannah was still sleeping. He eased into the room and removed his shirt.

"Where did you sleep last night?" she asked him.

Samson turned to face her. "I didn't know you were awake. I slept on the sofa in the den."

"Is this how you solve problems?"

"Savannah, I just fell asleep. It wasn't intentional."

She swung her legs out of the bed. "If you say so," she responded without looking at him.

"I'm not in the mood to argue or debate with you. Can we just have a pleasant start to our morning?"

"You act like all I want to do is fight with you. I have feelings too, and I want you to respect them."

"I do respect your feelings, sweetheart. Look, if you want to guide Trey on the path of enlightenment, do it."

"What I want is to stop all of this arguing. We haven't been married all that long, and we shouldn't be carrying on like this."

"I'm sorry if you feel I'm not being supportive. To be honest, I'm feeling the same way about you."

She appeared surprised by this. "I've tried to be as supportive as I can."

"I can't get you to go to church with me, Savannah, so how exactly have you been supportive?"

"We've already talked about this. I was under the impression that we'd settled that issue."

"I was merely pointing out that you haven't been as supportive as you'd like to believe."

She stood up and padded barefoot into the bathroom. Samson undressed, and then slipped into his robe.

When Savannah walked out a few minutes later, he headed inside to take a shower. He met her gaze straight on. She was still angry.

It was going to be a long weekend.

CHAPTER 15

$\mathscr{S}$amson arrived home to find Trey there with Savannah. And it wasn't the first time.

Since Trey expressed an interest in Buddhism at dinner the previous week, the two began spending a lot of time together. Savannah seemed thrilled that he displayed such interest in her faith.

She was wasting her time, Samson decided. Trey was just confused. He didn't know what he wanted. It had always been this way for him—trying this and then trying something else. Just a year ago, he wanted to be a Muslim. Eventually, Savannah would realize that this was just one of many passing phases for Trey.

"You two still talking about the path to enlightenment?" he asked, smirking.

"Honey, dinner will be ready in a few minutes. I put some chicken in the oven for you," Savannah told him.

Samson was shocked. He couldn't believe she'd actually cooked meat. Recovering, he said, "Thank you, baby. I appreciate that."

She gave him a smile, then turned to Trey. "Why don't you join us?"

"Yeah, join us," Samson said. "But no talk about the Buddha, okay? My sermon on Sunday is about worshiping false Gods. Trey, you might want to come to church and hear it. Better yet, I'll give you copies of the CD."

Savannah rose to her feet, saying, "Hmmm . . . you seem a little rough around the edges. What's going on with you?"

"Today just wasn't the greatest," Samson answered.

"I'm sorry about that, honey. Why don't you sit down and talk to Trey while I check on our dinner."

Samson kissed her. "Thanks for making the chicken."

"I'm really trying to meet you halfway," she whispered.

"I appreciate your efforts, in case I haven't told you so. I love you, baby."

"What's up with you?" Trey asked when Samson dropped down beside him.

"I had to deal with one of the deacons at Hillside. He was all over my uncle, about why his wife isn't teaching women's bible study anymore and I just had to set him straight. You can't go after my family like that."

"Church is filled with drama," Trey responded with a shake of his head. "Church politics are why I'm not a Christian."

"That's why Savannah became a Buddhist," Samson responded. "The problem is that you get some people who want to lead, and that's not going to work. My uncle is the leadership."

"Church politics have nothing to do with why I became a Buddhist," Savannah said, coming out of the kitchen. "To be honest, I feel that I maintain a mixture of both faiths."

Samson eyed her. "Really?"

She nodded. "Yes."

"I don't see how," he said. "Christ died for our sins. His dying offers us the free gift of salvation by simply believing and accepting what he's done on our behalf. There's nothing in Buddhism that compares to Jesus Christ. Your faith rejects that there is a God. Buddhism's ultimate goal is nirvana. Christianity's ultimate goal is eternal life."

"From the little bit I do know about Buddhism," Trey interjected, "I know that it teaches people to forsake all evils and practice only what is good. Isn't this also the essence of Christianity?"

"Not exactly," Samson replied.

"Samson, that's what I have a problem with," Savannah told him. "Buddhism is good, but when judged by Christian standards, it's not good enough."

"That's because Buddhism is atheistic," Samson responded. "Christians believe in one supreme God. You can't see the beauty of the world and the grace of God's creation if you follow only Buddha's teaching. You see this world as one full of misery, and everything in it as vanity."

"My beliefs didn't keep you from wanting to be with me," Savannah said. There was a sudden edge to her voice.

"Don't flatter yourself, Savannah. You came after me, remember?"

Trey discreetly left the room while Samson talked to his wife. Samson could see that his words had wounded her. "I'm sorry for the way that came out, sweetheart."

Aware that Trey was watching them, Samson surprised her by pulling her into his arms. He kissed her long and hard.

"What was that for?" she asked when they'd parted.

"We should be doing more of that and less talking," he said softly. "Maybe we wouldn't argue so much. Let's get through dinner and we'll talk later."

Trey cleared his throat noisily. "I think I'm gonna leave."

"No," Savannah said quickly. "Trey, you don't have to leave. We want you to stay."

He looked over at Samson, who nodded in agreement.

They had a great time during dinner, although they all felt an undercurrent of tension swirling around them.

After Trey left, Savannah resumed their conversation about Buddhism. "Samson, we talked about our faiths before we got married. I thought everything was worked out. I'm doing everything I can to make you happy, even going to Hillside, but things still aren't working out." She released a long frustrated sigh. "I just don't think it should be this hard."

"I'm not the one who's causing the problems," Samson snapped in anger. "I've been a good husband to you. It's easier to find a needle in a haystack than to get you to compromise. Frankly, I'm tired of doing things your way."

"Don't you ever talk to me in that tone again. I won't stand for it."

Samson grabbed her arm. "I will talk to you in any tone I please. You are my wife and it's time you started acting like it."

Her tone hardened, she retorted tartly, "Excuse me? I *am* a good wife to you, Samson, so don't even try to go there with me."

His grip tightened.

"Let go of me," she snarled, snatching her arm away. "You can't rough me up just because you're not getting your way." Savannah rubbed the spot where he had grabbed her. "I think we need to end this conversation right now." She headed to the door. "I need to get some air."

"Savannah, don't leave," he pleaded.

She shook her head. "I need to get out of here, and I think you need some time to yourself." She slammed the door as she left.

Frustrated, Samson picked a pillow off the sofa and threw it against the wall.

Savannah didn't return for almost two hours. When she walked into the condo, Samson was pacing. "Where have you been? I've been calling your cell phone."

"I didn't take it with me. I told you that I needed some space."

"When you said you needed some air, I thought you meant that you were going to sit outside for a while. I had no idea you were going to leave. I was worried about you."

She met his gaze. "As you can see, I'm perfectly fine."

"Where did you go?"

"I just drove around."

Samson didn't believe her for a second. "You've been driving for two hours?"

"I stopped at a doughnut shop. I wasn't aware that I needed to report every minute I was gone."

"Look, I was concerned about you. I'm not trying to interrogate you, baby."

"You didn't need to be. I'm going to take a shower and get ready for bed. I'm tired and I have a long day tomorrow."

She turned and left the room before Samson could utter a response.

• • •

Over the next few months things between Samson and Savannah appeared fine on the surface, but then he began to notice that she was becoming more and more distant. She made excuses when he wanted to make love, and she wasn't as talkative as she'd been in the past.

When she arrived home two hours after him one night, looking completely exhausted, Samson called her into the living room. "Honey, why don't you sit down here beside me and just relax for a moment. I'll give you a foot rub."

She gave him a tiny smile. "Honey, that would be nice."

"This case seems to be getting to you."

"It's a big lawsuit. My client has been accused of falsifying documents to conceal the role of two felons working for Carson Cobalt Properties. Their offices were raided and their bank accounts seized. That's why I was so late coming home."

"Sounds like this is one of many late nights."

Savannah nodded. "They're suing my clients for fifty million dollars."

"Wow."

"This case can make or break my career," she told him. "I'm up for partner, and I know that if I can get them to settle out of court, I'll make partner for sure."

Samson wanted to believe Savannah, but he couldn't escape the feeling that she wasn't being entirely honest with him.

• • •

Samson was booked on speaking engagements for almost every weekend in the month of September.

Savannah was still working long hours during the week and worked even when she was home. However, she still managed to have time for going to the temple with Trey.

Samson wasn't worried about their relationship because he was confident in Savannah's love. It frustrated him that she seemed to spend more time with Trey than with her own husband.

Samson wanted Savannah to join him on his upcoming trip to Las Vegas in the first week of September, but she refused, citing her heavy caseload.

"I really wish you'd reconsider," he told Savannah the Thursday before he was scheduled to go. "I think time away would be good for us. I don't like this distance between us."

"You're working, Samson," Savannah reminded him. "It's not a vacation."

"We can take a couple of extra days if you like."

"I really wish I could, but I have too much work. I'll be here when you return. Just think of me and how I'm preparing a very special homecoming for you."

"It better be a homecoming I won't ever forget."

Savannah broke into a grin. "You can count on it."

"I love you," he whispered in her ear.

"I'm really going to miss you while you're gone." She wrapped her arms around him and kissed him.

"You can always change your mind about going with me."

"I really have too much work to do," she told Samson, not quite meeting his eyes.

Samson took her by the hand and led her up to their bedroom.

"I thought you had some work to do," she said.

"It'll wait until later. Right now all I want to do is make love to my beautiful wife."

"Honey, I know that you love me, but I also know that you need to prepare for your trip. Go downstairs and lock yourself in your office. I have some research I need to finish. When you get back, we'll have plenty of time for us."

"You don't want to make love?"

"It's not that I don't want to, honey. I just have so much work right now. My research can't wait. I have to be in court on Monday."

He scanned her face. "Are you sure that's the only reason?"

"What other reason could there be?"

Samson pondered the question.

• • •

Samson arrived in Las Vegas on Friday and called his wife as soon as he checked into his hotel room. "Baby, I just wanted to let you know that I made it here safely."

"I'm glad," she told him.

"You okay?" Samson inquired when she didn't say anything else. "You don't sound like yourself."

"I'm fine."

"Do you have company?"

"No," she answered a little too quickly. "Why would you ask me that?"

"Savannah . . ."

"I have to go. I'm glad you made it to Vegas. I'll see you when you get home."

"I'll call you back tonight," Samson stated. Something was off with her. Savannah was usually the one wanting to talk for hours. She had never rushed him off the phone like that.

She probably had to be in court, he decided. They would talk later on that night.

In a few hours, he was scheduled to be the guest speaker at the young men's conference hosted by Omega Baptist Church. He needed to work on his sermon. Samson sat down at the desk and opened his laptop. He spent the afternoon trying to work on his sermon, but he couldn't fully concentrate because his mind was on Savannah.

CHAPTER 16

On Monday Samson was glad to be going home. He intended to sit down with his wife and get their marriage back on track.

He pulled into the garage and parked beside Savannah's car. When he got out, Samson noted the black Yukon sitting in front of his town house. Trey kept his SUV clean and shiny.

"Trey, I'm going to have to start charging you rent," Samson joked when he walked in and found his friend seated in the kitchen with his wife. "Lately, it seems like you're here more than I am."

"I came by because I thought it was time you and I talk man-to-man." Trey's voice had depth and authority.

Samson didn't like the sound of this. He studied Trey's face for a moment before glancing over at his wife, who was fidgeting and couldn't quite meet his eyes. A thread of apprehension snaked down his spine. "What's going on?"

"Why don't we all sit down?" Trey suggested.

Samson shook his head. "Just spit it out. What do you want to discuss with me?"

Trey was about to speak, but Savannah stopped him by interjecting, "No, I should be the one to tell him." Her voice sounded stifled and unnatural.

"Tell me what?" Samson demanded.

"Samson, there's been a lot of tension between us lately," Savannah began. "You can't deny that all we seem to do lately is fight a lot, and that things are different between us."

"I'm listening." He ground the words out between his teeth.

"This is so hard . . ." she said in a low voice. "Samson, I feel bad about the way things have turned out, because I know that you've tried to be nothing short of a wonderful husband. I need you to believe that I never meant to hurt you, but I owe you the truth."

"What are you trying to tell me?" he asked, looking from Savannah to Trey.

"Savannah and I are in love," Trey blurted. "We didn't plan this—it just happened."

"I don't believe this," Samson muttered, fighting to control his anger. "Are you kidding me? If this is a joke, it's not funny."

"No, it's not a joke." Tears rolled down Savannah's cheeks. "I'm so sorry, Samson."

A wave of fury overtook him. "Trey, I know what this is really about. I'm not stupid. I guess this is your pathetic attempt at payback for what you think I did to you?"

"That's not what this is about," Trey responded. "I never rolled like that, and you know it. Savannah and I didn't plan to fall in love. It just happened, and we care enough about you to be truthful with you."

Samson shook his head in disbelief. "This was never about Buddhism. You deliberately set out to seduce my wife." He couldn't believe that Trey had betrayed their friendship like this. "This isn't some girl I was just dating. *This is my wife, man*. How could you do this to me?"

"Savannah and I have been together only once. She was

upset and came to my house. It just happened, but then as we realized how strong our feelings were for each other, we knew that we had to tell you."

"You did what?" Samson spat.

"I did it too," Savannah interjected.

They both looked at her.

"The truth is, I had feelings for Trey from the very beginning," she said.

Samson couldn't believe what he was hearing. "Are you trying to tell me that you never loved me?" Samson glared sharply at Trey, his hands curling into fists.

"I handled this all wrong, and I'm sorry," Savannah said quietly.

"You're sorry," he repeated, his heart shattering into a million little pieces. "You think that makes this okay?"

She started to cry. "I'm so s-sorry."

Enraged, Samson punched the wall. His hand hurt like the devil, but he didn't care at the moment. Nothing compared to the agony he felt in his heart.

Savannah tried to see if his hand was okay, but he backed away from her. "Get her out of my house," he told Trey.

"Samson, we didn't want to hurt—"

He punched Trey square in the face, knocking him against the wall. Savannah stifled a scream.

Samson grabbed Trey by the throat, ignoring the throbbing pain in his hand. "I don't want to hear another word come out of your mouth. You betrayed me in the worst way when you went after my wife. Now get out of my house before I do something that will put me behind bars. Get out and take that Buddhist tramp with you." He released him.

Sobbing, Savannah headed to the door. It was then that Samson noticed the suitcases. The nightmare was real. She was actually leaving him for Trey.

Savannah wiped her face with her hands, and then said, "I know that you can't accept this right now, but I am sorry for hurting you."

"How could you do this to me?" His voice was filled with pain. Samson thought about the many times he'd professed his love for her, and Savannah remained silent or told him how much she cared for him. She would declare her love only in rare moments.

As if to confirm what he was thinking, Savannah said, "Samson, I tried to lo—"

He cut her off. "You *tried* to love me?"

"I know that you're angry and hurt, but, Samson, you're better than this," she responded. "If you just think about this, you'll see that I'm right. We don't belong together."

A flash of pain ripped through him. Samson glanced down at his hand, which was swelling, and muttered a string of profanities.

"You should get that hand looked at," Trey suggested as he wiped away the blood from his busted lip.

"You two should get out of my house," he snapped in response. *"Get out now."*

Samson opened the front door and tossed out the suitcases. Savannah ran out the door with Trey following. Trey paused, turned around, and opened his mouth to speak, but Samson slammed the door in his face, not wanting to hear another word come out of the traitor's mouth.

His back against the door, Samson slid down to the floor, his hand throbbing and tears in his eyes.

• • •

His aunt had the gift of discernment and she knew something was wrong the minute she picked up the phone.

"Hon, what's happened?"

"I just called to tell Uncle that I won't be in church tomorrow. I have some fractures in my left hand and I . . . I just need some time alone."

"Alone? Where's Savannah?"

Samson didn't respond.

"Son, what's going on between you two?" Hazel inquired. "I can tell by your voice that you're in pain."

"I hurt my hand," he mumbled, looking down at the splints. He had gone to the hospital, where X-rays showed that he'd fractured two fingers.

"It's much more than that," she responded. "Zachariah and I will be over there shortly."

Samson hung up the phone. He didn't want company, but he was too deflated to argue with his aunt.

They arrived thirty minutes later.

Hazel embraced him, then examined his bandaged right hand. "Son, please tell us what happened."

"Savannah's gone," Samson said. "Auntie, you were right about her. She never loved me. She was having an affair."

Hazel released a sigh of disappointment. "I'm so sorry, Samson. I never wanted to be right about this."

His uncle nodded in agreement. "How long has the affair been going on?"

"I'm not really sure," Samson responded. "The man is Trey."

Hazel gasped. "I never thought I'd see the day when you and Trey had a falling-out of this magnitude. I can't believe he'd do something like this to you."

"Go on and tell me what a big fool I was."

"Son, we know how hurt you are," Zachariah responded. "We're not going to kick you while you're down."

"I was a good husband to her and I thought Trey was my boy."

Hazel nodded. "I know, hon."

"I loved her more than my own life. Do you know what she said to me? Savannah told me that she tried to love me. *She tried . . .*"

"I'm so sorry," his aunt said.

"I'm so tired of hearing that word. There's no point in being sorry," Samson muttered. "I stood there and let Trey walk out with my woman. I wished I'd killed them both."

"Son, nothing is worth spending your life in prison for," Zachariah told him. His eyes traveled over to the hole Samson had made in the wall when he hurt his hand.

He followed his uncle's gaze. "I punched Trey too."

Hazel took his uninjured hand in hers. "Samson, hon, it's going to take some time, but your heart will heal and you'll be able to move on with your life."

"I'm furious with Savannah," he confessed. "But I still love her. She is my wife."

"Even though she wants to be with Trey?" asked Hazel.

"I know that, Auntie," he snapped. "I don't need you rubbing it in my face."

Zachariah sent him a warning glance. "Son, I know you're upset, but don't go taking it out on your aunt."

"You're right. I'm sorry, Auntie. I shouldn't be taking this out on you."

She stroked his cheek. "I know that you're in a terrible state right now."

"I'm angry. I feel like a fool for falling in love with Savannah. How could I be so stupid?"

"You weren't stupid," Zachariah told him. "You didn't destroy your marriage, and no one blames you."

"Forget about Savannah," Samson said angrily. "How could Trey do something like this to me?"

"That's what I'm not understanding," Zachariah said. "You and Trey have been like brothers."

Samson had never told his aunt and uncle how he came to meet Savannah. It was irrelevant as far as he was concerned.

I should have let Trey have you from the very beginning.

CHAPTER 17

*S*amson didn't hear from Savannah until the end of September when he was served with divorce papers at the church.

Zachariah entered his office and sat down beside him.

"She's divorcing me so that she can be with Trey," Samson announced. "My wife left me for my best friend. How clichéd is this?"

"I'm real sorry your marriage came to this, son."

"She didn't love me," Samson stated with a shrug. "I thought she did—she told me that she loved me. It wasn't in my head, Uncle."

Zachariah didn't say anything, choosing instead to let Samson vent his hurt and anger.

There was a soft knock on his door.

Samson was shocked to see Savannah. "What are you doing here?" he demanded. "Oh, that's right. You came to see my reaction to your little package. Yeah, I got the divorce papers today."

Zachariah rose to his feet. "I'll leave you two to talk."

Samson watched his uncle leave the office, closing the door behind him.

"My attorney called to tell me. That's why I came over." She paused for a moment, then said, "Samson, I had no idea they would be delivered today. I thought it wouldn't be for another week."

"And that would be a better time how?"

"Samson, it wasn't until I saw Trey again that I realized what it meant to truly be in love. I loved the idea of marriage and a family—it's what I wanted and I rushed down the aisle with you."

"Now you're rushing to divorce me."

"We never should've gotten married, and if you're honest with yourself, you'll agree."

"Your version and mine will never agree," Samson said, his tone chilly. "Yeah, we had some problems, but the truth is that you never really gave us a chance. Why not be honest and just say that, Savannah?"

"Because that's not what happened. Trey and I could've just had an affair, but we didn't want to do that to you. When we realized how we felt, we had to come to you."

Samson's dark eyes never left hers for a second. "Well, now you can leave."

"Samson, I don't want you to hate me."

"I don't care what you want," he snapped. "Just stay away from me."

Savannah nodded. "I'm sorry things turned out this way."

He sighed with exasperation. "I don't believe you, so please stop repeating that lie."

"Samson, please don't blame Trey," she said. "He feels bad about hurting you."

"I don't care how your lover feels, Savannah. I hate him as much as I hate you." She gasped at his anger.

He walked briskly to the door and opened it. "I have work to do."

Savannah rushed out of the office in tears, but Samson didn't care. He never wanted to see her again. He crossed the room in angry strides and sat down at his desk, massaging his temple.

An hour later, his aunt poked her head inside his office. "I just wanted to see if you were okay."

"I didn't know you were here."

"I got here about ten minutes ago. Hon, why don't you join your uncle and me for lunch?" she suggested, entering the office. "We're going to Pan Pan."

"I haven't been there in a while," he said.

"Then you should come with us."

Samson rose to his feet. "I think I will. The only good thing out of this divorce is that I don't have to eat all that vegetarian stuff anymore. I can enjoy my ribs, baked ham, or whatever without Savannah glaring at me."

Hazel chuckled.

Samson silently vowed to hurt Savannah the same way she had hurt him. He was going to make her pay for breaking his heart.

• • •

"Samson, wow. Long time, no see," a young woman said as she walked up to him in the parking lot of the Triangle Town Center Mall two months later.

He had been caught off guard by the sudden vibrancy of her voice but recovered when he realized who it was. "Hey," he murmured. "Kenya, how are you doing?"

She smiled. "I'm fine."

"I guess you heard what happened."

The tenderness in her expression amazed him. "I want you to know that I think my sister is making a huge mistake. I know you were a good husband to Savannah."

"I guess it really doesn't matter anymore," he responded with a shrug.

"So how are you really doing, Samson?"

"Actually, I'm fine. Just trying to get on with my life." He could barely keep his eyes off her; she was stunningly beautiful. At that moment, a plan formed in his mind. He knew just how to hurt Savannah.

"So what are you doing here at the mall?" Kenya asked. "Doing a little retail therapy?"

He chuckled. "I need to pick up a couple of suits, and then I'm thinking of grabbing a bite to eat."

"Hey, do you mind if I join you?"

The hungry way that she was eyeing him stroked Samson's bruised ego. "I have to warn you that I'm not exactly great company."

"That's okay. I'm not in the best of moods myself. My boyfriend and I split up. That's one of the reasons I came home this fall. I just needed to put some distance between us." She pointed toward the mall. "And do some retail therapy."

"How long have you been home?" Samson asked.

"Just a couple of days. I've applied to a couple of law schools, so I'm waiting to hear back. I'm planning on getting a job in the meantime."

"It's good to see you again."

Kenya broke into a grin. "I was just thinking the same thing about you."

His gaze met hers. "You know, I could use your help picking out some suits."

She looped her arm through his. "I'd be more than happy to do so. I'm a true fashionista."

Samson laughed, his eyes traveling from her face to her trendy shoes. "I can see that." It had been a couple of months since Samson had enjoyed the company of a woman, so Kenya was a welcoming sight.

In Saks Fifth Avenue, Kenya helped him pick out three suits. He tried them on and purchased all three.

"You looked so handsome in those suits, Samson," Kenya

told him after they'd left the store. "I'm glad you bought all three."

"Do you have time to have dinner with your former brother-in-law?"

"You bet," she responded with a grin. "I would love to."

They decided on the Twisted Fork.

When they were seated in the restaurant Kenya smiled at him. "This restaurant is a favorite of mine." She eyed him for a moment, and then said, "Samson, I don't like seeing you look so heartbroken."

"I really loved your sister, and Trey was my best friend. I'm so angry with them both right now. I don't know if I can ever forgive them."

"I would be angry too. Furious, actually."

"I was," he admitted. "But there's no point in staying angry. Besides, your sister and Trey are together and nothing's going to change that."

"You're a good man."

He chuckled and picked up his menu. "You don't know anything about me."

"I know that you were a great husband to my sister. I know that you love the Lord and that you didn't deserve what happened."

"Kenya, I really don't want to talk about this anymore. What's done is done."

"I'm sorry."

Samson laid down the menu. "I apologize for snapping at you like that."

She reached over and covered his hand with her own. "You have no reason to apologize. We're cool."

The waiter arrived, ready to take their orders. Kenya wasn't a vegetarian—she ordered baby back ribs for her entrée. Smiling, Samson ordered the same.

While they waited for their food, Kenya gave him an overview of her plans for the future.

"I thought you were going to be applying to med school," Samson stated.

"I was. But the truth is, I really like law."

"So you're going to be a lawyer like your sister."

"But I plan to specialize in criminal law," Kenya said.

He surveyed her for a moment. "I really can't see you as a criminal attorney. I would think you'd be more of a corporate attorney."

"I considered it, but I think criminal law is more challenging." Kenya sat back in her chair and studied him. "You look good, Samson."

He was about to return the compliment when their food arrived.

"Are you preaching tomorrow?" Kenya asked after they'd tucked in.

He nodded. "Why?"

"I was thinking about coming to Hillside."

Samson remembered that she had come a few times while he was married to Savannah.

"I always take away nuggets of knowledge whenever I hear you preach."

"Is that the only reason you come?" He was not one for playing games. He knew that Kenya was attracted to him.

"I like you, Samson. I'm sure you already know that."

He showed no reaction when he said, "Being subtle is not exactly a strong quality of yours."

Kenya met his gaze with her own. "How do you feel about that?"

"I'm flattered, but we can't forget I was married to your sister."

"She didn't want you, Samson. But I have always wanted you. From the first time I saw you. If you want to know the truth, it was torture for me to see you with Savannah."

"I'm not looking for a serious relationship. Just companionship."

Kenya leaned forward and said, "I don't want to rush you

into anything. I just . . . you asked, and so I wanted to be honest with you."

"I appreciate your honesty. Believe me, it's refreshing."

Samson's mind was busy at work. He knew that getting involved with Kenya would not make Savannah happy. She was very protective of her younger sister.

"Do you want to get out of here?" Kenya asked, drawing his attention back to her.

"What do you have in mind?" he asked, meeting her gaze.

"We can go back to your place and just get to know each other better."

Samson smiled. "I'll pay the bill."

Kenya followed him back to his town house.

As soon as they were inside, Samson's conscience got the better of him. "Kenya, I think that you should leave," he said quietly, his back to her. "This is wrong."

"I don't want to leave you."

He turned around to face her. "You're a nice girl. I don't want to hurt you."

"You won't," Kenya said. "We're just two people who need each other. There's nothing wrong about us coming together. My sister is the one who left, and she's the one who filed for the divorce."

Samson stiffened as though Kenya had struck him; he hated the constant reminder. But he couldn't resist Kenya. He pulled her into his arms, and his mouth covered hers hungrily. She moaned as his lips left hers to nibble at her earlobes.

He guided her into the bedroom and gently he eased her down onto the bed. Her dress crept up onto her thighs.

"You're sure about this?" Samson asked.

"I've been waiting for this moment a long time," she said huskily.

Samson felt a thread of remorse for his actions, but he didn't care. He wanted to hurt Savannah.

"This is wrong on so many levels, Kenya," he told her afterward.

"It doesn't feel wrong to me." She sat up in bed. "Samson, I'm in love with you and I've wanted to make love with you for a long time. I couldn't wait any longer."

He smiled. "You're great for my ego."

"I want this to mean a whole lot more to you."

It will, he thought. He could hardly wait to see Savannah's reaction when she found out he was seeing her baby sister.

CHAPTER 18

$\mathcal{K}$enya was in church on Sunday just as she promised. She sat in the second row to make sure Samson saw her.

He was thrilled to see her there, but he kept his distance. He didn't want his aunt getting even a whiff of what was going on between them. She and his uncle would not be happy to know he was sleeping with his former sister-in-law.

"Are you coming over for dinner?" Hazel inquired after the service ended.

"Not today," Samson answered. "Auntie, I'm going home and relaxing. It's been a long weekend for me."

"Oh, well okay, dear." She glanced over her shoulder, then back at him. "I was surprised to see Kenya this morning."

Samson tried to play it off. "We've always gotten along, so I'm not surprised."

Hazel surveyed his face. "Just don't forget who she is."

"What are you talking about? Kenya and I are just friends."

She looked around for her husband, then fussed, "Zachariah will stay here and talk to everyone in this church. He's been really tired lately. I need to get him home and force him to get some rest."

"Do you want me to go get him?"

Hazel shook her head. "I'll take care of it."

Samson kissed her on the cheek. "I'll give you a call during the week."

He drove home, full of happy anticipation.

• • •

"I brought dinner," Kenya announced when she arrived at his home an hour later. "I thought we might need some nourishment to keep up our strength."

"Really?"

She slipped into his arms. "I can't help it. I find you incredibly sexy."

He kissed her long and hard, then picked her up and carried her to the bedroom. They would eat dinner later.

• • •

"Are you sure you're ready to do this, Samson?" Kenya asked with a tinge of doubt. "We don't have to go to this Christmas party. I'm pretty sure Savannah and Trey will be there. Personally, I can do without the drama."

They had been seeing each other for five weeks, and to his knowledge, no one knew about their relationship. He replied calmly, "Just because my marriage to Savannah didn't work out doesn't mean we can't be friends, right?" Samson wanted his ex-wife to see that he had moved on, with her sister. It would kill her.

"I'm okay with it if you are," Kenya said.

"Well, what's wrong with two friends going out together on a Friday night? Savannah is dating my best friend, and everybody seems to be okay with that. The way I see it, there shouldn't be a problem with me going to a party with my former sister-in-law."

She scrutinized his face, not believing him. "You know that my sister is not going to be happy about us. I can handle her, though."

"I don't care how Savannah feels," Samson stated flatly. "She has no say in my relationship with you."

"Savannah certainly can't make any decisions for me."

He smiled. "Now, that's exactly what I want to hear."

Samson couldn't wait for Savannah to see him with Kenya. She was going to freak.

The thought made him grin from ear to ear.

He dressed in the black suit Kenya had picked out, then stood in front of the mirror admiring his reflection. He still couldn't believe that Savannah had actually chosen Trey over him.

An hour later, Samson and Kenya made their grand entrance.

Savannah came over almost immediately. "Kenya, I didn't think you were coming to the party," she said. Her eyes traveled to Samson. "It's good to see you out and about, Samson."

"I haven't been sitting home, if that's what you think," Samson replied nastily.

"Hey, bro," Trey said.

Samson ignored him. "Kenya, would you like something to drink?"

"Sparkling water with lime," she answered.

Savannah lifted her head. "Did you two come here together?"

"What does it matter?" Kenya asked her sister. "Aren't you here with the man you love? You and Samson are no longer together."

Savannah was speechless over Kenya's outburst, while Samson was secretly pleased. She glanced over at Trey, who was staring at Samson in disbelief.

"Samson, can I talk to you for a moment?" he asked.

"Trey, we have nothing to talk about." Samson walked away to get drinks for himself and Kenya.

When he returned, Kenya was alone. "Well, that went okay, I thought." She broke into a nervous chuckle. "Actually, that was awkward."

"I didn't think so," Samson assured her. He was well aware that Trey and Savannah were watching them from across the room. His ex-wife was visibly upset, which pleased him.

The next day, Savannah burst through Samson's front door like a blast of cold air. He'd expected to hear from her, although he hadn't expected to see her so soon.

"You're sleeping with my sister!" she shouted. "How could you do this to me?"

"Easily. Especially after the way you betrayed me. Besides, Kenya's been after me from the moment she first laid eyes on me. I just didn't buy into the opportunity out of respect for *my loving wife*." Samson downed the last of his iced tea.

"I never thought you could be so cruel."

He raised his gaze to meet hers. "I wasn't the one who violated our marriage bed, Savannah. You had no problems with the fact that Trey was my best friend. Clearly you weren't worried about boundaries, so why should I be?"

"You put me on a pedestal, Samson," she countered. "I told you I wasn't perfect. We can't help who we fall in love with."

He shot back, "I didn't want a perfect wife—just a faithful one."

"I'm really sorry for hurting you the way that I did, but why did you have to bring Kenya into this? She's my sister."

"I'm well aware of the relationship. I just don't care."

"Do you hate me this much?" Savannah asked. "You are only using Kenya to get back at me, but she thinks that you're in love with her."

He chuckled. "I never said that."

"What did you tell her?"

Samson wasn't putting up with her bullying any longer. "Savannah, I don't owe you any answers. You destroyed our marriage by sleeping with Trey. Our marriage is over and I am moving on with my life. I would think you'd want to do the same. Why don't you go meditate on it or something?"

Her nostrils flared with anger. "I don't want to see my sister with a broken heart. She does not deserve to pay for my sins. Trey and I—we fell in love. I don't know when or how it happened, but it did. He and I have more in common than you and I. He's even studying to become a Buddhist."

Samson was about to release a string of profanities, but contained his feelings before the words left his mouth. He strode to the front door, opened it, and said, "Get out of my house, Savannah."

"We're not d-done talking," she sputtered.

"Oh, we're done. You're not my wife anymore, so stay out of my life."

"Leave Kenya alone and you don't have to worry about seeing me again." She came closer, trying to be reasonable. "Samson, I'm truly sorry for hurting you. I hate seeing you like this—it's not the real you."

"How would you know?"

"I truly hope that one day you will find a nice Christian woman to settle down with. You deserve that and more."

"I don't need your hope." Samson broke into a grin. "*I have Kenya.*"

"Please leave her out of this," Savannah pleaded.

"Please leave *period*. I'm getting bored with this conversation."

"Samson—"

He cut her off by saying, "Good-bye. Savannah, do me a favor and don't ever come back to my house. In fact, that reminds me. Give me the key right now."

"Fine," Savannah said. "Have a wonderful life, Samson. Just please leave my sister alone."

"Oh, I will, when I'm finished with her."

CHAPTER 19

Samson continued to see Kenya over the next week, and she started pushing him to commit to her and take their relationship public now that her sister knew about them.

"I'm not ready for that," he continued to tell her.

He enjoyed her company, but now that he had accomplished what he'd set out to do, Samson decided it was time to end things with Kenya. He had no further use for her.

The sound of the doorbell pulled him away from his thoughts. Samson got up and walked across the room to see who his visitor was.

"Kenya, what are you doing here?" Samson didn't like the way she'd just showed up at his town house without calling. He would be leaving in a few minutes to help set up tables for the Christmas dinner being held the next day. Every year at this time, Hillside opened its doors to feed the homeless.

It was definitely time to put an end to their relationship.

"I'm sorry for just showing up like this," Kenya blurted out. "But I really need to talk to you."

"I have to be at the church to help set up for tomorrow. Can this wait until later?"

"This won't take long," she said in a choked voice.

He could tell she was upset. "If this is about your sister's little visit—"

Kenya interrupted him by saying, "I've told her to mind her own business. This is my life."

"I don't care what your sister thinks. Look, Kenya, we can discuss this later. Why don't you meet me here around seven? I'll make dinner."

"Samson . . ."

"Honey, I really have to be at the church tonight."

She released a long sigh. "Okay. I'll see you at seven. Waiting another five hours won't change anything."

Samson could tell that she was really bothered about something, but it would just have to wait. Maybe she had come to the same conclusion that they needed to go their separate ways. It would certainly make things easier.

Kenya crossed his mind a couple of times while he was setting up for the dinner. Samson couldn't shake the feeling that something was seriously wrong. He just couldn't figure out what it could be.

After he finished at the church, Samson went home and began cooking. He had planned a nice meal for them. They would eat, and then talk.

Kenya arrived a few minutes after seven.

"Dinner's almost ready," he told her.

She nodded, but couldn't get any words out.

"You okay?" Samson asked.

"I'm fine."

When they settled down at the table to eat, Samson asked, "Now, what was so important that you had to come running over here?"

"Savannah keeps saying that you're not in love with me." Kenya laid her fork across her plate. "Is she right?"

Samson wiped his mouth with the edge of his napkin. "I

care for you, Kenya, but it's not what I would call love. I've had enough of that particular emotion."

"What Savannah did was wrong, and I know she hurt you terribly, but you don't have to give up on love."

"We don't need to rehash this. Frankly, I'm tired of discussing Savannah."

A flash of hurt crossed her face. "That's not what I needed to discuss with you. However, I wanted to know where you were with your feelings for me, or lack thereof, before I said anything else."

Samson eyed Kenya, waiting for her to continue. She took a deep breath and exhaled slowly.

"Are you okay?" he asked again.

Kenya nodded. "I had a doctor's appointment earlier today. I thought that I had some type of virus—I'd been sick for the past couple of weeks."

"Well, what did the doctor say?"

"Samson, I found out that I don't have a virus. I've been sick because I'm pregnant."

Kenya's words hit him like a bag of bricks. "Okaay," he said. Samson pushed away from the dinner table and stood up. "I'm not sure what you want me to say."

She had a fragile look on her face. "How do you feel about it?"

Samson met her gaze. "*What?* Are you trying to say that this baby is mine?" He didn't wait for her answer. "Oh no, I don't think so, because we used protection each time. You were probably pregnant and didn't know it before you left D.C. Kenya, you're not going to pin some other man's child on me."

"I resent the fact that you would even think I'd do something like that. I don't know what kind of girl you think that I am, but—"

"How about we start with the kind of girl who was flirting with and eyeing her sister's husband the entire time they were married? Or one that didn't have a problem sleeping with a pastor. Kenya, I know my wrongs and I admit them freely, but here you are trying to play the sainted virgin."

Her eyes grew wet with tears. "My last relationship ended three months ago. Samson, I've been in love with you all this time. That's the only reason I had sex with you, and I told you that. I thought that you might one day feel the same way about me, but I see that I was wrong." Kenya wiped her tears away with the back of her hand. "Samson, I'm carrying your child. I know you don't believe me, but I'm willing to have a DNA test to prove it. I don't want anything from you. I just thought you might want to have a role in this baby's life."

Samson was not thrilled about the possibility of Kenya carrying his child. "When is your due date?" he asked cautiously.

"In August," she responded. "August twenty-fourth."

He couldn't imagine what his aunt and uncle, not to mention the entire church body, would say when this got out. "How did you let this happen?" Samson demanded. "You assured me that you were on birth control. And we used condoms."

"Except that one time," Kenya reminded him. "A month ago, remember? I guess you forgot that I told you I had to stop taking the pills. We didn't use a condom, but you told me not to worry, because I guess you thought I was still on the pill."

Samson recalled the conversation. "I guess you've decided to keep the baby, then."

Kenya lifted her chin defiantly. "Having an abortion never once entered my mind. I would imagine that you would oppose abortions."

"How is it going to look with me being a pastor and having an illegitimate child on the way?"

"It makes you human and flawed." She folded her arms across her chest. "Besides, you're always saying how you don't care what people think."

Samson didn't care, except when it came to his aunt and uncle. The news would kill them. He was the assistant pastor of Hillside Baptist Church—the very church that his uncle had founded. He was not willing to scandalize the church.

"I need some time to digest this news," he told her.

Kenya nodded in understanding. "Take all the time you need."

"What about school? You just applied to law school. How are you going to study and raise a baby?"

"I'll do what I have to do. If I have to put off school for a year, I'll do that. I'm having this baby."

He could not believe his bad luck. "I have to wrap my head around this, Kenya, so I hope you'll keep this just between us for now."

"I won't tell a soul, not even my sister. I'm pretty sure my mom suspects that I'm pregnant, but she hasn't said anything to me. Just so that you know, I didn't set out to trap you."

"So you're not expecting a marriage proposal?"

Kenya met his gaze. "To be honest, I would love to be your wife, but I know you're not ready for that. I would like for us to raise this child together—even a marriage of convenience would be an alternative to having a baby without a father."

He agreed in principle, but this was reality. "Thank you for being honest, Kenya."

She pushed away from the table, saying, "Call me when you're ready to discuss this further."

He walked her to the door. "I'll give you a call in a few days."

When Kenya left, Samson sank down on his living room sofa. What in the world was he supposed to do now?

• • •

Two days passed and Samson still had no idea what he was going to do about Kenya and the baby. Although she claimed to be willing to settle, he knew better. He didn't want to be trapped in a loveless marriage.

His heartbreak over Savannah had caused him to make some bad choices. Now the consequences he faced could not only hurt him but his aunt and uncle as well.

He met with Kenya.

"I wasn't sure I'd be hearing from you," she told him. "I know this is not something you planned for."

"Kenya, I care for you, but as you know, I'm not in love with you."

She nodded, looking very vulnerable.

"I know you want to keep this child, but the truth is, I'm not ready to have children."

A tear rolled down her cheek.

"I'm sorry, sweetheart. I know what I'm saying hurts you, but I want to be honest with you."

"So what am I supposed to do?"

"I thought about what you said about a marriage of convenience. I've given it a lot of thought and I guess that's what we'll have to do."

Kenya blinked in surprise. "Are you telling me you're going to marry me?"

"It's either that, or I'm leaving Raleigh, but I'll pay for your medical care and provide for the child. If you choose marriage, then I need you to understand that it's in name only. Once the baby is born, we'll see where we go from there. No matter what happens, I will provide for the child."

"You're going to marry me just to give our child your name."

He nodded. "It was your idea, Kenya."

"I know," she said. "That's fine. So when do we get married?"

"We can do it in a quiet civil ceremony as soon as my divorce is final." He scanned her face for signs of a response. "I thought you'd look happier."

"I guess I would be happier if I didn't feel that you're ashamed of me."

"I'm not ashamed of you, Kenya. I just prefer that we keep this matter between us, as I am a minister and this goes against everything I preach about. I know . . . I'm a hypocrite, but I don't want my hypocrisy to affect my uncle's ministry or the church." She remained silent, so he pressed her. "I need to know if we're in agreement in this. Are we?"

She stood up. "Well, I guess we're getting married." Kenya snatched up her purse and headed toward the door. "Even though our marriage will be in name only, I'm going to be a good wife to you."

"I believe you."

Samson followed her out to the car. He wrapped his arms around her and whispered, "Everything is going to be okay. You will want for nothing."

She wiped away a tear. "I only want you, Samson. I don't want your money."

"Please don't cry," he said, wiping her cheeks. She lifted her lips to his and kissed him. Samson instantly pulled away from her. "I still have an image to uphold," he whispered. "Some of the church members live in this area."

Kenya smiled and nodded. "If you want to have some type of legal agreement drawn up, that's fine with me."

"I will make sure you and the baby are well provided for," he told her.

"Just take care of this child. I don't need anything."

When she left, Samson got into his car and drove to his aunt and uncle's house. His divorce would be final in the next couple of weeks, so he wanted to prepare them for what was about to take place.

Hazel glanced up from her sewing when he entered the family room. "Hey, son. I thought I heard someone come through the front door. I thought it was Zachariah."

"How are you, Auntie?"

"I'm fine." She noticed the anxious look on his face. "But you look a little troubled."

"I need to talk to you and Uncle." Samson sat down on the sofa. "Is he here?"

Hazel nodded. "He's somewhere around this house."

"Who's looking for me?" Zachariah asked, strolling into the room. He paused to place his hand on Hazel's shoulder.

She reached up, giving it a loving squeeze. "Samson wants to talk to us."

Samson inhaled and then exhaled slowly.

Zachariah sat down on the sofa beside him. "What's going on, son?"

"I know that you're not going to like this, but I've been seeing Kenya."

"Savannah's sister?" his uncle asked.

Samson nodded.

Hazel didn't say a word, which wasn't like her at all.

"Anyway, we just found out that she's pregnant. She's carrying my child." He glanced in Hazel's direction, but she still didn't open her mouth. She simply looked at her husband.

"Auntie," Samson prompted. Her silence unnerved him.

"What do you want me to say?" Hazel said after a moment.

"I am still a man of God, Auntie, but I'm also a man with needs—needs in my weakest state that betrayed me. I never meant to get involved with Kenya," he lied. "She's Savannah's sister."

"I would think you would've had enough of that family," his uncle muttered.

Hazel shook her head in despair. "Samson, I honestly don't know what to say."

"That's why I made a decision," Samson said. "Kenya and I are going to get married as soon as my divorce is final."

Zachariah rose to his feet, clearly unhappy. "It sounds like you've made up your mind."

Samson met his uncle's gaze. "I have. I can't change the

past, but I can try and do the right thing for the future. I was angry. That's why I got involved with Kenya," he confessed. "I wanted to hurt Savannah."

His aunt gave a slight nod. "I figured as much."

"I was wrong to have involved Kenya in my plot for revenge. I wasn't thinking clearly, Auntie. I was so blinded by my anger, I just didn't care."

"And now?" Zachariah asked.

"We're getting married."

"Do you love her, son?" Hazel asked.

Samson shook his head. "I don't love her, Auntie. She's a nice girl and I've been honest with her. I know you and Uncle are disappointed, and I'm real sorry for that."

"Son, we love you," Zachariah said kindly. "We applaud you for trying to do the right thing by Kenya."

Samson nodded. "I'm going to straighten out my life, Uncle." He cared what Zachariah thought of him, and it saddened Samson to the core to see the look of disenchantment in his uncle's eyes.

This is all Trey and Savannah's fault, he silently raged.

CHAPTER 20

*S*amson and Kenya were married three weeks later. Her parents and his aunt and uncle served as witnesses to the civil ceremony.

Kenya looked beautiful in the ivory suit she was wearing. Her eyes filled with tears when he placed a platinum-and-diamond wedding band on her left ring finger. He couldn't ever remember seeing her look so happy.

Afterward, Hazel embraced her, saying, "Welcome to the family."

"Thank you, Mrs. Taylor."

She hugged Samson next, while Zachariah chatted with Kenya. Kenya's parents glared at Samson, but he didn't let it bother him.

On their way out of the courthouse, they were met by Savannah and Trey. Samson plastered on a smile before remarking, "Are you two here to get hitched?"

"No," Savannah answered, staring down her sister. "We came to see if it was true."

He wrapped an arm around Kenya. "We're married."

Samson thought he detected a flash of pain in Savannah's eyes, but when he blinked, it was gone.

"Congratulations," Savannah managed to get out. "I hope that you two will be very happy together."

"Do you really?" Samson asked with thinly veiled mockery.

"Samson, don't," Hazel told him.

Trey approached him. "Congrats, bro."

Samson glanced over at his aunt and uncle before turning back to face Trey. "Thanks," he muttered.

Kenya hugged her sister and then told Samson, "Why don't we get out of here?"

He nodded in agreement. Samson was more than ready to get away from his in-laws and ex-wife.

"Are you okay?" Kenya asked when they arrived home. "You were really quiet during the drive here."

Samson covered her mouth with his. She matched him kiss for kiss. When they parted, Kenya murmured, "Wow . . ."

He led her over to the sofa. "This is a marriage of convenience, Kenya. It's important that you remember that."

She was taken aback.

"We shouldn't confuse this with intimacy."

"What are you saying to me, Samson?"

"We're not going to be sharing a bed. I don't want to hurt you, so it's best that we abstain from sex."

"I see," she said quietly.

"I'm not saying that it's going to be this way forever. Who knows, Kenya . . . I may fall in love with you, but there's also a chance that we won't be able to stand each other by the time the baby's born."

She wiped away a tear. "I'm going to be a good wife to you."

"And I'll be a good husband to you."

He gave her the master bedroom, so she went to unpack, leaving Samson to ponder what his life would be like over the course of the next seven months.

• • •

Kenya was a wonderful cook, and she treated him like he was the only man in the world. She was in church every Sunday, being the dutiful pastor's wife—even his aunt and uncle were impressed. Things were going well between them. However, Samson was struggling with his determination to stay out of Kenya's bed.

Deep down, Samson wanted to be a better person. The fear of traveling down the same road as his father continued to haunt him.

"Father God, I need your help with this," he whispered. "I know what you have called me to do, but it's hard when I have all these women pulling at me. I married Savannah and I was happy, but she didn't want me. I married Kenya because she is carrying my child. She's in love with me, but I don't feel the same way about her. What do I do now? If we make love, I feel like it will only hurt her more if things between us don't work out the way Kenya wants."

When Kenya appeared in the doorway of his home office, Samson ended his prayer. "I thought you were taking a nap," he said with a hitch in his voice.

"I've been up for a while." Kenya patted her belly. "We're hungry, so I made a chef's salad. I came to see if you wanted to join us for a late lunch."

Samson smiled at her. "I'd love to," he said, rising to his feet.

Kenya waited for him at the door. Samson took her by the hand. "You've been amazing, sweetheart."

"It's because I love you, Samson."

He didn't respond, but he slipped his arm around her.

• • •

He made an earnest effort to be faithful in his marriage, but women were still a weakness for him. He was a man and he had needs. During the two months that they had been married, Kenya had tried to get him to make love to her on numerous occasions, but Samson held his ground that the marriage would be in name only. It was because he cared for her that he no longer wanted to use her for his own selfish needs. She was going to be the mother of his child and she deserved better.

Yet his celibacy vanished all in a few hours.

He was in the grocery store when a young woman approached him. She was a real estate broker and worked in the office with the agent who had assisted him in buying his town house.

They went to dinner afterward, and then back to her place. Before Samson realized what was happening, she had him in her bed.

When he arrived home a couple of hours later and found Kenya asleep on the sofa, he was filled with guilt. He thought about what had transpired earlier and silently added *I needed some relief from the sexual tension that seems to consume me most days.*

He bent down and gently shook Kenya. "Wake up, baby. Why don't you go get into bed?"

Kenya opened her eyes. "I was waiting for you to get home." She sat up and yawned. "Oh, I'm sorry."

He chuckled. "It's fine. You've been running around here like a madwoman. Kenya, I don't expect you to clean up this place—we can hire a maid. Baby, you're pregnant."

Kenya eyed him. "I'm more than capable of keeping the house clean and carrying your child."

"But you're tired all the time."

She smiled. "I love that you care, but I'm okay."

Samson felt uneasy beneath the warmth of her loving gaze. For a second, he wished he could return her love.

• • •

"Samson, I'm not a fool," Kenya snapped two days later. "I know that you've been seeing someone."

"What are you talking about?" he asked, trying to figure out if she'd found out about his indiscretion or if she was just fishing.

Kenya sank down in a nearby chair. "I thought we were going to be honest with each other. You agreed that we were going to be faithful during the marriage." She shook her head sadly. "I know you don't love me, but I thought you were a much better man than this."

"I'm not seeing anyone, Kenya."

"Are you really going to sit here and lie to me?" She folded her arms across her chest. "Samson, have more respect for me than that."

From the hurt expression on her face, Samson knew that she had found out something. He sighed, then said, "You're right. I do owe you more than that." He lifted his eyes to meet her gaze. "I'm not having an affair, but I did sleep with someone. It was a moment of weakness—a one-night stand."

Her large almond-shaped eyes filled with unshed tears.

"I haven't seen her since."

"That's not the way she made it sound."

Samson's mouth dropped open in astonishment. "How . . ."

"I ran into her at the hair salon and she was in there bragging about this hot pastor she was involved with. She described you to a tee." Kenya wiped away a tear that had rolled down her cheek.

"I'm sorry," Samson said. "Believe me, I know just how empty my apology sounds."

She started trembling uncontrollably. "I can't live this way."

"Kenya, I made a big mistake."

She looked at him. "You don't get it, do you? I love you and I've been nothing less than a good wife. I went into this marriage knowing that you didn't love me, but I thought you would at least keep up your end of the agreement."

"You have every right to be angry," he said, hanging his head.

"I don't need you to tell me that," she snapped in frustration. "Samson, I need you to be totally honest with me. Can you be faithful to me while we are married?"

"I don't know," Samson replied quietly. "I'm just not sure. I have needs and while I try to ignore them . . ."

She was sobbing now. "If it's sex you want, why won't you make love to me?"

"I want you," he said earnestly, "believe me, but I don't want to hurt you like that."

"Why can't we try to have a real marriage?"

Samson got up and sat down beside her. He had to tell her the truth. "When we got together, it was because I wanted to hurt your sister. You were a means for me to hurt Savannah. I've grown to care for you as the mother of my child, but I don't love you. Can you sit here and tell me that you want to be with a man who used you to hurt his ex-wife?"

Her shock turned to anger. "This was all about Savannah? You never . . ."

"I do care for you," Samson said, raising his head, "but only as a friend. But now . . . things are good between us—better than I ever expected. I don't know. Maybe there is a chance for us to build a real marriage, but are you willing to stay with me now that you know everything?"

He could tell that he'd deeply wounded her. Kenya removed the wedding ring and handed it to Samson. "I'm filing for an annulment in the morning. This farce of a marriage is over. I knew you didn't love me. I knew you weren't really into the marriage, but I thought that once we were together . . ." Her voice died.

"Kenya, I felt you deserved the truth."

"When we first got together I really thought you were into me. I never considered that you were just using me to hurt my sister." She stood up slowly. "Thanks for being honest. I'll be out of your home by the time you come back tomorrow."

"I will make sure you and the baby—"

Kenya cut him off. "I don't want anything from you. I will take care of my child. When I leave here tomorrow, I don't ever want to see you again."

Samson protested weakly, "The child is also mine."

"And? It's not like you really want him or her," Kenya spat. "Do me a favor and just let us go. Please." She rushed out of the room and into the master bedroom.

Samson thought of going after her, but decided against it. Kenya had been good to him and he'd just broken her heart. She hadn't deserved to be a pawn in his game of revenge. Now he was paying the consequences. Now he was losing her and his child.

He put his face in his hands and cried.

• • •

Kenya was true to her word.

When Samson came home the next day, she was gone. The house felt cold and lonely without her, but he refused to dwell on it. "It's for the best," he whispered.

In a little over a year, he had married two women. He was divorced and his second marriage was going to be annulled.

"Well, Dad, I think I might have you beat," he murmured.

Samson considered calling Kenya, but didn't think it was a wise thing to do. She was very emotional right now and hurting. He didn't want to make it worse or upset her to the point of putting his unborn child in danger.

He avoided telling his aunt and uncle anything for the rest of the week. But on the following Sunday, when Kenya didn't appear at church, his aunt cornered him after the service.

"Where's your wife?"

"Gone," he responded.

Hazel led him into his uncle's office. "Do you feel like talking about it?"

"I messed up again," Samson announced as he sat down on the leather sofa. "I cheated on her and she found out. We talked about it and I ended up telling her the truth—that I got with her only to hurt Savannah."

"Oh my goodness," Hazel murmured. "She loves you so much."

"I know, but she deserved the truth. Anyway, she left me and she's filed for an annulment. Our marriage was never consummated."

His uncle joined them and Hazel gave him a quick recap of what happened.

"I'm sorry, Uncle."

Zachariah remained silent, absorbing all he had been told. Finally, he said, "Son, I don't think you need to be in the pulpit ministering—you need to be ministered to, so I want you to step down for a couple of months. We'll tell everyone that you're taking a sabbatical."

Feeling numb, Samson gave a slight nod.

"There's a wonderful place in Florida called Beside Still Waters," Zachariah said. "I think it'll be a good place for you to rest and refocus. I'll call and make arrangements for you to spend some time there."

"It'll do you good," Hazel contributed.

Samson released a long sigh of resignation. "All I know is that I'm tired, Auntie. I can't keep living like this."

CHAPTER 21

*A*s it turned out, his retreat was cut short.

"Samson, I need you to come home," Hazel said two weeks before he was scheduled to leave Florida. "Zachariah has been diagnosed with prostate cancer."

"What?" Samson said in shock.

"While he's fighting that disease, we need you to minister to the congregation. They are going to need a leader."

He asked her all about the diagnosis and what it meant, and she answered all his questions. He was saddened by the news, but he decided that the call had come at exactly the right time. He'd been in Florida for a full week, enough time alone. He missed his aunt and uncle and was anxious to return to the pulpit.

"I'll take the next flight home," he said.

"I hate pulling you away from your sabbatical."

"You and Uncle come first," Samson told her.

After hanging up, Samson made an airline reservation, and then he packed up and prepared to leave.

Samson vowed to be a better man now that he had been

given a second chance. He was returning to Raleigh, and he was going to make his uncle proud. He was not going to make the same mistakes as before.

Samson returned to Raleigh early the next morning and drove to his aunt and uncle's house. Hazel met him at the door. "I'm so glad to see you, hon."

"I'm glad to be home. How's Uncle?"

"He's as well as can be expected. He's in good spirits and he never complains. He's sleeping right now, but I expect him to be getting up shortly."

Samson followed his aunt into the kitchen.

"I was just about to make some breakfast. Are you hungry?"

He grinned at his aunt. "Starving."

She began pulling out pots and pans.

"Have you spoken to Kenya?" he inquired.

"She left for California on Sunday afternoon," Hazel announced. "She's going to law school out there right after she has the baby."

"Good for her," Samson murmured.

"Trey and Savannah got married on Saturday," Hazel added.

Samson tried to keep his face void of emotion. "Yeah, I heard. I ran into one of Trey's cousins at the library." He had stopped in to find books on prostate cancer and treatment options before heading home.

"Auntie, how is Uncle really dealing with the diagnosis?" he asked, changing the subject.

She released a short sigh. "You know how Zachariah is when it comes to that. He says that there's healing on this side and on the other. Either way, he will be healed. He says that he's lived a good life and he's ready when the time comes for him to leave this place." Hazel's eyes filled with tears. "Me, I'm feeling a bit selfish. I want him with me."

Samson rushed to comfort her. "He's like a father to me. I've already lost one and I don't want to lose another, Auntie.

I know that sounds pretty selfish, but it's the way I feel. I can't picture the rest of my life without Uncle."

"God is a healer and we're going to just hold on to His word. I thank Him that Zachariah is responding to the hormone therapy. The tumor has shrunk some, so that's a good sign."

Samson nodded. The thought crossed his mind that maybe his uncle was suffering because of his sins.

Hazel's voice pulled him out of his reverie. "Zachariah is counting on you, Samson. Lorne stepped down from the ministry after his divorce, so we don't have anyone right now to take over except you. Joseph does a great job with the youth ministry, and Cal has been preaching for the last two Sundays."

"I'm ready to step in," Samson stated. "Wherever I'm needed."

"We're so thrilled to have you back home," Hazel said.

Samson crossed the room in quick strides and embraced his aunt. "I can't tell you what it means to me. You and Uncle have always been here for me. I don't want you to worry about anything. I'll even move in if you need me to help with Uncle."

She waved off his suggestion. "Samson, we know how much you value your privacy. I'll be fine and you're not that far away."

While his aunt finished cooking breakfast, Samson took his suitcase up to his old room and changed into a pair of sweats.

He strode into the master bedroom, where he found his uncle sitting up and reading the Bible. "What are you studying?" he asked.

"I was reading Leviticus."

"The book of sacrifices," Samson murmured.

"God impressed upon my spirit that we cannot fully understand the inheritance He has provided if we do not understand Leviticus. I don't think I've ever preached from this particular book in the Bible."

"Not many preachers have, Uncle. I guess they don't think the members want to hear about all the offerings and sacrifices."

"I think that the next time I preach, I'll be coming from Leviticus," Zachariah said. "I think I need to talk about the purpose of blood sacrifices in the Old Testament, and Christ shedding blood for our sins in the New Testament."

Struck by the parallel, Samson nodded in agreement.

"Son, God has placed it on my heart that we need to really teach the Word. The time has passed for recycled sermons. We need to really delve into the Bible and instruct the congregation to do so for themselves. They look to us for guidance, but what are we really teaching them? If we are doing our jobs, then why are so many people still bound? In the face of trials and tribulations we fall apart."

"You've really given this a lot of thought," Samson said. "What brought this on?"

"As the leader of a church, God will hold me to a higher standard. I have to give an account for my actions."

Samson silently considered his uncle's words.

"When I'm gone, you will become the senior pastor, son. Teach them, don't just stand up there in that pulpit and preach. Preaching doesn't empower people, but teaching equips them with the tools they need to weather the storms of life."

"I hear you, Uncle."

"Breakfast is ready," Hazel announced from the doorway. "Hon, you feel like joining us at the table?"

Zachariah nodded briskly. "Today is a good day. I feel stronger than I've felt in a long time."

CHAPTER 22

One month back in the pulpit, Samson was contacted about being a keynote speaker for a youth luncheon. Initially, he considered turning the offer down but decided to meet with the coordinator in person before making a decision.

They arranged to meet for lunch the next day.

Samson was the first to arrive. He had just been seated when Trey and Savannah entered the restaurant.

He breathed a sigh of relief when they didn't notice him and were seated on the other side of the restaurant. He didn't want to be anywhere near the *happy* couple.

A young woman entered the restaurant looking like a million dollars. From where he sat, Samson could see the huge rock on her left hand. She could be none other than Delinda Lewis-Hatcher, wife of NBA superstar Bobby Hatcher and the woman he was having lunch with.

She walked straight to the table. "Pastor Taylor, I'm Delinda Lewis-Hatcher. I apologize for being late."

He smiled. "It's nice to meet you, Miss Hatcher."

"It's Mrs. Lewis-Hatcher," she corrected.

"Thanks so much for agreeing to meet with me," she said, pulling out a leather notepad. "As I told you on the phone, I'm coordinating a youth event and would like you to be our keynote speaker." Delinda gave him a brief overview of her organization. "Hatcher Youth Foundation is an organization that serves an alienated, marginalized community of young men and women in North Carolina. We work to equip youth through building self-esteem, and through inspiring and mentoring programs." Then the waiter arrived to take their order.

Samson was entranced by her beauty and easy smile. She was even more beautiful than Savannah.

"So, I'm hoping you will say yes," she was saying.

"I'd be honored," Samson told her. "Thank you for considering me."

When their food arrived, Samson blessed their meals, then said, "How did you hear about me?"

"I heard you preach in Las Vegas, and when my husband signed with the NBA, we went to Hillside a few times. You were away then."

He wiped his mouth on the edge of the napkin. "Well, you two should come back."

Delinda smiled prettily. "We will."

Samson studied her expressions as they talked. There was a spark of interest between them. He felt it and was positive that Delinda felt it too.

She's a married woman, he reminded himself. He was not about to travel down that road.

Delinda went over the speaker contract with Samson before he signed it. She paid for lunch although he offered to take care of the bill.

"I invited you," Delinda told him.

"I'll agree to this only if you allow me to pick up the tab the next time," he said.

As they walked out of the restaurant together, Samson felt

the hair on the back of his neck stand up. He looked over his shoulder and found Trey and Savannah behind him.

"Hello, Samson," Trey said. "I didn't know you were back in town."

Savannah glared at him.

Samson looked them both up and down and then shook his head. He rushed out after Delinda.

He watched Delinda as she made her way across the parking lot and into a brand-new BMW 750iL. She was classy all the way. Samson was looking forward to seeing her again.

• • •

"Make God your one and only God, and everything will be plain and simple," Samson said to an audience of three hundred teens, ranging from thirteen to eighteen years old.

"Let's start with money," he told them. "Yeah, you have to work. After all, those nice clothes you're wearing, food, and life necessities cost money. You have to have money to survive in this world, right? I would agree for the most part. But examine your life. Is money a god for you?"

Samson paused for a moment before moving on. "Next item on the list is dating. Yeah, we all get crushes. As a teen, you've probably experienced your first real love. It's fantastic, isn't it? But God wants you to save yourselves for the person you marry."

"Thanks so much for agreeing to speak to the teens," Delinda told him afterward. "They really enjoyed listening to you, Pastor Taylor."

"Please call me Samson. It was my pleasure. We have to pour our wisdom into our youth. That's been a mission of mine since I started preaching."

Her cell phone rang. "Excuse me, please. It's my husband."

Samson gave a slight nod, wishing that Delinda had just let

the call go to voice mail. He was extremely attracted to her, and it bothered him that she was married. Her words caught his attention: "Bobby, I understand that, but we were supposed to have dinner together. I thought you were coming home this afternoon. I miss you and I want you to come home."

Samson could tell Delinda was upset by her husband's sudden change of plans. He turned away so she couldn't tell that he was listening to her conversation.

"I'm sorry about that," Delinda said at last, putting her phone away. "My husband's plans have changed and he's not coming home today."

"Are you okay?" Samson inquired.

She was still stewing. "Just disappointed. I wanted to try out this new restaurant . . . I hate eating out alone."

"Why don't you and I go?" Samson suggested. "I was just trying to decide where to eat dinner anyway. I was getting bored with the same old places, so I'm in the mood for something new."

"Samson, you don't have to do this. I'll grab something on the way home."

"I'm serious. Look, I'm hungry and I'm not a big fan of eating out alone, either. Think of it as you doing me a huge favor."

She considered it for a moment, then consented. "I'll follow you in my car."

He smiled. "Great."

When Samson got in his car, he was smiling. What man in his right mind would treat his wife that way? Bobby Hatcher didn't deserve Delinda. That thought got on him the entire way over to the restaurant.

In the restaurant parking lot Delinda parked beside him and got out of her car.

"You okay?" he asked.

She nodded.

"No, you're not," Samson said. "You look a little nervous. What's wrong?"

She glanced around. "I'm not sure I should be here with you."

"You just had lunch with me a couple of weeks ago. Delinda, there's nothing wrong with two people having dinner together. We haven't done anything wrong."

"I know that. It's just that Bobby—"

Samson interrupted her. "It's just dinner."

Delinda allowed a pained smile. "You're right. I don't know why I'm overreacting like this."

They went into the restaurant and were immediately seated.

"How long have you been married?" Samson inquired while they were waiting for their food to come out of the kitchen.

"Three years," Delinda answered. "But I dated Bobby for almost five years before that."

"I'm divorced," he said. "My marriage didn't last even one year."

"Really? What happened, if you don't mind my asking?"

"My wife left me for my best friend."

She looked genuinely sad for him. "Oh, Samson, I'm so sorry."

He shrugged. "It had me down for a while, but I'm getting myself back on track."

"Do you still love her?" Delinda asked.

"Not anymore."

"I think Bobby's cheated on me," she announced unexpectedly. "At least a couple of times."

"Why are you staying with him if you know he's unfaithful?"

"I love him. And I don't want to give up my lifestyle. I've earned it."

"Don't you believe that you deserve a man who will love you and treat you like a queen?"

She met his gaze with a level stare. "My life is fine, Samson."

"Is it?"

"Yes," she said tightly.

He decided to back off. "I'm sorry to sound so surprised, but I have to be honest with you, Delinda. You just don't seem like a happily married woman."

She abruptly pushed away from the table. "I knew this was a bad idea. I have to leave."

Samson reached over and grabbed her hand. "Please don't leave, Delinda."

"Why are you so concerned with how my husband treats me?"

"I like you, Delinda," he said mildly. "I think that you're a nice person and I want to see you happy. That's all."

"I still don't understand why you care one way or the other."

"I care about anyone who is unhappy."

After dinner, Samson escorted Delinda to her car.

"Thanks for indulging me. I really enjoyed your company," he told her.

She smiled at him. By this point the awkwardness between them had long since passed. "I had a great time too."

Samson decided to put his true feelings out there. "I know this sounds inappropriate, but I hope to see you again real soon."

"How about now?" Delinda responded, surprising him.

"Did you just say—"

"Yes," she interjected. "Let's go to your place."

"Are you sure about this?" Samson asked. The last thing he wanted was to get her to his house and have her suddenly start freaking out.

Her gaze met his. "I've never been more sure about anything in my life."

She followed him to his town house.

"You have a beautiful home," Delinda said when he showed her around.

"Thank you."

They settled down on the sofa in the den. "Delinda, why are you here?" Samson wanted to know. He needed to make sure they were on the same page.

"I don't know," she responded truthfully. "I guess I didn't want to be alone."

Samson shifted closer and placed an arm around her shoulders. "I don't want to be alone either."

He drew in for a long kiss and she didn't slap him or try to fight him off. Encouraged, Samson took her by the hand and led her to the bedroom.

CHAPTER 23

*S*amson was in a great mood the next day. He was grinning from ear to ear when he arrived at the church administration building.

"You're looking quite chipper this morning," Zachariah said. "What's going on?"

"Nothing, Uncle. Just a new lease on life, I guess."

Samson went to his office and turned on the computer to check his appointments. He was meeting with two newly engaged couples to schedule premarital counseling, one at eleven o'clock and the other at one o'clock.

Samson spent his time before the first meeting working on a proposal for a summer sports camp. He was pretty sure his uncle would approve, but he didn't know what the advisory board would say. He planned to invest some of his own money and hoped the funds would help to sway the board in his favor.

The church secretary entered his office. "Booth and Sasha are here to see you, Pastor Taylor."

He smiled. "Send them in, please."

A minute later, a couple walked through his door and Samson greeted them.

When they sat down, Sasha said, "Pastor, I would like for you to explain why attending premarital counseling is important. Booth doesn't think so—he thinks it's just a waste of time."

"Is it really a must?" Booth asked. "Because I don't think people value premarital counseling as much as you think. It's just another way for someone to force their opinions on you." Before Sasha could protest, Booth added, "Babe, I don't want you to judge me by the dos and don'ts given in these counseling sessions. Let's just be real. This pastor ain't even married. What can he tell us?"

"I was married," Samson interjected. "It didn't work out, however. I should add that we didn't attend premarital counseling sessions. Maybe things would've been different if we had." He didn't mention his second marriage. He thought about Kenya and how much he missed her. Samson now regretted not ever giving their relationship a real chance.

"What are we gonna be talking about?" Booth asked.

"We cover lots of stuff taught in these counseling sessions," Samson said. "From financial management to communication to sex. Many people enter marriage for different reasons, and we tackle the issues that matter to you."

"Do people still get married after counseling?" Booth wanted to know.

"Some couples do decide not to go ahead with the marriage," Samson admitted. "It's better to call off the wedding if you're not sure of each other."

Sasha nodded in agreement.

After a moment, Booth said, "Okay, when is the first session?"

"How about tomorrow evening?" Samson suggested.

Samson made notes and then keyed in an appointment for Sasha and Booth. He had known Sasha since they were in preschool together and wasn't sure she was ready to get married. She was on the immature side in his opinion.

He caught himself. *What right do I have to judge them? It's not like I haven't been messing up every so often. I'm involved with a married woman.* Samson thought of Kenya and what he'd put her through. He didn't want to allow himself to dwell on the fact that she would give birth to his child without him.

Samson tried to shake away the troubling thoughts.

Why am I so messed up? He had pondered that question over and over again. He never wanted to be like his father, but that's exactly who he had become. *Maybe it's just the way I was made,* Samson rationalized.

Bothered, he got up and went across the hall to the break room, where his uncle was pouring himself a cup of coffee.

"Hey, I hope you're not overdoing it," Samson commented. "Auntie will be all over me if I let you exhaust yourself."

Zachariah laughed. "I'm having a good day today. I'm feeling pretty good."

Samson was relieved to hear that. "Let me know if you need help with anything. I promised your wife you'd be home before three today. She wants you to take it easy because you have chemo tomorrow."

"I know." Zachariah frowned at the prospect. "That woman is going to worry herself sick."

They talked for a few minutes more before Zachariah retrieved a bottle of water from the refrigerator and headed back to his office.

Samson decided to end his workday shortly after four. Before he left his office, the telephone rang.

"Samson, this is Delinda."

"Hey . . ." He could feel the struggle going on inside him.

"I was wondering if you wanted to get together tonight,"

she said, her voice a sexy purr. "My husband's going to be away for the rest of the week. I thought maybe I could come over to your place."

Samson knew that his response should've been no, but instead, he asked, "What time should I expect you?"

"I'll be there around nine."

"See you then," Samson said before hanging up.

He glanced upward. "Lord, I know what you must be thinking . . . despite how this looks, I really believe that my life is about to change forever because of her."

• • •

The next morning, Samson drove his uncle to his chemo treatment. Hazel was in the backseat, singing softly.

He glanced over at Zachariah. "Can I ask you a question, Uncle?"

"Sure, what is it?"

"How does it feel? This treatment."

"I guess you can say it's sort of like a cross between having stomach flu and just being completely out of it," Zachariah told him. "Some days you feel like you don't really care if you live or die."

Samson didn't want to hear that. "I know you're going to beat this cancer."

"I intend to give it all I got. I'm not going down without a fight."

Shortly after they arrived, a port was placed in his upper left arm where the treatment would be administered.

Zachariah had to see his oncologist before every other chemo treatment. Samson and his aunt went with him when he met with the doctor. They insisted on being present because they wanted to know everything about the cancer. Usually, the meeting was so that the oncologist could feel the nodes and just let Zachariah vent if needed, but Zachariah never once uttered a complaint.

After leaving the doctor's office, Zachariah gave Samson a pat on the arm. "I'll be out shortly."

"We'll be right here."

While his uncle was in the back receiving treatment, he and Hazel sat in the waiting room. Samson put his earphones in to listen to his iPod and then closed his eyes. His uncle would be hooked up for about three hours.

He applauded his uncle's courage through this battle with cancer. The chemo was so powerful, at times the cure seemed worse than the disease.

Usually after treatment, Zachariah felt terrible, so he always went home and straight to bed to sleep through the nausea that plagued him. Although he never actually threw up, he would complain of feeling awful for a few days and not want to eat. By the time he felt more like himself, only a few days were left before the next treatment.

"God, please save my uncle," he whispered. Samson didn't know what he would do if something happened to Zachariah.

"You look like you have something heavy on your mind," Hazel said, intruding on his thoughts.

"I hate not being able to help Uncle," he said. "I know that God is the ultimate healer, but I can't bear the thought of losing him."

"I know how you feel, so I don't think about it. I simply give thanks for each day that he's here with us."

Samson nodded in understanding. "I have to do that."

She reached over and grabbed his hand. "Your uncle is doing well. He's a strong man."

"I love you both. I want you to know that." Samson kissed her hand.

"Hon, we know. We've always known."

Images of Delinda floated in his mind as he said, "I really want to make you and Uncle proud of me."

CHAPTER 24

$\mathscr{S}$amson finished his morning workout and headed for the shower. His mind was working overtime as he washed himself. Delinda dominated his thoughts these days.

Samson was falling in love with her, and he found it increasingly hard to handle his jealousy where Bobby was concerned. He hated the way the man treated his wife. Delinda deserved better. She was the type of woman he needed in his life, Samson decided. *She should be mine completely.*

He made sure that he was extremely careful in his pursuit of Delinda. He couldn't afford another scandal, and he didn't want to upset his uncle.

They had been seeing each other for more than a month now. Delinda was skittish at times, and she often felt like she was being watched. Samson was constantly assuring her that their secret was safe and that no one knew about them.

It was Zachariah's chemo day, so he went over to pick him up. His aunt surprised him when she decided to stay home to take care of some housecleaning. This was the first time only he and Zachariah had gone.

Three hours later, Samson took his uncle home and helped his aunt get him settled in bed.

"I'm going to pick up some lunch for us," he told her. "You look like you need to lie down and get some rest. Auntie, I think you're trying to do too much."

"I put in my paperwork to take a leave of absence from the job," Hazel announced. "I want to spend more time with Zachariah."

Samson called in an order and then left ten minutes later to go pick it up.

He ran into Delinda as he walked into the restaurant. She had just exited the bathroom.

"Samson, what are you doing here?" Delinda asked, her eyes as big as saucers. She glanced around the restaurant. "My husband is here with me."

"I came here to pick up lunch for me and my aunt," he said innocently. Yet he caressed her with his eyes.

"Samson, I'm a married woman," she said in a low voice. "Please get your food and leave before Bobby sees you."

"You're married to a man that obviously doesn't make you happy," Samson returned. "You're not first on his list of priorities. Delinda, you shouldn't settle for less than what you deserve."

"And I supposed you're the man for the job," she responded. "Samson, I live a life most women dream about. I'm not about to give that up."

"Is it worth being miserable for the rest of your life?"

Delinda was quiet for a moment. A man suddenly appeared by her side. He grabbed her arm, asking, "Who is this, Delinda?"

Delinda suddenly looked afraid. She swallowed hard before responding, "Honey, this is Pastor Taylor. He was the keynote speaker for the youth luncheon last month. I told you about him, remember?"

"Oh yeah," Bobby said, checking Samson out from head to toe. He shook Samson's hand roughly. "Nice to meet you, Pastor."

Samson noted that Bobby's smile didn't reach his eyes.

"I heard that you turned it out at the luncheon. I'm disappointed I couldn't be there to hear you myself."

Samson itched to wipe the smug look off the man's face. He didn't like the way he was gripping Delinda. He toyed with blurting out that she was in love with him. Instead, he picked up the bag off the counter and said, "It's nice to meet you, Bobby. Mrs. Lewis-Hatcher, good to see you again. Enjoy your lunch."

He was furious by the time he reached his car. He didn't like Bobby Hatcher and that condescending attitude of his. He didn't deserve Delinda, and Samson vowed that she would be his before the year was out. He just had to convince her that she was better off without her husband.

• • •

Two days later, Samson was mildly surprised to find Delinda at his door. He stepped aside to let her enter the town house. Without a word between them, Samson and Delinda fell into each other's arms. He picked her up and carried her to his bedroom.

Samson's lips descended on hers. He reveled in the pleasure of being so close to Delinda. He had been trying to reach her for the past couple of days via a private web-based email account she had set up just for them.

"What am I doing?" Delinda murmured as she lay in his arms later. "I am going straight to hell if I keep this up." Her head turned toward his. "I thought for sure Bobby suspected something was going on between us, but he never said anything."

"Why did you think that? We've covered all of our bases."

"He's not stupid. But if he knew anything, he wouldn't be able to keep it to himself. Bobby's got a terrible temper. He's been in legal trouble for fighting."

"I'm a black belt in karate. I'm not afraid of Bobby."

"But this can't happen again."

"Why not?"

"I have a husband. A very jealous husband, and if he finds out, I don't know what will happen. He can't get in trouble again, Samson. If he does, then he could lose his contract, endorsements, and well, that just can't happen. We've worked too hard for everything we have. I won't give it up. I won't.

"I love my life and I'm not interested in giving it up. Bobby is a pain at times and he can be the biggest jerk, but I'm not ready to end my marriage."

"I'm free and I want a woman in my life. I'll treat her like a queen and she'll want for nothing," Samson said. "That woman is you."

Surprised by his plea, Delinda laughed. "That's sweet, but there's only so much you can do on a pastor's salary."

He didn't respond. He wasn't about to reveal the fact that he was worth millions. Samson didn't want a woman who just wanted a man with money. He hoped Delinda wasn't really as shallow as she sounded right now.

• • •

Delinda called the next day wanting to see him, and Samson met her at his house.

"After what you said yesterday, I didn't think I'd see you again."

She gave him a seductive look, then responded, "I couldn't resist temptation."

They went to his bedroom and made love. Afterward, Delinda said, "I want ice cream."

"You're as bad as a ten-year-old," Samson said, kissing

her. She didn't answer but merely buried her fingers in his hair. "I'm crazy about you," he told her in a low voice.

They showered together.

After getting dressed, they drove to the ice cream parlor two blocks away from his house. Samson told her how much he enjoyed spending time with her, and he desired that she commit to him. When he told her so, she said, "I have strong feelings for you, Samson, but I still love my husband."

"Cut the crap, Delinda," he responded tersely. "You love Bobby's money. If he wasn't playing in the NBA, I doubt you would stay with him."

She sent him a sharp look. "If you really think that, then you don't know me at all."

He shrugged. "I call a spade a spade, Delinda."

"I've earned every penny. After everything Bobby's put me through, he owes me big-time and I'm not going to just give it all up."

"You must have signed a prenup," he retorted.

She looked offended. "Samson, you can be so cruel at times."

"It's not my intention. I just don't see why we need to skirt around the issue."

She was silent on the way back to his place. When they pulled into the garage, Samson expected her to leave, but she surprised him by following him into the condo. She made her reasons clear soon enough. Delinda stood in the middle of the living room, lowered the straps on her top, and eased the bodice down, baring her body to the waist.

Samson's breath quickened. "What you do to me, baby?" he said, his voice rough with passion.

He allowed her to unbutton his shirt.

"No more talking," she told him. "I just want to enjoy what we have right now."

Samson kissed her, holding her close. After a moment she breathlessly pulled away and removed the rest of her clothes. He did the same.

They made love in front of his fireplace.

Afterward, Samson and Delinda lay there, still intimately joined, each pondering what was going on between them.

Neither spoke.

There was no need.

There was no excuse.

• • •

"I'm not sure Uncle is doing well," Samson told his aunt a few days later. "He never complains or anything, but he's so weak. I don't think he's getting any better."

"We must have faith, dear. We can't waver—either we believe he is going to be healed or we don't."

"Auntie, I understand what you're saying, but there is healing on this side and the other. Uncle says he's made his peace with God. He says he's ready to go whenever the good Lord is ready for him."

Hazel looked away, discouraged. "He's tired."

"I know, Auntie. That's why I'm worried. I don't know if he's strong enough to keep fighting."

Hazel met his gaze. "Zachariah has never been one to just give up, Samson. It's not in his DNA, so you don't have to worry about that."

He wasn't reassured, though. "I can't imagine life without him. I need my uncle."

"I need him too," Hazel admitted.

"Why all the doom and gloom?" Zachariah asked, surprising them both when he entered the dining room.

"You should be resting," Hazel told him severely. "Let me help you back to bed."

He shook his head. "I'm fine. I want to sit out here and have dinner with my family."

"Are you sure you feel up to it, Uncle?" Samson asked.

He nodded. Hazel prepared a plate for him and brought it to the table.

"What's going on with you, son?" Zachariah asked, taking a seat across from Samson.

He wiped his mouth with a paper napkin. "I'm not sure what you're talking about."

"Is there someone special in your life?"

"Not really," Samson responded cautiously. His uncle was always so perceptive. "Why do you ask?"

"You're acting the way you did when you met Savannah. I just thought that the light I see in your eyes was because you'd met someone."

"I'm dating, if that's what you mean," Samson said. "But nothing serious. At least not yet."

"So there is someone," Hazel said with a tiny smile.

"If things continue to progress, then you two will be the first to know." Samson took a long sip of lemonade. "I promise you."

He stole peeks at Zachariah as they ate. His uncle looked thinner than ever. Samson sent up a silent plea. *Father God, I will give up Delinda if you'll just let my uncle live. Please don't make him pay for my sins.*

CHAPTER 25

*D*elinda called Samson and asked him to meet her. They had been sneaking around, seeing each other for three months now and he hoped she had finally made up her mind to leave Bobby. Thrilled at the prospect, he raced out of his office and drove across town to the address she had given him, a location where they wouldn't be recognized. He parked in the driveway of the house.

"Whose place is this?" Samson asked when he walked inside.

"It belongs to a cousin of mine."

"I almost thought I'd written down the wrong address when I didn't see your car."

"My cousin and I switched cars at the mall. Samson, I think someone is following me."

She looked so scared, Samson felt compelled to ask, "Did you see anyone on the way here?"

She shook her head. "My cousin and I look a lot alike. We have on the same clothes and she's still at the mall. I can't stay long, but I wanted to talk to you face-to-face."

Her voice was trembling. In fact, she was shaking all over. Delinda seemed really frightened.

"I think you're overreacting, honey."

"No, I know someone is watching me. I think Bobby's hired a private detective."

"Delinda, I love you and I want to be with you." He pulled her into his arms, holding her close. "I won't let anything happen to you. I want you to know that. If Bobby is having you followed, just leave him."

She stepped away from him. "Samson, we really need to talk."

"We can talk later. I've missed you so much." He reached out and touched her face.

Delinda pushed his hands away. "No, I have to do this now. Samson, I can't see you anymore. Bobby and I are committed to saving our marriage."

"The man doesn't respect you, Delinda. He doesn't appreciate you."

"It doesn't matter," she shouted. "I love him. I love Bobby."

Samson shook his head. "I don't believe you. If you truly loved him like you want me to believe, then you wouldn't be here."

"I came here today to end things with you," Delinda said, meeting his gaze straight on.

She had gone back and forth so many times, he didn't believe her. "You don't mean that."

"Samson, it's over."

"You love me," he stated firmly. "I can see it in your eyes."

Tears rolled down her cheeks. "I'm sorry. I can't see you again. Now, I need you to leave."

"Delinda . . ."

"Samson, please leave and don't contact me ever again. I mean it."

He left the house feeling depressed. He wasn't going to let Delinda go without a fight, but for the moment he did as she asked and left.

I need to get her away from Raleigh. We need to go some-where where she doesn't have to worry about Bobby, he thought as he drove home.

Samson pulled out his cell phone and called a travel agency.

"I need two plane tickets to Nassau, Bahamas," he told the agent. "First-class tickets."

As soon as he hung up, he called Delinda. "Meet me at the restaurant in about an hour."

She replied harshly, "I can't do this with you. I've already said all I need to say. It's over."

"Please," he said. "Baby, I really need to see you. I just need you to hear me out."

There was a slight pause.

"Delinda," Samson prompted.

"All right, I'll meet you for drinks, but I can't stay. I have to hurry up and get back home."

"That's fine. Meet me at the church. You can tell him I've asked you to help plan an event for my youth ministry if you need a cover."

"I'll be there within the hour."

Satisfied, Samson smiled. She'd jump at the chance to go with him to the Bahamas.

When Delinda arrived, she said, "Samson, I can't stay long. Bobby's coming home at any moment. He—"

"I bought two first-class tickets to the Bahamas," he inter-rupted. "For next Friday. Your husband's going to be away that weekend, right?"

She was stunned. "You did what?"

"I think we need to have a weekend where you're not worried about being followed. We need this time so you can really figure out what it is that you want. I'll be flying out on Thursday. Once we get there, we—"

Delinda cut him off. "I can't go with you. I've already told you that what we had is over. I'm not going to leave Bobby."

"You don't love him. You love me."

"It doesn't matter," Delinda responded. "I am choosing him over you."

"Meet me in Nassau, please. Let's spend some time together, and if you still want to go home to Bobby, then fine. I will let you go without a fight. But I have a feeling that next weekend is going to change both our lives forever."

• • •

Samson paced back and forth across the marble floor of the hotel room. Delinda's plane had landed almost an hour ago. He tried her cell phone but got no answer.

She wasn't coming. The realization made his heart drop and he pressed a hand to his temple as he felt a headache coming on. *She loves me. Delinda is in love with me. But she's not here. She didn't come, so I guess I have my answer.*

In the middle of his disheartening thoughts, he heard a knock at the door.

Samson rushed to open it.

"Where is my wife?" Bobby demanded, brushing past him.

"Obviously, she's not here with me," Samson said. He glared at the huge basketball player standing in front of him. "Shouldn't you be playing somewhere?"

What in the world was going on? he wondered. Where was Delinda?

"It's none of your business what I have to do. I know that my wife was supposed to meet you here," Bobby said as he stormed through the suite, opening doors and checking everywhere.

Fury at the basketball player's arrogant behavior threatened to choke Samson and he balled his hands into fists. "You have no right to barge into my suite like this."

"Oh, I have every right," Bobby snarled. "You've been sleeping with my wife and I'm pissed!"

"You're such a hypocrite," Samson said coolly. "You've been cheating on your wife—it's been in all the tabloids. I love her."

"She's mine until I decide to let her go," Bobby told him. "Now where is she?"

"Delinda was right. You were having her followed, but as you can see, she's not here with me. Hopefully, she's had the good sense to leave you."

Bobby's face transformed into a glowering mask of rage. "You tell me where she is."

"Get out," Samson demanded. "While you still can."

Bobby chuckled nastily. "You think you can take me on? Really?"

Samson swung at him. Bobby dodged Samson's blow and punched Samson in the face.

Samson struck back, his punch landing on Bobby's chest. The two men fought hard, knocking over a table and a chair. Samson was a black belt in karate, but he was no match for a man of Bobby's size. He avoided the last two swings and even clipped Bobby on the cheek. Samson was glad to see blood squirt from the man's busted lip.

Enraged, the basketball player picked Samson up and threw him forcefully toward the glass patio door. The force of the impact caused the glass to shatter into a million pieces. An explosion of glass blasted fragments into Samson's face.

Excruciating pain ripped through him before everything went black.

• • •

"He's coming around . . ." A female voice penetrated the fog enveloping Samson's mind. He was shrouded in darkness.

Machines were beeping amid other distinct hospital sounds. An antiseptic smell permeated the air. Samson felt a firm pressure around his head. He reached up to touch what felt like bandages that covered his eyes. A feminine hand stopped him.

"Mr. Taylor, my name is Rose. I'm a nurse here at Doctors Hospital in Nassau."

"Hurt," he muttered. Pain throbbed behind his eyes when he tried to open them. Samson was in so much agony, he thought that dying might be better than what he was going through right now. He silently begged for the pain to end. "Can you tell me what happened? Why am I h-here?"

"You were in an accident," she responded. "We had to rush you to surgery to remove shards of glass from your eyes."

"G-Glass . . ." Memories flooded Samson's mind. Images of him fighting with Bobby. Patio door shattering, fragments of glass blasting into his face. Excruciating pain ripped through him. "I remember . . ." he groaned in agony.

"The pain medication should take effect pretty quickly," the nurse told him.

Samson grimaced. It wasn't working fast enough as far as he was concerned. "Delinda . . . where is she?"

"I haven't seen anyone," Rose responded. "But I just came on a couple of hours ago."

Samson swallowed his fury. He had never been in a fight that ended with him getting the worst of it. "Do you know if another man was brought in with me?"

"No, you were the only one."

Samson put a hand to his face again, feeling the bandages covering his eyes. He moaned in pain.

"The doctor will be in shortly," Rose said before leaving the room.

He listened every time he heard footsteps slowing outside his door. "Where are you, Delinda?" he murmured. There was no way she was going to stay with Bobby after this.

The man was violent and would end up killing her if she didn't leave him. Maybe she was in a hotel somewhere getting some rest before coming back to the hospital.

Samson didn't want to consider that Bobby had forced her to leave with him. He didn't want to think about that possibility.

A pained sigh left his lips as a floating dizziness came over him. That must be the painkillers.

The soft sound of his door opening and closing announced that he was not alone. "Who's here?" he asked.

"Mr. Taylor, my name is Doctor Jones. Your body going through the glass door propelled glass shards with such force that they sliced through your cornea. You were in surgery nearly eight hours but we were fortunate to be able to remove all the glass. There was more corneal damage than I expected."

The doctor's conclusion sent a shred of fear down Samson's spine. "Will I be able to see anything when the bandages come off?"

"There were severe tears in your retina. It's too soon to tell how extensive. You may recover some of your vision, but it will be muddy at best. I'm sorry, but I can't guarantee that your eyesight will ever return to anywhere near normal."

Samson couldn't imagine going through the rest of his life without being able to see. "Even with more surgery?"

"It would be a slim-to-none chance."

The word *blind* screamed through his brain, reverberating over and over again. "My God can handle those odds," he told the doctor. "I've never let anything beat me, and I won't start now." Samson wanted to cling to the hope that he would regain his eyesight. "I know that I won't have perfect vision, but I will settle for decent eyesight. I can't live my life as a blind man."

"I wish I had better news for you." The doctor told Samson he'd be back later and left the room.

Left alone, Samson wrestled with what the doctor told him.

"Father God, I know I haven't done much to bring honor to your name lately," he whispered. "I know the call you have upon my heart and I am eager to do your bidding, but this flesh of mine . . . it's betrayed that calling. I tried to control it on my own, but I should have asked for Your help. Beauty and lust are my weaknesses. Father God, I repent of all my sins and I ask for Your forgiveness. Please spare me of such a harsh punishment and give me back my eyesight. If you do this for me, I will honor You in all that I do. In Jesus's name I pray. Amen."

He placed trembling hands to his temples, willing the pain to stop. *This is not happening to me. This can't be real.*

Samson could hear the footsteps long before they stopped in front of his room. He knew somehow that they did not belong to a nurse or a doctor—the rhythm of the footsteps was almost hesitant.

The door to his room opened and Samson turned his head in that direction, although he could see nothing.

"Hey there, bro."

Hot anger swelled inside him at the sound of Trey's voice. Samson clutched the sheet in his fists. "Trey, what are you doing here? Did you come all the way to Nassau to gloat?"

"I heard about what happened, so I came to see you," he responded quietly. "I thought that you shouldn't be alone to deal with all this. I thought that maybe you could use a friend."

"Then I definitely don't need you," Samson snapped. "You are not a friend of mine."

Trey walked up to the bed and said, "I messed up. I can't even lie about it, but I want you to know that Savannah and I really love each other. Even though it was foul the way we came together, it doesn't matter. I know that she is my soul mate."

The hole in Samson's heart caused by their betrayal had

never healed and it didn't help that Trey offered the same reasoning Samson had given him for going behind his back to snag Savannah in the first place. He wanted Trey to leave so that he could be alone. A feeling of bitterness and fury burned inside him. "So why don't you leave and go back home to your soul mate? I don't want you here."

"Samson, I still consider you my best friend despite all that's happened between us."

"I don't consider you anything but a traitor. I never would've done something like that to you, Trey."

"Look at where you are now," Trey snapped out of frustration. "Even a blind man can see that you're here because of your own actions. You're not perfect, Samson. *Sin is sin, bro.*"

Samson didn't want to be lectured. "Why don't you go back home?"

"You may not want to admit it, but you need someone right now. Your aunt and uncle couldn't come because your uncle isn't well—that's why I offered to come. Savannah wanted to come too, but I thought you and I needed this time alone."

"We're not a couple," Samson replied. "We just need to go our separate ways."

"Fine," Trey said with a sigh. "After I get you back home, you can do whatever, but until then I'm not leaving your side."

Samson thought that Trey's eagerness and devotion bordered on the extreme. It was as if he had a motive for wanting to help him.

"Why are you doing this?" he demanded. "Are you trying to assuage your guilt?"

"I'm here because I miss my best friend," Trey said evenly, "and even though he's not going to admit it, he needs help and I'm sure he misses me too. You've lost your wife, now your sight, and you're angry for a lot of reasons."

"Where's Delinda?" Samson asked. "Is she here at the hospital? She's the only person I want by my side."

Trey broke the bad news. "No, she's not. She went home with her husband. At least, that's what I was told. She did leave you a letter. The nurse gave it to me just before I came in here. Do you want me to read it to you?"

The last thing he wanted was Trey reading a private note left for him, but he couldn't read it. "Sure," he grunted.

He could hear Trey ripping open the envelope and the slight ruffling of paper. His mind played back the seconds just before he was thrown through the patio doors. He was worried that Bobby would try to harm Delinda and vowed to find a way to save her from her violent husband. Samson also wanted vengeance against the man who had done this to him.

"'My dearest Samson,'" Trey began. "'I want you to know that I'll never forgive myself for what happened. I never wanted any harm to come to you, but I've always told you that my husband is quick-tempered and a man who doesn't know his strength. Despite his faults, I love him. I'm not willing to give up on my marriage. I am going to do everything I can to get him to forgive me and give us a second chance. Getting involved with you was a mistake. It may have cost you your sight, and me my marriage. I pray you will be well and I ask that you never try to contact me again. What we had is over and never should have started in the first place.'"

"Don't read any more," Samson said wearily. "I don't want to hear another word. Take the letter and rip it up."

Trey did as he was told.

"The only reason she's staying with him is because of his millions," Samson said after a moment. "Delinda doesn't love him."

"It's *her* choice. And she's made it. I think you need to respect her wishes."

Samson didn't respond. He had never felt as defeated as he did now. Savannah didn't love him and neither did Delinda. His mind traveled to Kenya. She loved him, but he had used her to get back at her sister.

Trey interrupted his thoughts. "I'm sorry for the way things have turned out for you."

"*Go to hell, Trey.*"

"I'm not going anywhere, Samson."

"I'm blind and there's nothing you can do about it."

"It may not be permanent."

"I guess you haven't spoken to the doctor. There is a strong chance that I will be blind for the rest of my life."

"Don't think that way. I know the man that you truly are—not the man you've been pretending to be. You have some radical faith, bro, and I need to see some of that. God needs to see it."

"This is a consequence of my actions," Samson said with a sigh of resignation. "I've been playing around and now I have to pay for everything I've done. Well, God's gotten me back big-time. I guess I deserve to be in this position."

Trey tried to make him see the bright side. "You're still alive, and you have your health. You have a lot to be thankful for."

Samson didn't agree. He was not in a grateful mood and didn't know if he would ever be in one again.

"Would you like for me to read from the Bible?" Trey offered.

He shook his head firmly. "What I'd like is to be left alone."

"I'll go down to the waiting room to give you some time to yourself, but I'm not leaving this hospital and that's final."

Samson would never admit it to Trey, but he was relieved to have someone there with him. He had hoped Delinda would've stayed around, but she chose to go after her husband, a man who didn't appreciate her, yet acted as if he owned her.

Two women he had cared deeply for had betrayed him. Samson clenched his fist, the sting of their faithless ways poisoning his blood. He vowed that he would never allow another woman to steal his heart.

The cost of love was too high a price to pay.

CHAPTER 26

*B*obby's lawyer came to visit Samson later that day.

"Mr. Hatcher wants you to know how badly he feels about this situation. Emotions were running high and . . . well, it was unfortunate."

"What did you come here for?" Samson demanded. "Just get to the point."

"Mr. Hatcher would like to cover your medical expenses—"

"That's a given," Samson stated.

"In appreciation for your not telling the police what really transpired. He would like to spare everyone, including your uncle and his church, embarrassment."

Furious, Samson gritted his teeth. "And he thinks paying the medical expenses is thanks enough? I'm sure there's more."

"He is offering you a settlement of two million dollars. He never wanted you to lose your eyesight."

"You can tell your client that if he wants to pay me off for my silence, then he'd better come correct. I won't accept anything less than five million. I will never get my eyesight back. He still has that skank of a wife, so he hasn't really lost anything—well, except his trust in her. But it doesn't matter to me. Those two deserve each other."

• • •

Trey was true to his word. He stayed in Nassau until Samson was ready to leave the hospital a couple of weeks later. They would be heading to the airport to catch a flight home to North Carolina.

When the bandages were removed, Samson could no longer live in denial. He could see only darkness. According to his doctor, his blindness was most likely a permanent condition. He didn't like to wallow in self-pity, but at the moment, Samson was powerless to prevent its onslaught.

"Are you ready?" Trey asked him while they waited for the doctor to sign the release papers.

"Yeah, I'd like to go home. I've been here way too long already."

Trey positioned Samson's hand just above his elbow and said, "Now follow the motion of my body. I'm going to help you get into the wheelchair."

"I never envisioned my life turning out like this," Samson said, feeling miserable. It bothered him that he was going to be wheeled around the airport and onto the plane like an invalid.

"Samson, I know you, and you are a fighter. I know this isn't going to hold you down."

"You have to lose sometime, Trey, and I guess this is it for me." Samson felt a wave of depression engulf him. "I've lost big-time."

"You still have your life."

"Yeah, I'm alive. So what?" Samson snapped. "I can't see a thing—how can I enjoy what I can't see?"

"It's possible, man. Think about the people who were born blind. They still manage to have full lives."

Samson scoffed. "They can't miss what they never saw."

The nurse walked into the room. Samson could hear the soft shuffling of papers. His postsurgery instructions, he assumed.

She spoke to Trey like Samson wasn't even there, which irritated him to no end, but he kept his mouth shut. He just wanted to get out of Nassau.

When they were cleared and ready to go Samson fumbled around, feeling for the wheels of the wheelchair. "I don't know how to wheel myself to the door. Hey, I can't even see the door." Samson muttered a string of curses.

"Whoa, bro. It's okay. That's why I'm here. I'll get you out of here."

As Trey wheeled him out of the room, Samson said, "I guess she didn't know I still had my hearing."

"The only reason she was talking to me was because of the instructions. She wanted to make sure I understood everything."

"I don't care," Samson muttered. "I just want to get out of here."

"Your aunt and uncle are looking forward to seeing you," Trey said, striking a positive note. "They were ecstatic when I called them last night to tell them you were being discharged."

Samson wondered what they really thought of him after everything that had happened. He knew they had to be sorely disappointed.

"Your aunt wanted me to tell you she loves you."

Samson smiled, glad to hear it. "I bet she told you the same thing."

Trey chuckled. "Yeah, she did. She said that she loves us both. Miss Hazel is really happy I was able to be here with you."

Samson wasn't going to let that go by unanswered. "I appreciate all you've done for me, but this doesn't really change things between us."

"I know that."

"I keep forgetting how well you know me."

Trey gave him a brief pat on the shoulder. "I know that you can hold a grudge forever, but that's okay. I can still be here for my friend even though he may hate my guts right now."

Samson remained quiet as he wheeled out the main door of the hospital.

In the car the sounds of car motors and trucks passing them came from all around him. He had never noticed just how noisy it was inside a car. He heard a siren coming from behind them. *We take so much for granted,* he thought.

When they arrived at the airport, Trey requested another wheelchair.

"I don't need a wheelchair," Samson grunted. "I can walk."

"You just got out of the hospital."

"I feel fine," Samson stated flatly. "I'm sure I can make it to the plane without a wheelchair."

"Okay, but let me know if you start to get tired." Trey lowered his voice. "Man, you don't have to prove anything."

"Yeah, I do," Samson whispered back. "I have to do this for me."

"All right. Place your hand on my shoulder and use the cane with the other," Trey instructed.

Slowly they made their way through the busy airport; the steady tapping of the cane was a constant reminder that he would never see again.

Trey was right about how weak he'd become. Samson felt like he had walked a mile by the time they reached their gate. He was tired but refused to let on.

As Trey guided Samson over to one of the seats in the waiting area, he was careful to provide visual cues about obstacles in their path.

"Thanks," Samson mumbled.

He was grateful to feel the hard seat of the chair beneath him. Spending all that time in a hospital bed had turned him into a vegetable.

Trey sat down beside him. "Samson, I know that we probably won't ever be as close as we used to be, but I want you to know that I love you like a brother. Will you ever be able to forgive me, bro?"

Samson considered Trey's question for a moment. He had to be honest with his friend. "I have to, Trey. Like you told me—sin is sin. What I did to Bobby was much worse than what you did to me. I did sleep with his wife. Several times. If I'm to be honest, I broke most of the Ten Commandments."

Trey laughed. "We all have broken at least one or two."

Samson shook his head, not willing to agree. "Man, I really messed up."

"Don't beat yourself up, bro." Trey changed the subject to lighten the mood. "Hey, you remember the last time we flew overseas? That time we went to Mexico . . ."

Despite himself, Samson chuckled. "We said we'd never talk about that."

Trey kept the string going. "I guess you wanted to sow all your wild oats in a week. I'd never seen so many girls coming in and out of a room. I practically had to schedule an appointment just to talk to you."

"I know you're not trying to act all innocent. Don't forget that I walked in on you and the two cousins."

"Man, it wasn't even like that," Trey said, bursting out laughing. "We were just hanging out."

"Is that why one of them was doing a striptease and the other was trying to take off your clothes?"

They kept trading barbs about their past trip as they waited to board the plane.

"We had some good times together, didn't we?"

"We did," Trey confirmed. "They don't have to end."

Samson's former gloom returned. "I won't ever be the same man that I was before."

"Actually, that in itself may not be a bad thing, bro."

Samson nodded in agreement. "You're right about that."

When it came time for them to board the plane, Trey guided Samson onto the plane and to his seat. Samson swallowed his pride as he clumsily made his way down the narrow aisle. He was glad to hear Trey say, "We're here. Slide into your seat." He hit his leg on the arm of the seat, but he managed to sit down without too much fumbling. Samson had new appreciation for others who had to deal with living in darkness.

"How is my uncle really doing?" Samson asked as they waited for the plane to take off.

"He has good days and bad ones, but every time I visit, he's always smiling. He never complains."

"That's my uncle—always a smile on his face."

"He's not giving in to the cancer. He's fighting it at every turn." He clasped Samson's hand and gave it a little shake.

"I hear what you're saying. It's just not that easy for me to be a fighter right now." He settled back against the seat cushions and closed his eyes. He was exhausted.

• • •

Trey woke Samson up right before the plane was about to land at the Raleigh-Durham Airport.

It took him a few minutes to adjust to his blindness. His eyes were open, but only darkness surrounded him. "How long was I asleep?"

"For almost four hours. I knew you were tired, so I let you sleep. We can grab something to eat after we leave RDU so that you can take your meds."

"I'm not hungry," Samson said. He hadn't had much of an appetite since the accident. "I just want to get to my aunt and uncle's house. I want to see—" He stopped short. "I need to make sure my uncle is doing okay."

"You need to put something in your stomach before you take your pills."

Trey and Samson slowly made their way to the baggage claim area. In an ever irritating reminder, the tapping of the cane signaled their progression.

After securing their luggage, Trey said, "Sit here and wait for me. I need to go get the car."

"I'll be right here," Samson stated dryly.

He sat in the chair, clothed in darkness, listening. He'd never noticed before, but people had different rhythms when they walked. Some woman walked by him at a fast pace, her high heels tapping out the hustle and bustle of her life. Samson imagined that she was always in a hurry.

Then he heard the persistent crying of a baby. A new baby.

Samson hadn't allowed himself to think about Kenya until now. He wondered how she was faring. He thought about the baby. Samson knew the child had been born.

I never should have hurt her like that, he thought.

Trey was gone a good fifteen minutes. Breathless, he returned, saying, "Okay . . . let's go."

"What did you do?" Samson asked. "Run all the way there and back?"

"Something like that."

A few minutes later, they were in the car and heading away from the airport. "You're sure you don't want to stop anywhere?" Trey asked.

"I'll eat when I get to the house," Samson said, his tone final.

Twenty minutes later, Trey announced, "We're here."

Samson was exhausted. Traveling had proven too much for him. Still, he was glad to be back in Raleigh. He reached out, trying to locate the door handle.

He heard his aunt's voice as she opened the door and

rushed out of the house. "Thank you, Jesus, for bringing my baby home. Thank you, God. Thank you!"

Trey had come around the car and was helping him out. Hazel wrapped her arms around him and held on to him with all her might.

"It's good to see you too, Auntie."

"Samson, I wanted so much to come to that hospital to be with you, but I couldn't leave Zachariah."

"I understand." Samson turned to where he thought Trey was. "Trey stayed by my side even when I wasn't real nice to him. He made sure I had everything I needed."

"I hope you two took that time to hash out everything. You two have been friends for such a long time."

Samson truly was grateful for Trey's being there for him in Nassau. That's what friends did. "We're working through it, Auntie. Taking it one day at a time, you know."

"God is so good," she said. "Well, let's get you inside the house. Your uncle has been asking when your plane was due to come in. He needs to see for himself that you're okay."

Samson nodded doubtfully. He was alive, but as for being okay—that was another story.

Trey led him down the hall toward his old bedroom. He could hear his aunt's footsteps a few feet ahead of them. From the sounds of it, she was wearing her favorite slippers.

"Okay, we're here at your old room," Trey said. "Now we're walking through the door."

"The bed is centered in the room," Samson stated, remembering how the room was decorated. His aunt never changed it after he moved out. "On my left, there is a green sofa against the wall."

"Good," Trey said. "You're doing great. Picture the room in your mind."

First he wanted to see Zachariah, though, so Trey and Hazel assisted him down the hall.

"Son, you made it home."

"Uncle, how are you feeling?"

"This is a good day. Samson, I'm glad you're here. I was terribly worried when we first heard what happened."

"I've made some terrible choices for my life."

His uncle didn't comment on that. Instead he said, "Son, go and lay down in your room. You just got out of the hospital, and then you traveled all the way home. Get some rest and we'll talk tomorrow."

Samson was still weary from his travel, so he didn't argue. "You do the same, Uncle. You need to preserve your strength."

He could feel the warmth of his uncle's smile.

"It's real good to have you back home, son."

"Thank you, Uncle."

Trey helped Samson settle down on the bed in his old room. Hazel had insisted that he get into bed while she went to the kitchen to prepare something for him to eat.

"Why did you mention the pills in front of Aunt Hazel?" Samson asked Trey when she had left. "That woman is going to drive me crazy about taking my medicine. She's the pill police."

"That's what you need," Trey responded with a chuckle. "You've never liked taking meds. You used to spit out your vitamins when we were kids."

Samson chuckled. "Do you ever forget anything?"

"Not the important stuff," he responded with a laugh.

Hazel strolled into the bedroom, saying, "I made you a ham and Swiss sandwich and a bowl of my chicken soup."

"Thanks, Auntie."

She set the tray down on his lap.

"Trey, you are officially relieved of duty," Samson said. "I'm sure you want to go home to your wife."

"Okay, but don't you go giving your aunt a hard time. I'll be back tomorrow to help you shower and shave."

"He'll be fine. I can help him brush his teeth and get to the bathroom," Hazel told Trey. "Give Savannah my best."

Trey hugged Hazel. "I will."

When Trey left, Samson told his aunt, "Oh, so now you can be pleasant to Savannah."

"Yeah, I can," she responded. "She's not the wife of a Baptist minister. Better yet, she's no longer your wife."

Samson had reached a decision. "I can't keep blaming her for everything that went wrong in our marriage. I really should've listened to you, Auntie."

"It no longer matters, hon. Stop looking back, and look to the future."

"I would give anything to be able to *look,* period."

She stroked his forehead. "God is a healer, Samson."

He nodded. "I know that to be true. I'm just not sure He'll do anything for me after all that's happened. I certainly don't deserve anything."

CHAPTER 27

$\mathcal{T}$rey returned to the house the next day, shortly after nine, ready to assist Samson with bathing and shaving.

"I can't tell you how humiliating this is for me," Samson said. "I'm not an invalid."

"No one is treating you like one. I'm just here to guide you. That's all."

Samson realized Trey had made the effort to come over. "I don't mean to sound so unappreciative. I just can't stand living like this."

"I can understand that. I'm sure I'd feel the same way."

"How am I supposed to get dressed? How do I pick out my clothes?" Samson huffed. "Man, I hate being in this position."

"Samson dear, I will help you get dressed," his aunt informed him as she walked into his bedroom. He almost said something about knocking on the door before coming in, but checked himself. He was a guest in her home.

"That's the point. You shouldn't have to, Aunt Hazel. I'm a grown man and I shouldn't need help."

"Samson," Trey pointed out, "you should pay attention to identifying characteristics such as buttons, collars, and pleats when you go through your clothes. Your aunt can attach all of the outfits and suits that coordinate."

Samson didn't respond. He had always been very independent and now he was blind and wouldn't be able to live alone.

"I know this is hard for you," Hazel said tenderly.

"Aunt Hazel, you can't even imagine. I can't live in my own home, I can't pick out my own clothes—I'm not sure I can even buy my own food anymore. Let's face it. My life is over."

"You still have a life, but things have changed," Trey corrected him. "You are now a blind or visually impaired man, but that won't stop you from being in control of your own life. Samson, you can live comfortably and safely almost anywhere you choose. I have a very good friend who is an instructor at the Raleigh Academy of the Blind. I called her and she's interested in working with you. I've arranged an appointment for you to meet."

"That's never going to happen," Samson declared. He was never going to regain his eyesight, so all this effort was a waste of time. "You and I both know that, so tell your friend not to waste her time. I don't know why you arranged this in the first place—I thought you were helping me."

"Just give it a chance. You'll like Meagan."

"I'll love Meagan if she can restore my sight."

"Samson, you know she can't do that," Trey went on, trying to make Samson look ahead. "Meagan's good at her job, but only if you let her do that job. The academy offers counseling sessions in addition to classes to help you adjust. You will benefit greatly from attending the academy and talking to one of the counselors."

Samson didn't feel the need to respond. He was too tired to argue.

"Trey has really come through for you, hasn't he?" Hazel said after he was gone.

Samson sent a sightless glare in her direction. "Auntie, he's guilt-ridden. That's why he's doing this. He's trying to make up for betraying me."

"He's not the only one who's betrayed someone," she responded tartly.

"Excuse me?"

"Your uncle and I know all about your affair with that ballplayer's wife. It's been all over the news. There's lots of speculation over what happened between you and Bobby."

He couldn't deny that she'd made a valid point. Samson had already admitted as much to Trey. "I guess you think I deserve what happened to me, then."

"How could you say such a thing?" Hazel asked, outraged. "We wouldn't want something so tragic to happen to you or anyone else, Samson."

"I know that, Auntie. The truth is that I did deserve it. I was no better than Trey. Don't you think I knew that what I was doing was wrong? I never should've gotten involved with Delinda, but I fell in love with her. Like Savannah, I thought she loved me just as much. I was willing to risk everything to be with her."

"Is it really love that you feel for these women? I don't think so. Love is selfless."

Her question gave him pause for thought, but he couldn't come up with an answer. "I'm tired," he said in the end. Samson didn't want to continue this discussion. She'd spout off a list of religious instructions, and he wasn't up to that.

She sighed in resignation. "Okay, I'll let you get some rest."

After Samson woke up from a nap, he swung his legs off the bed and rose to his feet. With hands out front, he made his way to the door and down the hall. Trey was in the living room.

"I didn't expect you to come back here today," he said to Trey.

"I brought over some stuff to help you gain back some independence. I know how much you hate to depend on others."

"I don't see where I have much of a choice right now."

"I brought over a device called Talking Prescription Bottle. It will attach to your prescription bottles. I've recorded all the necessary information about your medication."

"That's interesting," Samson said, intrigued. "I never knew there was anything out there like that."

"I also bought you an atomic talking clock. According to the box, it's a full-function talking calendar alarm clock that will never need setting or adjusting. All time and calendar functions are spoken in a clear female voice."

The feeling that he could become more independent brought a smile to Samson's face. "That's nice. Trey, how much do I owe you?"

"Nothing at all."

Samson cleared his throat. "I will never have to worry about money. Let me pay you back, because I imagine that clock had to have set you back a lot."

"We're cool. These are my gifts to you. You can get more of the talking prescription devices if you need them."

His encouragement made Samson feel better. "Thanks, Trey. I appreciate all you've done for me."

"And all I will do. Come on, we're going out."

Trey took him for a short walk around the neighborhood. Samson tired easily, so they didn't stay outside long. They returned to the house and found his uncle sitting on the porch.

"I'm going to sit out here and talk to my uncle for a while," he told Trey. Samson could feel the warmth of the sun and a soothing breeze brushing against his face.

"Okay, well, I'm going to leave. I need to get home, but I'll check on you later."

"He's always been a good friend to you, Samson," Zachariah said.

He nodded. "Even when I wasn't that great a friend to him. What goes around truly does come around."

"Samson, you can get through this trial. I know the man you are."

Samson frowned. "I always thought I could handle anything that was thrown at me, but I don't know about this." Samson hated sounding so weak and scared.

"Son, you know that God comes in the face of disaster. You hold on to that."

"That's easy for you to say. You still have your eyesight."

"But I also have cancer," Zachariah reminded him. "You might not have your eyesight, but you have your health." He paused to let that sink in. "Samson, you can either ride the storm or you can struggle against it, but you're not going to change a thing in the end. The Lord is in control, and when things look their bleakest, just look around, Jesus is about to show up."

Samson knew that his uncle was right, but right now his situation was just too awful for him to grasp. "I'm blind and it could be permanent. Don't you get it? I'm being punished."

"There are consequences for every action, but I wouldn't say that God is punishing you."

Samson heard the front door ease open. He knew that he and Zachariah were no longer alone. His aunt had joined them.

"The next thing I know, you're going to tell me that I'll have a testimony."

"You will," Hazel interjected. "The storms of life are God's means of testimony."

"I know all the verbiage, Auntie. But it doesn't matter when all I see around me is darkness. I'm sorry, but I can't find joy in my situation. I can't."

"You will pass this test," Hazel stated firmly. "You will.

Hon, thank God that Jesus came with a message of peace and of power. He came with a word of power."

That wasn't helping him. "I don't care what you and Uncle say right now," Samson said. "God gave me plenty of chances to do right. I made choices and now he's punishing me. It is what it is."

"Samson—"

"Let the man be," Zachariah said, cutting her off. "This is his cross to bear, and Samson has to do it the best way he can."

He heard his aunt sigh in resignation.

When Zachariah was ready to go back into the house, Samson followed him inside with Hazel guiding him.

While she saw to her husband's comfort, Samson decided to explore the house by touch. He needed to become more familiar with where the doors were, how the furniture was positioned, and the flow of each room. He was determined to do this with the use of a cane.

Later that evening, Samson received a surprise visitor. From the disapproving tone in his aunt's voice, he initially thought Delinda had shown up until the woman said, "Hello, Samson. It's me, Teà."

He smiled, hiding his disappointment. "Teà, how are you?"

"I'm fine. I heard about what happened to you in Nassau, and I wanted to come by and make sure that you were okay."

"News travel fast, I see. You're my fifth visitor this week."

"It's been all over the news and in the tabloids," Teà told him. "They keep saying you were attacked in your suite by some locals trying to rob you and that Bobby and his wife were in the one next door, and that he saved your life. The only problem I see with this story is that I've seen you out with Bobby's wife. And I know Bobby—he's very jealous and he likes to fight. I understand why y'all would want to keep this under wraps, but tell me the truth. Samson, weren't you involved with his wife?"

He didn't respond. In the end, Bobby had paid him a five-million-dollar settlement for the loss of Samson's eyesight. It had brought him little satisfaction, but he would respect the terms of the agreement.

"That's fine if you don't want to tell me—I'm pretty sure I'm right. I know the type of women you like."

He allowed a smile. "I suppose you think you do."

She moved closer to him. "Samson, can you see anything at all?"

He shook his head. "I'm totally blind."

"I'm so sorry."

"It's not like you did it," he said. "I'm so glad you came by, Teà. I've missed talking to you."

"I've missed you too. You know I care about you."

"That's good to know," Samson said. "I've lost a lot of my so-called friends. I haven't really heard from anyone outside of Trey and people from church since I came home."

"It's not that they don't care about you. They just don't know what to say to you," Teà said. "I have to confess that I'm at a loss for words myself. I want to comfort you, but I don't know what to say."

"I just need you to be here for me."

He heard her stand up. "I don't know if I can do that. I have to be honest with you. Seeing you like this freaks me out. I can't handle it."

Samson wasn't sure what he was hearing in her voice but it sounded as if she were saying good-bye. "What exactly are you saying?"

Regret filled her voice. "I don't know how to be here for you. I can't bear seeing you like this. I'm sorry."

He could tell that she was getting ready to leave. "Teà, don't leave. Let's talk this out."

"I really have to go," she said.

"Where did Teà go rushing off to?" Hazel asked when she entered the family room. "She looked upset."

"She had an appointment," he said. But Samson knew the real reason she went flying out of the house. Teà couldn't bear to look at his pathetic eyes any longer.

She pitied him.

CHAPTER 28

"Hi, Mr. Taylor, my name is Meagan Montgomery. I'm an instructor at the Raleigh Academy of the Blind. Trey is a friend of mine and he asked me to come out to talk to you."

Samson didn't respond. He had woken up in a truly black mood this morning. He had told Trey last week not to waste the woman's time by sending her. Irritated, he intended to call his friend and get on him for butting into his life.

"Mr. Taylor, did you—"

"I heard you," he snapped. "I'm not deaf."

If he had offended her, Meagan didn't act on it. "You're visually impaired, Mr. Taylor, but you can't let—"

"I'm blind," he said, rudely cutting her off. "Let's just call it what it is. No need to be politically correct around here."

"Mr. Taylor, why don't we sit here and talk?" Meagan suggested.

"Talk about what?"

"Why don't we let you get some stuff off your chest? For instance, why do you hate being blind?"

Her cheerful tone grated on his nerves. "You're kidding, right?"

"No, I'm very serious. You're angry and you need to get it out, so do it. Mr. Taylor, why do you hate being blind?"

"I can't see!" he shouted. "That's why. And please stop calling me Mr. Taylor. Just call me Samson."

"Okay, that's number one," she said, completely ignoring his outburst.

Samson calmed down some. "I hate that being blind restricts my mobility and that I can no longer drive myself anywhere. I don't like being dependent on other people."

"What else?" Meagan prompted.

"I can't pick out my own clothes or look in a mirror anymore," Samson said, recalling all the things he used to enjoy. "I miss seeing the stars, moon, and trees. The trees in North Carolina are beautiful in the fall. I won't see them change colors ever again. I wish I could roll all by myself sometimes, without having to be bothered with anyone."

"Life doesn't have to end for you."

Samson couldn't wait for Meagan to leave. Her optimistic view of life and sunny disposition frustrated him to no end. "For your information, my life is over, Meagan. All I want is to be left alone."

"That's not possible right now."

"So everyone keeps telling me," he muttered. "Blind people can't live on their own."

"Mr. Taylor, I understand the hardest thing about losing your vision is fighting the anger and the depression. It's difficult to adjust to something that is so unexpected—something that has now affected every aspect of your life. I'm sure I would be angry and frustrated at times just like you, but you have to realize that losing your vision doesn't mean you can't still function. Life doesn't end when you lose your sight; it just gets more complex," Meagan told him. "I have a couple of students who live alone."

He remained stonily silent.

"If you let me, I'll help you address the complex issues and continue to live your life independently and fully." She released a soft sigh. "But I can't help you if you won't let me, Mr. Taylor."

"I told you to call me Samson," he said, fed up. "If you can't follow that simple request, then what do I need you for?"

A bout of silence followed. "I don't think I'm the person for you," Meagan said quietly. "I know that you're scared and angry, but I will not allow you to continue to be rude to me or verbally abuse me. It's time you stopped wallowing in self-pity and learned to deal with your life, Samson. Trey can find someone else to work with you."

"Wallowing in self-pity!" Samson snapped. "You're crazy, lady. Look, I don't need you."

"No, you don't. You're certainly right about that. You need Jesus! I pray the Lord continues to bless and keep you during this transition. I'll show myself out."

Samson muttered a string of profanities under his breath. He could feel the sting of her gaze as she eyed him a moment before storming out of the house.

"You were wrong and you know it," his aunt stated.

"I didn't hear you come in."

"I've been standing here a good while, Samson. I can't believe you treated that poor girl like that. All she came here to do is help you."

He was tired of being scolded. "I'll tell you like I told her, Aunt Hazel. I don't need any help."

"Look here, boy. Don't you go thinking that I give a fig about you being blind. Ain't no cause for you to talk to me like this, and I for one won't be taking it. I still have my bat, and I will bring down the law of the Lord on your head with every strike. Now, I know you hurting, but you better get yourself together."

He faltered under her stinging words. "You don't understand."

"Oh, I understand, all right. You're having yourself one good pity party, and you're not ready for it to end." She made a tapping sound, like she was knocking on the door frame. "Samson, your uncle needs me, so I'm going to him. You can stay here in this room by your lonesome."

"I don't need anybody," he growled.

"We'll just see about that," Hazel responded. "I always told you that a hard head makes a soft behind. You should be ashamed of the way you treated Meagan. She's a sweet girl and was doing everything she could to help you."

Nobody can help me except God, but we're not on speaking terms at the moment.

• • •

Samson carefully eased his body to the edge of the bed, and then slowly rose to his feet. He put his hand out in front of him, inching a step forward, then another, until his foot got caught on the bottom of the overstuffed chair in the bedroom, tripping him. His knees connected painfully with the hardwood floors.

Hazel rushed into the room. "Oh, dear Lord in heaven," she shrieked. "Hon, are you okay?"

Samson ran his fingers over the smooth surface of the floor. "I'm okay," he grunted.

His aunt helped him to his feet. "Zachariah wants to see you," she told him. Hazel took him by the hand and led him into the master bedroom, where his uncle lay.

"Hey, Uncle," Samson said. "I heard you wanted to talk to me."

"Son, I need you to hear me out," his uncle said. "Now, I know that you're frustrated. I know you want to go back to your own house and be independent, but it's going to take time for you to readjust your living and working skills to your new situation." Zachariah was straining to speak. "The only way to accomplish this is through specialized training. You shouldn't have been so mean to that young woman. She was only trying to help you."

Irritated, Samson sighed. "I can't believe Aunt Hazel came to you about that. You have enough to deal with."

"I'm still the man of my house and, son, I need to set you straight. You're a man now, and it's time you start acting like one. A real man recognizes when he needs help and isn't afraid or too proud to accept assistance."

His uncle sounded like he was getting weaker, Samson realized. He was not about to upset the man he loved like a father. "I know you're right," he said softly. "I feel betrayed, angry, and so many other emotions."

"I imagine anyone facing what you are would feel the same way. You lost your sight, son, but you still got your life. Try to enjoy every minute of it."

Samson couldn't imagine how his uncle could remain so upbeat in the storm he was battling. He was getting weaker every day, but still he never uttered a negative word. "Do you have any regrets, Uncle?"

"Yeah," he admitted with a sigh. "I didn't spend as much time as I would've liked with your aunt. She never once complained, though. She has been a good wife to me."

"She loves you dearly," Samson told him.

"I know. I can see it in her eyes, feel it in her touch, and hear it in her voice. Son, I want you to promise me that you're going to take care of my Hazel when the Lord calls me home. She's gonna need your strength."

Samson felt badly about snapping at her earlier. She was dealing with a lot herself. "I promise I'll make sure she's okay."

"I've already told the board members that I want you to be the senior pastor and they are in agreement."

Samson did not respond. There was nothing he could really say. He could not tell his uncle that he did not intend to ever set foot into another pulpit.

• • •

Zachariah Turner stepped from earth into eternity the very next day, on the first of October. Homegoing services were held at Hillside four days later.

Samson wrapped an arm around his aunt, giving her a comforting squeeze as they headed to the waiting limo at the cemetery. "I guess Uncle's up there grinning because he got to see Jesus first."

Hazel chuckled. "Yeah, he would love that."

"I'm going to miss him," Samson said.

"Me too. I feel like a huge part of me is missing." Her voice broke and Samson knew that she was crying. He hugged her, feeling how frail she'd become.

"He loved you more than anything else in this world, Auntie."

"Zachariah loved you like a son. I hope you know that."

"I do. He was a great dad to me. When my parents died, I had never felt more alone, but you and Uncle, you welcomed me into your home and your hearts. Thank you for that."

"We're at the car," Hazel said.

She got into the limo first, and then he followed. Samson had become better at navigating around.

They rode back to the church in silence. The house was too small to host a repast, so Hazel decided to hold it at the banquet dining hall. Samson got out of the limo and assisted his aunt. She guided him toward the doors.

"Sounds like the entire congregation is here," he whispered.

"And some," Hazel confirmed. "Zachariah was well loved by the members and the community. The mayor is here, Congressman Burns, and a few other high-profile officials."

One of the ushers guided them to a table that had been reserved for the family. Samson heard familiar footsteps and caught a whiff of Savannah's fragrance as she approached him.

Samson instantly became guarded. He and Trey had made peace, but this was his first run-in with Savannah since seeing them at the restaurant when he was seeing Delinda.

"I see some people I need to say hello to," Hazel said. "I'll leave you two to talk."

"Savannah . . ."

"I'm so sorry for your loss, Samson," she said. "I really liked your uncle and I had a lot of respect for him."

"Thank you," Samson responded stiffly. "He liked you, too."

"How have you been?" she asked, taking a seat beside him. "I've been worried about you."

"I'm not your problem anymore, Savannah. You don't need to worry about me."

"I know that you don't want to believe this, but I still care what happens to you. I know that a lot has happened, but I really hope that one day we'll be able to get past it and be friends."

Samson shook his head, canceling out the possibility. "I have to be honest with you, Savannah. I don't know if that will ever happen."

"You and Trey are working through everything. Why is it so hard for us to try and build a friendship?"

He had never considered the idea of having her as a friend. "Trey and I are like family. He betrayed me, but I know his character and so we were able to get past this. As for you—I loved you more than my own life, Savannah. I really thought that I'd take my last breath with you by my side. That won't happen now, and to be honest with you, I'm not interested in being your friend. I'm sorry, but it's too much to expect."

"I'm sorry you feel that way," she said, her voice barely above a whisper. "Since you and Trey were working through your issues, I had hoped we could do the same."

"It's still too soon, Savannah," he told her, then he remembered what his uncle used to say about unforgiveness. It poisoned the heart. In a more tolerant voice he added, "Savannah, it's still too soon for me, but maybe in time . . ."

"I understand," she said. "Please let me know if I can do anything to help you."

"We'll be fine, Aunt Hazel and I."

She released a soft sigh, then said, "Okay. Well, take care of yourself."

"I always do."

"From the expression on your face, I have a feeling that your conversation with Savannah didn't go well."

Samson hadn't realized his aunt had returned. "She has decided she wants to be friends. Can you believe that? Savannah actually thinks that we can just lay the past to rest and start a friendship. I know I have to forgive her, but I'm not ready to be her friend."

"You and Trey are moving in that direction," Hazel said. "I guess she figures that you and she can do the same. I thought that maybe you had gotten past all this."

"I have, but I don't need people like her in my life. She is Trey's problem now."

Hazel covered his hand in hers. "For what it's worth, she does look repentant."

He prayed his aunt wouldn't keep pushing him. "I don't care how she looks, Aunt Hazel. She wronged me and I won't apologize for not rushing to forgive and forget. She took vows with me, and apparently they meant nothing to her."

Hazel kept patting his hand, and he remembered he was there to honor his uncle.

"Let's change the subject," he suggested.

"I couldn't agree more," she said. "Actually, there is something we need to discuss. Hon, you know that Zachariah would want you to take over as senior pastor."

His body stiffened and Samson shook his head. "I can't do it."

"What are you talking about? Preaching is what you've been called to do. Before he died, Zachariah spoke with the advisory board about you becoming the senior pastor. Pastor Greene has agreed to be your right hand. I will be your eyes."

Samson's insides tightened with hostility. "Aunt Hazel, look at me. I am in no condition to get up in a pulpit and talk about the goodness of God. I'm angry and I don't want to preach ever again."

"I'm so sorry that you feel this way," Hazel said quietly, sounding disappointed. "I know that you're dealing with a lot right now, but God still loves you."

"I'm not feeling the love," he said rigidly. Acid anger burned inside him. "Sometimes I think it would've been better if I'd died that day."

"I hate when you talk like this, son. It grieves my spirit."

"I wish Uncle was still here. I miss him."

"So do I," Hazel murmured softly. "I don't sleep well at night because he's not in bed beside me. We've been married forty years, and I can't help feeling like there's a big chunk of me missing."

Samson put his own troubles aside and asked, "How are you doing, really?"

"I'm sad," Hazel confessed. "Really sad and heartbroken. The love of my life has passed from time into eternity. I know that I should be rejoicing that he's gone to be with the Lord and no longer suffering from pain . . . I just pray for God's peace."

"I feel like God has taken everything from me," Samson said.

"It's easier just to blame Him, I suppose."

"Aunt Hazel, this is God's doing. He allowed me to lose my sight, and for what? If this is what happens when you serve Him, I want no part of it."

"I see."

Samson waited for her to go on, but she didn't. "That's all you're going to say?"

"It sounds like you've made up your mind. Anything I tell you won't mean anything."

Samson noted how tired she sounded. "I've never known you to go down without a fight, Auntie."

"Hon, you're a grown man. I can't change the way you feel. When you're ready to take a nice long look in the mirror, even a blind man will be able to see the truth."

Some of the fight was back.

"I accept my part in what's happened. Believe me, I do. But to lose my eyesight along with everything else . . ."

She did not respond.

"I know that you think I'm wrong," Samson said. "You might as well say it."

"Hon, this is the path you've chosen to take, but I know that at some point you'll turn around and come back to where you belong. The call is much too great and there's no escaping it."

Samson decided to give voice to what he really wanted. "I need God to give me back my sight. If He does this for me, I will go back into the pulpit fully committed."

"Do you think you can bargain with the Lord, Samson?" Hazel asked frostily.

He didn't care. "I just want to be able to see again. What's wrong with that? He's called me to the pulpit . . . well, I need my eyes to do it."

Later at home, Samson thought about Meagan and felt bad for the way he had treated her. She had done nothing to deserve his rage. He stuck out his hand, searching for his cell phone. When he found it he activated the voice dialing. "Call Meagan Montgomery."

She didn't answer. Samson left a short message asking her to return his phone call.

Two hours passed.

He tried a second time. Still no answer.

"Do you need some help?" his aunt asked. "Are you trying to call someone?"

"I was trying to call Meagan. I wanted to apologize to her, but she's not answering and she won't return my phone call."

"Maybe she's busy with her clients, Samson. Meagan will probably give you a call later."

He didn't want to be pushy, but he needed to make things right between them. "You think so?"

A little of her iciness from the church returned. "Hon, I believe the woman is out trying to make a living. She's not sitting at home waiting on you to call."

"That I don't doubt," Samson said. He decided to make a grim joke. "Auntie, when I had my sight I was juggling women, but since the accident, I don't think I've heard from anybody except Teà, and she can't handle my blindness. Well, I take that back. I did hear from a couple of women— they wanted to check to make sure I was fine and wanted to know if the blindness was permanent. When I told them that it might be, I never heard back from them."

"There is a woman out there somewhere who will love you regardless," Hazel reassured him.

He was eager to hear the words. "You are forever the optimist."

"You are a wonderful man, Samson. You deserve some-one special."

He wanted to believe her, but he no longer trusted himself when it came to women. Changing the subject, Samson asked, "What time is it, Auntie?"

"It's almost three."

"Should I try Meagan again?"

"Wait until the end of the day," Hazel advised. "She could be in meetings, with a client, or taking care of paperwork. Meagan will call you when she's done."

"I was really mean to her."

"I'm sure you weren't the first client to react negatively. You were still in shock over the accident and losing your sight."

"I need her. If I'm ever going to learn to do things for myself, then I need Meagan to help me."

Hazel agreed.

Samson tried once again to reach her later that evening, but she still didn't answer. He was pretty sure Meagan was avoiding him.

CHAPTER 29

$\mathcal{H}$azel spent most of the next morning trying to get Samson to reconsider returning to the pulpit.

"I'm sorry, but I can't do it," he told her.

"Before he died, Zachariah told me that God pressed upon his spirit that you were the one to replace him as leader of Hillside."

Samson knew she was telling the truth because God had placed that on his heart as well, but he was still angry. He was not in the right mind-set to step up as pastor. He was not worthy.

"God looks at the heart, Samson."

"He still judges harshly."

Samson was glad when Trey showed up. It would get his aunt off his back.

"I can't get Meagan to return any of my calls," Samson told Trey when they were alone in the den. "Have you talked to her?"

"I spoke to her last night," he responded. "Samson, she's not coming back here. But don't worry, I found someone else for you. Maybe you and Charles will be a better fit."

Samson shook his head. "No, I want Meagan. I only want to work with her."

"I understand that, but the fact of the matter is that she isn't interested in working with you. She finds you rude."

"I was," he admitted. "But I'm feeling better. I'll be nicer this time around. Trey, I know I was a big jerk to her, but I need you to get Meagan to come back to me."

Trey was baffled by his insistence. "Why her?"

"I don't know," Samson answered. "I guess I feel bad about the way I treated her and I'd like a chance to make it up to her."

"I can't force her to work for you. If you've apologized already, then just move on."

Samson could feel his old stubbornness come back. "I liked Meagan's style. I would feel comfortable with her, and she won't care about my attitude."

"Your attitude is one of the reasons Meagan left."

He knew his friend was right, but he wasn't going to give up. He hadn't been nice to Meagan, but there was something about her—maybe it was her peace, the calmness of her spirit—that drew him to her. "Just do me this favor, Trey," he pleaded. "Talk to her."

A change appeared in Trey's voice. "Samson, are you interested in Meagan?"

His question surprised Samson. "No. Why would you ask me that?"

"Well, when she was here, you didn't want her around and now all of a sudden, you're dying to work with Meagan and only her."

Samson hardly thought it was a sign of interest. "I think you'll agree that I wasn't exactly in my right mind when she was here. Trey, I need you to get Meagan to come back."

"I can't promise you anything, but I will see what I can do."

"Thank you," Samson said.

Trey changed the subject. "Hey, I hear that you're refusing to take over the reins at Hillside."

"Aunt Hazel told you right," Samson said. "I'm done with preaching."

Trey grabbed his shoulder and held it. "I've known you for a long time. You were born to be a minister. We both know this."

"That was before I ruined my life."

"You've always talked about how God is so forgiving." His grip grew tighter. "Are you telling me that He doesn't forgive you?"

"Forgiveness comes with consequences. We still have to pay for our actions, Trey. I just never thought mine would come at such a high price. Living in this darkness is pure hell."

Trey let go at last. "Samson, I don't think you should view this as a punishment. Losing your sight is a tragedy, but one that you can overcome."

"I don't know about that, but I do know that I have to adjust my lifestyle to fit my disability, and I need Meagan to help me do that."

"Like I said," Trey said, laughing at his insistence, "I'll see what I can do."

• • •

"I sent the flowers to Meagan along with a note expressing your apology," Hazel announced two days later when she entered the den, where Samson sat listening to the television. This was one of the things he missed—just the simple act of watching TV.

"Did you mention that I want her to come back to work with me?"

"I did."

"Thank you, Auntie. I appreciate you taking care of this for me."

"I didn't mind it at all."

"Auntie, are you cooking collard greens?" Samson asked, sniffing the air.

"I am. You've always had a good nose when it comes to food. You know, you're getting around this house pretty good without assistance."

Her words pleased him. "I can see the way this room looks in my mind. I hope you don't plan on moving the furniture around anytime soon."

"I won't," Hazel said. She hesitated, then made a suggestion. "Samson, why don't you rent out your place or put it on the market and just move back here with me? I wouldn't feel good about you living alone."

"Right now I can't go anywhere. I've been trying to decide what I want to do with the place, though. Speaking of which, I need you to write out some checks for me. I need to pay my mortgage and some other bills."

"Okay."

"I'm thinking about having someone manage my finances for me."

"Hon, if you want me to, I'll take care of them for you. I don't mind."

"Are you sure?" He trusted his aunt but didn't want to burden her with taking charge of his expenses.

"Hon, I will do anything I can to help you."

Samson nodded. Then a familiar rumble started in his stomach. "Auntie, when are those greens going to be ready?"

She laughed. "Not for a half hour. Would you like for me to make you a sandwich or something?"

"I'll wait for the collards."

The telephone rang. Hazel left the room to answer it.

"It's not her," Hazel said when she came back in. "It's Deacon Byrd."

Samson rose to his feet and tentatively made his way to his bedroom, using the walls as a guide. He had learned to recognize every nuance of the doorways; he even knew where the light switch plates were located even though he didn't need them.

Once in his room, he sat down on the edge of his bed, his face in his hands. Samson was miserable with the way things were going for him. He hated living in darkness.

"Help me, Father God," he whispered. "Please help me. I can't live like this. I need some help, and if Meagan won't help me, then I guess I'll have to find someone else."

Samson removed his shoes and crawled into bed. He fell asleep as soon as his head touched the pillow.

Samson thought he had dozed off when he heard someone knocking on the door. "Come in."

"I wanted to make sure you were up," Hazel said. "I checked on you earlier but saw that you were sleeping."

"How long have I been asleep?"

"About two hours. If you're ready to eat, I'll fix your plate."

He gave her a grateful smile. "Thank you, Auntie."

Samson felt renewed by his sleep. Right then and there he decided, he needed to start building a life for himself.

CHAPTER 30

The doorbell rang and Samson stumbled forward, his hands out in front of him. He shuffled his feet forward along the floorboards. Samson found the knob by sliding his hands across the wood grain surface of the door.

He experienced a small measure of triumph in being able to open the door.

"Good morning, Samson. Good job."

He smiled broadly. "Meagan, thank you for coming back." Samson moved aside to let her enter. "I am truly sorry for the way I behaved. I was in a depressed state, bitter, and I struck out at anyone around me. This hasn't been easy for me, but I had no right to be rude to you."

"I recognize that, totally," Meagan responded. "But having said that, Samson, I'll warn you, I won't allow you to mistreat me in any way. I know that you're going to have good and bad days. I know that you won't always be in the best of moods, but I do expect you to temper your rage when it comes to me. I'm not your enemy. I'm here to help you adjust to your new lifestyle."

He nodded emphatically. "I understand."

She took Samson's hand and guided him back into the living room. The scent of Meagan's perfume stayed with him.

"So where do we start?"

"It might be helpful if you got a Seeing Eye dog."

His lips turned downward. "I'm not about to become the poster child for pity."

"I notice you have lots of books, so you must love reading."

"I did," Samson confirmed. "It's one of the things I miss most—reading. I have audio books, but it's not the same. I love books."

"That doesn't have to change. You can still enjoy a good book. You can learn Braille."

He had thought about that before. He didn't know how he'd ever learn all the little bumps, though. "Is it really that difficult?" he asked.

"There are different versions of Braille," Meagan explained. "The first version consists of the twenty-six standard letters of the alphabet and punctuation. People who are first starting to read Braille mostly use this. The second version consists of the standard letters of the alphabet, punctuation, and contractions, and the third is used only in personal letters, diaries, and notes. It's like shorthand, with entire words shortened to a few letters."

Samson thought about that. "I guess it's worth a shot," he said. "This is about empowerment, right?"

It was time to leave for the Raleigh Academy of the Blind. Meagan assisted him into the car. While she drove, Samson could hear her humming softly to the music playing on the light radio channel.

The everyday sounds of the road captured Samson's attention. Horns blowing, sirens blaring, and engines revving. With the window down, whenever they stopped at a light, he could hear people talking as they walked across the street.

"How am I supposed to handle money?" Samson suddenly wondered aloud.

"If it's a dollar, you leave it unfolded," Meagan instructed. "For a five, fold it widthwise; for a ten, fold it lengthwise; and for a twenty, you fold it lengthwise, then widthwise."

Scratching his head, Samson muttered, "You make this all sound so easy."

"Samson, I know that it's not, especially when you have just recently lost your sight. But I promise that you will find a way to handle all sorts of problems."

"What if I don't want to?" he asked, feeling overwhelmed. "What then?"

"I don't know. I guess you have to find a way to make peace with your situation."

He didn't like that answer, but he didn't want to argue. "Meagan, I want you to do something for me," Samson said. "When you leave here this evening, take a few minutes to admire the trees and the flowers all around. As you drive, take note of your surroundings—the beauty of God's landscape designs, which He entrusted to our care. The weather's nice, so make sure you soak in the spectacular sights. The colors are usually breathtaking this time of year."

"It's beautiful outside," Meagan said. "Just as you remember."

"I'm trying to hold on to those memories. I've always known that we live in a world of senses—hearing, smell, sight, and sound—and we take them for granted. I know I did."

"I know this is hard on you, but you have to accept the change. I'm not saying you shouldn't have faith that God will heal you—there is always that possibility—but you have to live your life in the meantime."

He cracked a wary smile. "You have more confidence in me than I have in myself right now—that's unusual for me."

She chuckled. "I'm sure."

"I guess you think I'm arrogant."

"You have your moments."

Samson gave a short laugh. "Don't bother holding back, Meagan. Tell me what you really think of me."

"Actually, I think that you are a nice guy who has gone through something life-altering, and you're trying your best to stay afloat."

"I was arrogant," Samson admitted. "I thought a lot of myself."

"And now?"

He sighed in resignation. "I feel worthless, like damaged goods. I used to have women all over me, and now they seemed to have all lost my number."

"Why? Because you're blind?"

"Yeah. I actually had one woman tell me that she didn't have time to lead me around. I see her point. I can't see, which means I can't drive or go anywhere. How can I have a social life? I won't ever go back to a restaurant, because I can't see the menu."

"You can still have a social life, Samson. As for that woman . . . she was a jerk."

"I'm not about to let a woman drive me around or order for me—"

Meagan interrupted him by saying, "Now, that's your ego talking. There's nothing wrong with needing some assistance."

"I'm a man."

She released a soft sigh. "You will still be a man, but a man who is visually impaired—at least for now."

Her statement didn't sit well with him. "What woman will want someone like me?"

"You're being too hard on yourself, Samson." Meagan made a right turn. "We're here," she told him.

They got out of the car, and he felt Meagan come up behind him. "Okay, there are exactly twenty steps to the front door," she said as she took his elbow. As they walked, he silently counted every step he took.

A strong burst of air greeted him when the door opened automatically.

"We're approaching the elevators," Meagan told him. When they reached them, she took his hand so that he could feel the raised dotted surface.

"Braille," Samson murmured.

"There are Braille dots near the numbers designating each of the floors."

The loud ding of the elevator bell let them know that one had arrived. Samson turned in the direction of the sound.

"Very good," Meagan said. "You're doing a great job, Samson."

They got off on the fourth floor.

"You'll attend a brief orientation," she told him. "I'll come back and get you when you're done."

"Okay," Samson murmured. He could feel and hear people moving around him. He wondered how many of them were blind; some brushed by him, walking fast. He heard the steady rhythmic tapping of canes on the tile floors.

In a room set up with desks, the director of the academy welcomed everyone and quickly outlined the curriculum.

When orientation was over, Meagan entered the room. Samson knew because his heightened sense of smell picked up the scent of her perfume.

She gave his hand an encouraging squeeze as she guided him down the corridor for his first session.

• • •

Mobility training helped Samson adjust to his blindness, and he developed more confidence in his ability to get around. He sat at the dining room table at his aunt and uncle's house practicing the Braille symbols he'd learned in the first two weeks at the academy. He was learning so much at the school.

Samson didn't want the seeing eye dog; instead he decided

to continue using his cane. He had learned to use it to help him locate steps, curbs, streets, driveways, doorways, bicycles—anything or anyplace.

With Meagan's help, he was also learning how to identify his clothes. Although he had never paid much attention to small details such as buttons, pockets, or fabric and texture, they had suddenly become very important to him. Meagan had given him some Braille labels that his aunt was sewing into his clothes. He had her sew a button into his blue suits and cut the corner of the tag on his black ones. He had two buttons sewn in for his gray suits.

Coming to the academy was the best decision he could've ever made, Samson decided. Later today, he had a class that would help him get back into the kitchen. He missed cooking for himself and didn't want his aunt to feel as if she always had to make dinner.

Samson needed his independence. He needed to feel more like himself again.

CHAPTER 31

"*Y*our aunt tells me you're not preaching anymore. Why not?" Meagan said one day.

By now Samson had learned how spiritual Meagan was, and he had an excuse ready "It's not easy to prepare a sermon when I can't do the research or even read the Bible. Aunt Hazel bought me an audio Bible, but it's not the same."

"Samson, there are Bibles and religious study aids published in Braille," she pointed out. "You have people around you who want to help you. The associate pastor of Hillside has offered to help, but you're letting your pride get in the way."

Apparently, she wasn't buying his excuse. "I see my aunt has been giving you an earful of what's going on with me," he said curtly.

"She really loves you, and she's worried about you."

His tone softened. "I know she does. I just wish she could understand that it's frustrating for me, dealing with all of this."

Meagan was getting better at reading him and she exclaimed, "I hope I don't upset you by asking this, but are you angry at the Lord?"

"Yeah," he responded heatedly. "No point in lying about it. I'm very angry at Him. I admit that I've made some big mistakes over the past couple of years, but I really feel like He's punished harshly. I messed up, but it's not like I killed anyone."

"Sin is sin," Meagan said.

He nodded. "You're right and I know that, but it doesn't help."

He had a petulant strain in his voice that she picked up on. "You look tired. How are you sleeping?"

He shrugged. "Some nights are good, and then other times I don't sleep. I lay in my bed just listening to the sounds of night."

She remained silent. Samson waited for a reply, and then he realized her silence was trying to tell him something.

"Come on, what's on your mind, Meagan?"

"Are you sure you want to hear what I have to say?"

"I know you probably think I'm suffering from a depression. You're most likely right."

"It's not just that. I think that what you're going through is more about your relationship with God."

His voice rose a notch. "We're not talking to each other."

"That's a big part of the problem."

"Meagan, I'm going to be really honest with you. I never wanted to be like my father, but in the end, I turned out to be just like him—maybe even worse."

"In what way?"

"I love women," Samson stated. "And because of that love, I'm blind. I just couldn't keep my hands to myself."

"The fight between you and Bobby Hatcher—that was over his wife?"

Samson nodded. Her lack of a response seemed like a condemnation.

"Meagan, say something, please."

"When you accepted that call on your heart, you were

supposed to abstain from fleshly lusts and attain self-control, which from the sound of it, you didn't. By giving in to your lust, you renounced your convictions. Now that I think about it, your life is very similar to Samson in the Bible. For all of his strength, he was weak."

Samson didn't know if he should be offended or not. "Samson was one of the most arrogant and disobedient characters in the Old Testament," he said.

"He typifies the natural man whose mind has not been renewed by the Word and, when given power prematurely, he can use and abuse it for his own advantage," Meagan observed. "Delilah represented worldly temptations that had become Samson's Waterloo."

"I had one of those in my life," Samson allowed. "Only her name was Delinda."

"Samson, we all at one time or the other fall to temptation. We have to ask Him to help us stay on the right path. We often make the mistake of thinking we can fix ourselves—we don't ask God for His divine help."

"That's why I feel the way that I do," Samson said sadly. "We are God's temple and his Spirit lives in us. If we destroy His temple through sexual immorality, then we desecrate His temple and create hostility toward God. As a result, God will destroy us like He did Samson. He took away his strength and allowed his enemies to pluck out his eyes." Samson pointed to his eyes. "He allowed my sight to be taken away from me."

"Samson, you could follow Samson's lead."

He frowned in confusion. "What are you talking about?"

"Some people drown in self-pity, but not Samson. He did the right thing. He prayed to God for the grace of giving him back his strength, so that in his handicap he could still serve God's purpose till death."

Samson nodded at that comment. "In a weak moment, Samson ended up breaking all his vows, yet God still used

Samson to defeat the Philistines. He could've done much more if he had obeyed," he said, more to himself than to Meagan.

"God made each of us for a reason," Meagan said. "He made us exactly how he wanted, but remember that God doesn't make mistakes. Your life might not be perfect, and it may not have turned out the way you think it should be, but He wants you to learn and grow with what you have."

All of a sudden he realized they were having a remarkable conversation. "Are you always so positive?" he asked her. "Maybe you should be a pastor."

"It's not my calling, but I do try to be optimistic. It doesn't do any good to be negative."

Samson chuckled. "I can see why you and Trey are friends. Why is it that I never met you? I've known Trey most of my life."

"We actually met once," she told him. "You had just graduated from Duke Divinity School."

This news surprised him. "Really?" He searched his memory, thinking back to the different women he'd seen Trey with. "Meagan, I don't remember that."

"You were too focused on my friend Vanessa."

He remember Vanessa, with her fine self . . . she was with a full-figured girl . . . that was Meagan?

As if she heard his thoughts, she said, "Yeah, I was the big girl with her."

"I think I remember that day," he said. He didn't want to reflect back to when he could see and appreciate beautiful women. The last woman he saw was Delinda, and look how that turned out.

He decided to change the subject. "I'll have you know, I made my own dinner last night. My aunt helped, but I cooked most of it myself."

He could feel her smiling at him.

"That's wonderful," she said. "I'm so proud of you, Samson." The awkward moment had passed. "You've become proficient enough to move on to the next part of your rehabilitation," Meagan said. "I'm extremely proud of you and all that you've accomplished in a short time."

"I couldn't have done it without you," Samson told her. "Thank you for your help. I really hope that you and I can become friends."

"I'd like that."

"So, friend, how about helping me prepare dinner?"

She tapped his hand. "C'mon, take me to your kitchen."

Meagan took time to explain to Samson how to use his nose and his hands to determine if fresh fruits and vegetables were ripe. She also offered tips on identifying spices.

"Smell this one," she told him.

Samson sniffed. "This is cinnamon."

"How about this one?"

He took in the pungent scent. "I have no idea."

She laughed. "It's thyme."

"Yeah, it's *time* to stop this lesson," Samson said, feeling a bit foolish. "Let's get this chicken in the oven."

"You're the boss."

Samson found that he loved the sound of her laughter. He enjoyed her company—mainly because she never made any demands on him outside of the academy. He had never really had a platonic friendship with a woman, so this was something new to him.

They sat down to dinner with Hazel forty-five minutes later. As his aunt said grace, Samson waited for them to try the chicken and prayed he hadn't overdone it with the seasonings.

"Hon, this chicken is delicious," Hazel told him.

Meagan agreed.

Samson sliced off a piece with his fork. He stuck it in his mouth and chewed. "It did come out pretty tender, didn't it? Actually, I think it's better now than when I could see."

They made small talk while they finished their dinner.

Afterward, Hazel refused any help to clean up the kitchen so Samson and Meagan sat down in the den.

"Meagan," he confessed, "I wish that I could see what you look like," he told her.

"You can," she said. "With your hands. Put your fingers on my face and tell me what you see."

He raised his hands to her face.

"Your skin feels smooth, almost silky," Samson said as his fingers explored. "What color are your eyes?"

"Brown. I would say a medium brown."

"You have soft curly hair that seems to fall past your shoulders, medium brown eyes with long lashes, high cheekbones, and full lips. From the texture of your hair, I would say that you're mixed with something."

"My mother is white," she told him. "I have my father's coloring, which is what I would call a coffee color."

Samson felt he had been bold enough and pulled his fingers away. "I knew that you were beautiful, but I wanted to see for myself."

"Thank you for the compliment," she said shyly.

He felt her getting up. "What's going on? Are you leaving?" Samson didn't want Meagan to leave. He was enjoying their time together.

"I have Bible study tonight. I'll see you tomorrow at the academy."

He rose to his feet. "I'll walk you to the door."

When he returned to the den, Hazel said, "I think you've taken a liking to Meagan."

"I have," Samson confessed. "She's a nice girl."

He stayed in the den with his aunt for a while before making his way to his bedroom. Yet, Samson didn't lie down. He prowled the confines of the room, walking back and forth. His insides were in turmoil over his feelings for Meagan.

He had finally found the right woman for him, but Samson was afraid that he'd blown it by confessing his sins.

Meagan was not the type of girl who would be interested in a man like him.

• • •

The more time they spent together, the closer he felt to her. Three weeks after joining the academy, Samson decided it was time to be completely honest with Meagan.

Hazel had gone to the church for a meeting, so he and Meagan were alone. He pulled her into his arms, kissing her. When she responded by kissing him back, Samson slowly released her, but not before he felt her trembling. "I've been wanting to do that for a while now."

"What are we doing, Samson?" Meagan asked with a tinge of apprehension.

"I want more than friendship," he told her. "You've become very special to me."

"You're special to me too," she pointed out, "but you told me that you wanted to just be friends."

"Not anymore. I would like to pursue a relationship with you. Whatever exists between us really feels right."

Her voice trembled. "Maybe you should take some time to really figure out what you want."

"I know what I want. I want to be with you. Now, if you don't feel the same way, then just tell me."

Meagan didn't respond right away. When she spoke, she said, "I'd like to see where this goes."

"You have no idea how happy you've made me. I finally feel like I'm getting my life back. All the good parts."

Meagan reached over and took his hand in hers. "Let's take it one day at a time."

CHAPTER 32

$\mathcal{O}$n Sunday morning a few days later, Samson sat outside on the patio. The November weather was still on the warm side. He couldn't stop thinking about Meagan.

She was everything a man could want in a woman. She could be sweet but also brave enough to set him straight when he needed it.

Lately, she had been on his back about returning to the pulpit. God had been dealing with him as well. Samson thought about a sermon he had preached a couple of years ago. He had talked of how Jesus and His men were on their way to the temple on the Sabbath, and happened to notice a man who had been blind since birth. The disciples posed a question to Jesus: "Rabbi, who sinned?" They wanted to know whose sin caused the man's tragic condition.

In his sermon, Samson had explained the historical implications to the congregation. "During the time of Jesus, any physical illness or ailment was seen as punishment by God. He was punishing you because you had sinned. That man spent his entire life believing that he was blind because he had committed a sin.

"Jesus replied that neither this man nor his parents sinned. The purpose for the blindness was in order that the work of God might be displayed in the man's life."

Samson further explained that the man was not just physically blind but blind to seeing God's love for him. He was blind to knowing his own innate goodness by believing that he was a sinner and being punished.

As he thought back on that sermon, Samson realized that he had a very similar issue. He had been blind to his own self-worth and blind to God's unconditional love for him, despite the sins of his flesh.

The words from "Amazing Grace" flowed into his mind. *I was blind but now I see . . .* "There is nothing we can do to change the eternal love of our Heavenly Father," he whispered. "All of us are worthy of unconditional love because God created us worthy, and that can never change."

Samson began to pray for the first time in a long time. He prayed for God to give him the strength to accept his condition, but he also repented of his sins and asked for forgiveness.

When he was done, Samson felt something he hadn't felt in a long time.

Peace.

• • •

The next day, Samson met with the interim pastor of Hillside. "Thank you for seeing me, Pastor Burkette."

"I'm glad you called me. Zachariah is up there smiling in Heaven."

Samson said forthrightly, "I've made so many mistakes, Pastor."

"Who hasn't? Surely you don't think you're the only one."

Samson laid out the truth right up front. "I blamed God for what happened to me and for taking my uncle away when I needed him most. After everything that happened,

I left the church. As far as I was concerned, me and God weren't on speaking terms."

"Son, we've all had moments like that. But the good news is that God is persistent. He doesn't just wait around for us to come back to him. He keeps pursuing us, loves us passionately, and goes to great lengths to help us see our situation with clarity and wisdom."

Samson nodded in agreement. "One thing I learned was that without him, I stay in trouble."

Pastor Burkette sounded glad Samson was being so honest. "When you go home, I want you to read . . . I'm sorry . . ."

Samson smiled. "I have an audio Bible. Please go on, Pastor."

"Check out the book of Hosea. It's a perfect example of God's loving heart and persistent nature."

"I know the book well," Samson told him. "I did a paper on it when I was in Divinity School. My topic was 'God Will Find You in Your Worst Moments.'"

"Son, it's time to ignore Satan's whispers that you have to be good enough to come back. God doesn't wait to buy you out of whatever slavery you've created for yourself. God helps you where you are. Losing your sight was not what you bargained for, but instead of looking at it as a tragedy, try looking at it as a hidden blessing."

Samson had never considered that idea. "I'm not sure I believe that."

"Ask God to reveal it to you."

He considered the man's words. "Pastor Burkette, I really appreciate your taking time out to see me."

"I want you to know that it's time."

Samson nodded in understanding. "I think you're right."

When he left Pastor Burkette's office, Meagan was in the lobby talking with the secretary. She instantly joined him.

"Thanks for driving me over here," Samson told her as they walked to the car.

"I didn't mind at all."

She didn't ask any questions regarding his visit with Pastor Burkette and he didn't volunteer any information. Samson wasn't ready to say anything prematurely to either Meagan or his aunt.

At home, his aunt had to leave to run some errands, so Meagan stayed with him. They made lunch together and sat down to eat.

When they finished, he helped her clean the kitchen, then he went to lie down.

He was surprised when Meagan came to his room thirty minutes later to tell him, "I didn't know if you were sleeping or not, but you have a visitor."

"Who is it?" he asked, taking a sip of the water he kept on his nightstand.

"Delinda Lewis-Hatcher."

Samson nearly choked on his water. He couldn't hide the surprise in his voice. "D-Delinda's here?"

"Yeah, she's here and she wants to see you. I guess she wants to see how you're doing."

Although she displayed no emotion in her tone, he was pretty sure she was bothered by the fact that Delinda had come to see him. Samson reached out and grabbed her hand. "I love you, Meagan."

"I know. I'll send her in."

"Okay."

A minute later he heard Delinda enter his room. "Hello, Samson."

"Delinda, what are you doing here?"

"I came to see you."

"Why now? It's been what? Four, almost five months since your husband burst into my hotel suite and tossed me through a patio door. He was looking for you. So was I."

"I told you that I wanted to work on my marriage. I went to Ashville that weekend because I needed some time alone."

"Why didn't you tell your husband where you were going to be?"

"Samson, that's all in the past." Delinda sat down beside him. "I was very confused back then."

"And now?"

"I did everything I could to make my marriage work, but Bobby . . . he's leaving me for a younger version. They're expecting a baby."

He didn't comment. Her visit was starting to make more sense.

"I know that you tried to tell me that Bobby and I weren't going to work out, but I wouldn't listen. I—"

Samson interrupted her. "Delinda, why are you here?"

"Because I never stopped thinking about you. Samson, I love you and I want to be with you."

"Come again?" Samson couldn't believe what he was hearing. He had just recommitted his life to the Lord, and now Delinda showed up. What was this about? He silently prayed for God to give him discernment.

She took his hand in hers. "I know that you still love me."

Samson hastily removed his hand. "Delinda, I got over you a long time ago."

"You're just angry," she told him. "I hurt you deeply and I'm sorry about that. Honey, what we had was beautiful."

"What we had was lust."

She went on as though he hadn't spoken. "After Bobby came home from the Bahamas, he really turned on me. All we did was fight, and then he met the tramp that's carrying his baby," she said bitterly. "She got pregnant on purpose but he can't see it. Bobby's divorcing me and he's not giving me a cent. I'm going to be penniless."

"So that's why you're here," he said. "You know that your husband paid me five million dollars to keep my mouth shut. Now you suddenly find me worthy of being your man."

"It should be mine. For putting up with him—I deserve that money."

He saw her in a new light. Delinda didn't care about him. She was driven by greed. She didn't even care that he lost his eyesight because of her. "I don't know how I could ever have loved you," Samson told her.

Delinda gasped in surprise. "I don't understand."

"Yeah, you do. You don't love me. The only reason you showed up here today is because you need another millionaire in your life to support your shopping habit." Realization dawned on Samson. "You arranged for him to find out about our trip to the Bahamas. You knew that he and I would fight and that he would probably pay me off. That way, when he kicked you out, you could come running to me, right?"

"You're crazy," she protested weakly. "I had no way of knowing what would happen."

"You know your husband. That's what you kept telling me."

"I haven't seen you in months."

"Oh, you weren't going to leave until he ended things—Bobby did tell me that. He said that you wouldn't leave until he was done with you. I guess he really knows you too."

"I do love you, Samson." She sounded almost desperate.

He shook his head. "You love money, Delinda. The funny thing is, you thought I was just some poor little pastor. You had no idea that I was already worth millions."

Delinda gasped louder this time.

"I wasn't good enough for you back then," he continued.

She grasped his hand, kneading it into hers. "Samson, I want to be with you. Just give me a chance to make it up to you."

"You don't have to do anything, but try and find a way to move on with your life. Money isn't everything."

Her hand stopped abruptly. "It's because of you that I lost everything," she accused nastily. "If I hadn't let you seduce me, Bobby and I would be happy now. This is all your fault."

"You are just as much to blame. Delinda, you came here for money and you can have it—the five million dollars. Meet me at the bank tomorrow, and we'll transfer the money into your account. I want nothing from you or Bobby."

She shifted by his side, and he could all but hear her shout with joy. "You're going to give me all of it just like that? Exactly how much money do you have?"

"You don't need to be concerned with that." Delinda hugged him, and tried to kiss him passionately but he turned his head. "I'll meet you at Wachovia at nine a.m. sharp."

"Thank you, Samson."

"Good-bye, Delinda."

She stood up. "Honey, we could have a good life together."

"I already have a good life."

"Is there a woman in your life?"

He smiled for the first time since Delinda's arrival. "In fact, there is. You met her earlier."

"The woman who opened the front door?" She gave a harsh laugh. "Samson, you're kidding me, right?"

"No, I'm not," he stated coldly. "She's the best thing to ever happen to me and I love her deeply."

He could hear Delinda stand up. "I'll see you tomorrow," she said.

Meagan and Hazel joined him after Delinda left.

"You okay?" Meagan inquired.

He passed his hand over his forehead, like he'd just gotten rid of a big headache. "I need you to take me to the bank tomorrow. I'm giving her the five million dollars her husband gave to me. I don't need the money."

"You're doing the right thing," Hazel and Meagan said in unison.

Samson chuckled. "After tomorrow, I will finally be free of the past."

• • •

"How are things going?" Trey inquired.

He had pulled up shortly after they returned from the bank. As promised, Samson gave Delinda the money and felt no regret in doing so. "As well as they can be," Samson responded. "I have an audio Bible that I like to listen to, so I'm staying in the Word."

"Good for you," Trey told him. "I knew you wouldn't let this keep you down. God has called you to greatness. I always told you that."

"Yeah, you did," Samson murmured. After a moment he said, "I never thought a woman would come between us, but then, I never thought a woman would come between me and God. I've done some thinking. Savannah and I were never supposed to be together. I think that the real reason I wanted her was because I wanted to beat you. It was you that she wanted the entire time."

"She cared for you, but she couldn't handle the pressure of being your wife and everything that meant. Her belief system is not and has never been the same as yours."

"You're a Buddhist now, I hear."

"I am."

"That's a conversation for another day," Samson remarked with a chuckle. Trey laughed too. "I'm surprised you and Savannah aren't pregnant yet. I know how badly she wanted to have children."

After a brief pause, Trey responded, "She is, Samson. We're going to have a baby in about four months. I wanted to tell you, but I wasn't sure you were ready to hear the news."

"Congratulations. I'm happy for you."

They shook hands like true brothers. "I think you should

know that Kenya is in town," Trey announced. "She and Jamie arrived yesterday."

Samson's breath caught in his throat. When he was finally able to speak, he said, "She had a little girl?"

"Yeah. They're going to be here for a couple of weeks."

"I'd like to see her. I want to apologize to Kenya and ask for her forgiveness. I know she doesn't want my help, but I want to work something out with her regarding Jamie's care." He was saddened at the thought that he would never get to see his little girl.

"Samson, I don't know if she'll come to see you, but I'll ask her."

"Thank you, Trey." After a moment he asked, "Who does she look like?"

"Bro, she looks like you mostly, but she has Kenya's eyes. She's a beautiful little girl."

"Kenya's a good mother, isn't she?"

"She is, and she loves Jamie to death," Trey responded.

CHAPTER 33

Two days later Samson was in his town house when he heard someone enter. He could tell that it was Trey by the way he walked, slightly dragging one foot, and the woodsy cologne he was always wearing. He was accompanied by another set of footsteps, tentative and cautious.

Trey announced himself. "Samson, it's me and I brought Kenya with me."

"Kenya, hello."

She did not respond, but Trey said, "I'm going to sit out on the patio while you two talk."

"It won't be a long conversation," Kenya said, her words full of venom.

Samson decided not to waste time with pleasantries. "Kenya, the reason I wanted to see you is so that I could tell you how sorry I am for the way I treated you. It was wrong and cruel. I know how hurt you must be—"

"You *know?*" she interrupted. "How can you possibly know how much hurt you inflicted on me? You can't feel a thing because you don't have a heart."

Kenya's words pierced him deeply.

"Samson, you didn't have to listen to everyone talk about how stupid I was for running after a so-called pastor—not to mention my own sister's ex-husband. Then I humiliated myself by marrying you when I should have known better. I actually thought that if I was a good wife to you, you'd fall in love with me. I made a complete fool of myself."

"I'm not going to make excuses, because I was dead wrong. I really am truly sorry, and I hope that one day you will be able to forgive me."

"I don't think that will ever happen."

"I do understand how you feel," Samson said, his heart heavy. "I know all too well that seed of unforgiveness, but I don't want it to taint your spirit like it did mine."

"Don't you dare try to preach to me," Kenya hissed. "No real man of God would've done what you did to me."

"I'm not," he responded quickly. Samson could hear the hurt and anger in her voice. "Kenya, you're absolutely right. No godly man would've treated you like that. Like I said earlier, I make no excuses for the way that I acted. One day I hope you will see that I've changed."

"Why? Because you're suddenly blind? If you hadn't been chasing a married woman, maybe you'd still have your vision."

"Kenya, that's enough," Trey told her when he walked back into the room. "Samson, I think we'd better leave."

"I'll leave when I'm done, Trey," Kenya nearly shouted. "You pleaded for me to come over here, and I'm not leaving until I've said everything I need to say to Samson."

"Trey, let Kenya have her say," Samson said. "She needs to get this out."

He could feel the heat of her gaze on him.

"I hope you didn't think I'd come here and feel sorry for you," Kenya said. "Because I don't. As far as I'm concerned, I think you got exactly what you deserved."

"I couldn't agree with you more," Samson responded.

"This was the only way that God could get my attention, and I have to be honest—it worked."

"Oh, so now you're supposed to be saved for real this time? See, that's the very reason I don't go to church anymore. There are too many people like you up in there—fake Christians."

"I have a heart for the Lord. But I am flesh and blood. I made some terrible mistakes, and now I'm suffering the consequences. However, I am striving to become a better man."

"Tell it to someone who actually cares."

They weren't getting anywhere, and he wanted to settle another point with her anyway. "I would like to help you with Jamie," he said. "I can arrange to have monthly payments sent to you."

"I told you before that I don't need your money. I can take care of my daughter myself."

"You're in law school," he pointed out reasonably. "Don't let your hatred for me keep you from securing a better life for Jamie."

"I told you that we didn't need you or your money. I can take care of *my* daughter."

Samson acknowledged the hit. "I've been doing a lot of thinking back on my life. I made a lot of mistakes, but I'm trying to do better now. I know you don't want to deal with me, but I can set this up where the checks are sent automatically. When my parents died, I was left very well off. Jamie will want for nothing."

"Children need the love of their parents—not money."

He also wanted to discuss this issue. "I wasn't thrilled about having a child in the beginning, but she's here and I want to get to know Jamie. I'd like to have a place in her life. I think about her all the time and I hate that I will never be able to see her face."

"I will not ever let you near my child. I'm sorry, but that's not going to happen."

His eyes filling with tears, Samson nodded. "Well, I understand why you would feel that way. Thank you for coming to see me. I appreciate your hearing me out."

"Trey, I'm ready to leave," she shouted.

He entered the room. "Kenya, you can go on out to the car. I need to speak with Samson for a moment."

When she walked out of the house, Trey said, "I'm sorry, man."

"She has every right to be angry. I just hope that she'll be able to get over those feelings before they take root in her soul."

"Kenya's still hurting, but one day those wounds will close. Hopefully, her being able to face you today will help her heal."

"That's what I want," Samson said. "I really hope that she'll let me help her out financially and that she'll let me meet Jamie one day. Or at least let my aunt get to know her."

"I'll talk to her," Trey said. "Well, I'd better get going. I'll give you a call later."

Samson nodded. "Thanks for getting Kenya to come. I'm sure it wasn't an easy task."

"You don't know the half of it. It was Savannah who actually persuaded Kenya to come see you."

"Tell her I said thanks."

"I will." Trey headed toward the front door.

After Trey left, Samson broke down and cried. He felt an incredible loss and a world of regret for the way he had handled things with Kenya. He had heard in her voice the hatred she felt for him.

He wiped his face when he heard the front door open and close.

"Samson, it's me, sweetie."

"I'm so glad that you're here, Meagan."

"What's wrong? Did something happen between you and Trey? I just saw him leave with a young woman in the car."

"That was his sister-in-law," Samson responded. "Nobody

really knows about this, but Kenya and I were married for a short time and she is the mother of my daughter."

"You have a child?"

He could hear the surprise in her voice. "Jamie's three months old."

Her voice gained an edge. "Do you want to talk about it?"

"I was angry when I found out about Trey and Savannah. All I could think about was hurting her the same way she hurt me, so I got involved with her sister."

"Ouch," Meagan muttered.

"It was wrong, I know. I ended up not only getting Kenya pregnant but causing her pain. She hates me now. She said that I deserve to be blind."

Meagan tried to reassure him. "She didn't mean it. She's still very angry. In time she'll come around."

"She won't even let me see . . . she won't bring Jamie to see me and she doesn't want me to help her out financially."

"Give her some time."

"You really think Kenya will come around?"

Meagan took his hand in hers. "I do. She just has to see how much you've changed."

His heart yearned for his daughter. "I never thought I'd feel this way, but I really don't want Jamie growing up without me."

"She's your daughter. You have a connection."

Samson wanted to be a part of his daughter's life. He didn't want her growing up without a father. "Meagan, how can I make this right?"

"Just give Kenya some time. I'm sure Trey will tell her how you've changed for the better. This is something she needs to work through."

"I really hope so, sweetheart."

"Would you like me to fix you something to eat?" Meagan asked.

Samson shook his head. He felt hollow inside. "I'm not hungry."

"Then, would you like to work on your reading?"

"Sure," he responded with a shrug. His heart grieved for the child he'd never wanted. Now that she was here, he couldn't see his life without her in it.

CHAPTER 34

"Meagan, sweetheart, I need to talk to you and Aunt Hazel," Samson announced. "It's really important." Two weeks had passed since his encounter with Kenya.

His aunt sat down across from him while Meagan dropped into the empty chair beside him.

"What is it, hon?" Hazel asked.

"I've been spending a lot of time in prayer. God and I have been having some great conversations, actually. Pastor Burkette and I have been communicating as well. God spoke into my spirit two words—'it's time.' The first time I met with Pastor Burkette, he said those same words to me."

His aunt began praising God softly at first, and then she began to sob.

"I know what I'm supposed to do. Although I lost sight of my calling many times before, in the last couple of weeks I've learned some things about God."

"Do you feel like sharing?" Meagan asked.

He reached over and took her hand in his. "I don't mind at all. The first thing I learned is that sometimes God allows the world to beat us down before He has that life-changing meeting with us."

"Amen," Hazel murmured.

"God took me through His Word and showed me how Moses had spent the first forty years of his life in the palace of the Egyptian pharaoh, where he had the finest of everything. Nothing was withheld from Moses and he didn't have to work for any of it. This reminded me of myself. I have all this money and I didn't work for it."

"Hon, you lost your parents and so you deserved every penny."

"Like with Moses," he went on, "everything changed one day. I didn't lose money, but something much more valuable—my eyesight. Sometimes God allows our situation to humble us before He chooses to meet with us. I've been humbled, and for a while I lost heart. Not until recently did I realize this was the perfect time for God to meet with me."

"When God calls you to meet with Him, your attendance is required, but it is not forced," Meagan said.

Samson agreed. "Exactly. God had been wanting to meet with me since the accident, but I wasn't interested. I was too angry. I failed to remember just how holy God is. But when I did, I realized that it was His holiness that caused me to see how far short I fall of being the person God wants me to be. Now that I'm blind, I can see what God expects of me."

"So what is your next step?" Hazel asked. "Now that you've received revelation."

He broke into a big smile. "I guess you'll see come Sunday."

• • •

Samson returned to the pulpit for the first time since before his accident. Before giving his sermon, he opened up by singing a couple of verses of "Amazing Grace."

"Good morning, Church," Samson said when he finished the song.

"Good morning," the congregation responded in unison.

"Good to see you in the pulpit, Pastor," someone shouted. "God is good!"

Samson flashed a grin. "Thank you," he said. "It's great to be back, and yes, God *is* good. I know that some of you are probably shocked to see me standing up here, for various reasons. I'm sure some of you believe that I should never ever grace another pulpit after all that I've done. I know that I swore never to return to the pulpit after I lost my eyesight and then lost my uncle, but God had other plans."

He paused for a moment before continuing.

"This morning I'm going to tell you about another Samson. When Samson fell for Delilah, a woman from the valley of Sorek, it marked the beginning of his downfall and eventual demise. You see, Samson was judge over Israel, and the Philistines, hoping to capture him, offered Delilah a sum of money to uncover the secret of Samson's great strength.

"Using her powers of seduction and deception, Delilah persistently wore down Samson until he told her that his strength would leave him if a razor were to be used on his head. While Samson slept on her lap, Delilah called in a coconspirator to shave off the seven braids of his hair. Subdued and weak, Samson was captured.

"I'm sure you all know the rest of the story, but if not, then I'd like for you to read Judges. Samson was humbled and his heart now turned to God in spite of his failures and sins. His strength was restored when his hair grew back, and he destroyed the temple, killing all of the people in it and himself."

He paused a moment, listening as God spoke to his heart.

"When you think about this account of Samson's life, and then his downfall with Delilah, you might tend to think Samson wasted his life—that he was a failure. Yet even still, Samson accomplished his God-assigned mission. He is named in Hebrews chapter eleven among those who through faith conquered kingdoms, administered justice, and gained what was promised . . . whose weakness was turned to strength. This proves that God can still use people of faith, no matter how imperfectly they live their lives."

"Amen to that," he heard someone say.

Samson continued. "We might look at Samson's relationship with Delilah and consider him gullible. His lust for Delilah blinded him to her lies and her true nature. He wanted so badly to believe she loved him that he repeatedly fell for her deceptive ways. You can ask, Why didn't he get a clue when she kept coming back wanting to know his secret? I'll tell you why. Because Samson is just like you and me when we give ourselves over to sin. Because of our sinful nature, we can easily be deceived. In this state, the truth becomes impossible to see.

"I was like Samson. It took losing my eyesight for me to realize my total dependence on God. I once was blind, but now I see. Church, I want you to know that no matter how far you've fallen away from God, no matter how big you've failed, it's never too late to humble yourself and be dependent upon God."

Samson heard movement and knew that people were standing up. Clapping followed, until the applause became deafening.

"Thank you," he murmured. "Thank you so much. It's a blessing to have your support."

The clapping subsided enough that his voice could be heard. "Church, I ask for your forgiveness and your prayers. I made some terrible choices and some pretty bad mistakes."

"Pastor, you ain't the only one," a man shouted. "I did some things, but I know my God is a forgiving God. If He can forgive, then we can too."

"Amen" rang out around the sanctuary.

Samson sent up a prayer of thanksgiving when he was told that ten people came up to the altar that day to give their life over to the Lord. "God, I thank you for using me," he whispered.

"Samson, there's someone here who wants to meet you," Hazel said when he walked into his office with Meagan after the service ended.

He smiled. "Who is it?"

"There's this sweet little angel in my arms and her name is Jamie."

His mouth dropped open in surprise. Samson swallowed hard. "J-Jamie . . . you have Jamie with you?"

"I sure do," Hazel said. "Samson, your daughter is beautiful and she's so sweet."

"But how?"

"I brought her," Kenya piped up. "I wanted your aunt to see her, and I also wanted to hear what you had to say in the pulpit. You were always a good preacher, but there was something more this time. I believe that you've changed." She paused before adding, "For the moment anyway."

"Thank you for bringing Jamie," Samson said. "And for coming to service this morning."

"I've always liked Hillside," she responded.

"I'm going to take this little girl and show her off while you two talk," Hazel told them.

"Samson, I'll be with your aunt," Meagan said.

God had answered his prayers. Samson couldn't have been more overjoyed. "I really appreciate you coming today and bringing the baby. You've not only made my day but my aunt's too. She really wanted to see her niece."

When Kenya responded, her voice was muted. "Samson, I don't hate you. Not really."

"I'm sorry for hurting you, Kenya."

"I was just as much at fault. I practically chased you down."

"Can we please start over? We have a child together and I want to be in her life."

"Start over as friends?"

"Yeah."

"Samson, I want you to know I'm involved with someone and . . . I don't hate you, but I don't love you either."

He nodded in understanding. "I don't want to come between you and your man. I think you've met Meagan, and she and I—we're dating. I care a great deal for her."

"She seems really nice."

"She is," Samson confirmed.

"I know that you want to be in Jamie's life, but you do know that we're going back to California. We're going to be living there for a while, maybe forever."

He was taken aback by the news. "Am I allowed to visit?"

"Sure. You can see . . . I'm sorry. I mean, you can visit with your daughter. I'm sorry for saying that you deserve to be blind. I really didn't mean it."

"You did mean it, but it's okay. There are times when I feel the same way."

Samson felt so much better that they could talk again.

"If you're going to be home tomorrow, I can bring Jamie over so that you can spend some time with her. My parents are having a huge family get-together later this afternoon, so we need to get going."

"Thank you. I'd like that."

An odd note entered her voice. "Do you need some help getting to your car?"

"I can make it. I've gotten used to moving about on my own."

"Here's Meagan," she said.

"Am I interrupting?" Meagan asked Kenya.

"No, we're done. Have you seen Miss Hazel?"

"She's outside talking to some of the ladies," Meagan replied.

"Kenya is going to come by tomorrow, and she's bringing Jamie over for a visit," Samson announced.

"That's wonderful."

"I'll see you all tomorrow, then," Kenya said before walking away.

When they were in the car Meagan said, "What did I tell you? Praise God . . ."

"I still can't believe it," Samson said. "Thank You, Father God . . . thank You."

• • •

Kenya and Jamie arrived shortly before noon the next day.

Samson held the wiggling baby in his arms. A small hand touched his cheek. "Hey, little one," he whispered. "I'm your daddy."

She gurgled in response.

"Yeah, I am. I'm so sorry I wasn't there from the very beginning. My head wasn't right, but I promise you that I will be here for you until my last breath leaves my body."

Kenya allowed him to feed Jamie, guiding him without making him feel ill at ease. Samson was amazed at how well she and Meagan were getting along. He was glad because he planned on Meagan becoming a permanent fixture in his life—only this time he wasn't going to rush into another marriage.

When the time came, Samson hated having his daughter leave. It was going to be hard for him when Kenya took her back to California.

"Before we leave, I'll have Savannah draw up an agreement between us," Kenya said. "We'll outline visitation and support payments. Samson, now that I know you really want to be a part of Jamie's life, I won't keep her away from you. Who knows? When I graduate law school, we may eventually come back to Raleigh."

"I hope so," he said, and he really meant it.

Kenya hugged him. "Take care of yourself, Samson."

"You too. If there comes a time when you need to focus on school . . . I . . . we . . ."

"I appreciate that, but I'll be okay."

"Thank you for my daughter."

He could feel the warmth of her smile. "She is a beautiful little girl."

"Would you please tell Jamie every day that her daddy loves her?"

"I will." She embraced him a second time. "We have to go, but you take care of yourself."

"Kenya seems like a nice girl," Meagan said when she sat down beside him.

"She is."

"Your daughter is adorable."

He smiled. "I would give anything just to see her face one time. I haven't laid eyes on her, but she already owns a piece of my heart."

"Kenya seems willing to work out an arrangement. That's a good sign."

Samson agreed. He reached over and grabbed her hand. "I'd like to take a walk."

"Let's go," she said.

Samson stood up without assistance. He felt Meagan rise to her feet and gently grabbed her by the arm.

He had so much to be thankful for.

CHAPTER 35

Over the next five months Trey continued to come by the town house regularly to check on Samson.

When he came by Meagan would usually excuse herself, leaving the two men alone.

"How are you adjusting?" Trey inquired.

"Okay, I guess," Samson responded. "Meagan told me that Savannah had the baby. How are *you* adjusting to fatherhood?"

"Lots of sleepless nights, but it's worth it. Samson, when I first laid eyes on him . . . it was love at first sight. I love my son with my entire being."

Samson swallowed his pain and said, "I hope he has his mother's looks."

Trey laughed. "He does."

They both grew quiet for a moment.

"Samson . . ."

"What is it?" he asked Trey. "I feel like you want to say something to me."

He hesitated a moment before saying, "We've been boys forever. Actually, more like brothers. I don't know how you're going to feel about this, but I can't think of another soul I'd want for this—I want you to be my son's godfather."

Samson did not respond. He hadn't expected Trey and Savannah to want him to have such an integral role in their son's life.

"Savannah and I both agree that you are the perfect choice. Her best friend Lana is going to be godmother."

"After everything that's happened between us, you want me to stand as godfather to your child?"

"Yeah, I do. Your daughter and my son are first cousins. We're family. At least, that's how I still think of you. I love you and I pray one day we'll get back to the way things used to be between us. We used to be so close. I love you, flaws and all, Samson."

Samson was touched by Trey's words. "I feel the same way about you."

"Does that mean you will be T.J.'s godfather?"

Samson nodded vigorously. "Thank you for the honor."

Trey asked, "Have you heard from Kenya lately?"

"Yeah. She called last night so I could talk to Jamie. I think she called me Daddy."

Trey chuckled. "Jamie's got you wrapped around her little finger."

"I love her so much," Samson confessed. "I would give anything to see her little face just once. I have tried to imagine in my mind what she looks like."

$$\bullet \ \bullet \ \bullet$$

"So you're saying I will never get my eyesight back?" Samson asked the doctor. "That the most I'll get is these shadows and glimpses of light from time to time?"

"I'm sorry. There was so much damage . . ."

Samson swallowed hard. He was sorely disappointed in the news. "The doctors told me that before I left Nassau, but I chose not to lose hope."

He was going to spend the rest of his life as a blind man. Samson thought he'd made peace with the possibility, but clearly he hadn't. He swallowed his disappointment and tried to concentrate on the good things in his life. His mind traveled to Meagan, Jamie, and his aunt. He was grateful for each of them.

Back at his town house Meagan asked, "Samson, what are you thinking about? You were unusually quiet on the way home."

"That's the third doctor I've seen, and like the others, he doesn't believe that my sight will ever come back. He says there's a slim chance of my regaining partial vision at best."

She reached over and took his hand in hers. "I'm so sorry."

"Don't be. Meagan, I know how great my God is, and even when there is no hope, I still hope."

"Amen to that," she said. "God can do all things, and you just hold on to that promise."

Samson laughed. "I've never met a woman outside my aunt who was so on fire for the Lord the way you are."

"I know what God has done in my life, and there's no way I can forget about Him. I can't just go around giving lip service—He is the head of my life and the source of all I have."

"You better quit, Meagan. I'm not a shouting type of man, but you're about to make me have a praise party over here."

She laughed. "I'm trying to restrain myself. I just really love the Lord."

He nodded in understanding. Samson couldn't keep his mind off Meagan. She was a wonderful woman and his biggest cheerleader.

She went to the kitchen to make lunch for him.

"I don't know if I've ever told you so, but you are a wonderful cook," Samson complimented her. "I'm glad I had the good sense to snatch you up before somebody else did."

She laughed. "If you had your sight, Samson, I know that you would never have given me a second look. My weight offends some people, but the thing is, I don't want to be thin. I never have. I simply want to be healthy. I eat right and I exercise. I'm happy with my body."

"If I were the old Samson, you would probably be right, but that's not me anymore. All those women I thought were so exquisite brought me nothing but trouble." He shook his head. "I was so stupid back then."

"You allowed your flesh to control you," Meagan replied. "We all make that mistake from time to time."

"I should have known better, though. I stand up in that pulpit and preach from the Word of God, yet I was breaking every Commandment except one, and I probably would've broken that one if my parents were still alive."

"You're not alone, Samson. We all fall short, but we just have to pick ourselves up and try to do better. You've done that."

• • •

Samson turned away from the computer, smiling, when he heard footsteps. "Ladies, I've just finished my first document," he said proudly.

"Congratulations," Meagan and Hazel said in unison.

"Meagan, you might want to read it to make sure I haven't made a mess of it. It's in the printer."

Hazel patted him on the shoulder while he waited for feedback from Meagan.

"Samson, you did a great job with this," Meagan exclaimed. "I see only one typo."

"Praise the Lord," he murmured with a chuckle.

"I guess I need to go scrounge up something for dinner," Hazel said.

Samson heard the weariness in his aunt's voice. "Auntie, you go get some rest. I know you haven't been sleeping well.

I hear you moving around at night. Why don't you take a nap? Meagan and I can handle dinner."

"Are you sure?" she asked.

"We'll make dinner," Meagan said.

"I'm just going to lie down for a few minutes."

When she left the room, Meagan asked, "Is there something going on with Miss Hazel?"

"She really misses my uncle. I heard her moving around all night long. I don't think she sleeps well now that he's gone."

Samson and Meagan were the original odd couple in the kitchen.

Every now and then, Samson forgot and asked for the knife, forgetting that he could no longer chop, slice, or dice. Meagan had bought him an electric chopper to handle all that.

Samson tried to hide his aggravation about not being able to see what he was doing.

"I know you're frustrated," Meagan told him. "But let's try and have some fun anyway."

Samson peeled onions and garlic, while Meagan chopped. He stirred in the spices. Meagan guided him, telling him that he would soon be able to smell when to turn the chicken.

When dinner was ready, Meagan fixed the plates and brought them to the table.

"Samson, your chicken is at four o'clock, the rice at seven, the green beans are at ten, and your rolls are at twelve."

Samson knew that his iced tea was at two, so he followed the rim of the plate and picked up the glass to take a sip. He enjoyed cooking with Meagan. There was never a time they didn't dissolve into laughter over something.

For him, cooking wasn't only a passion; it had become a therapy that was fun and comforting. He felt victorious in the kitchen.

• • •

He and Meagan had been dating for eight months now and Samson had never been happier. He had moved back into his own place and had settled in comfortably, but he was worried about his aunt.

Meagan came up with a wonderful suggestion, so after church on Sunday, they took Hazel to brunch. Samson was surprised to find that they had menus in Braille.

"How are you doing, Aunt Hazel?" Samson wanted to know.

"I'm okay," she said, subdued. "I miss Zachariah more and more each day."

"Why don't you come live with me?" he suggested. "I could use another pair of eyes around the place after Meagan leaves in the evenings."

"I don't know . . ."

"I have more than enough room," Samson said. "You're alone in that big old house. If you won't move in with me, then do you mind if I come back to live with you?"

"I don't want to uproot you. You just moved back home a couple of months ago. I'll give some thought to moving there. You're right. The house is too big for just one person. Maybe I should consider selling."

"I could get a bigger place," Samson said. "I hope to have a family one day. We can all live together."

"You might want to wait and ask your wife about that," Hazel responded.

"I'm pretty sure the woman I plan to marry won't mind," he said with a smile. Samson could feel the heat of Meagan's gaze. "You don't mind if Aunt Hazel comes to live with us, do you?"

"If we get married, I don't have a problem with it, but since you haven't asked me, it's not something we have to discuss right now." She rose to her feet. "If you will excuse me, I need to go to the ladies' room."

He heard Meagan walk away.

"She wasn't upset, was she?" he asked in a low voice.

"I don't think so, but what in the world are you waiting for?" his aunt wanted to know. "You're not getting any younger, Samson."

He chuckled. "I'm on it, okay? I need to work out some things with the Lord first. As much as I want Meagan to be my wife, I can't let that be a distraction. I'm trying to learn from my past mistakes."

"Don't pressure him, Miss Hazel," Meagan said when she returned. "Samson told me how he rushed into his first marriage, and then the one with Kenya. I like our pace. It's nice and we're really getting to know one another."

"I love this girl," Hazel declared. "This is the one for you, Samson. I know it in my spirit, and if you let her get away, well then, you deserve to be alone."

"You see how she talks to me?" he told Meagan.

"I'm afraid I agree with her," she remarked with a laugh. "I know I'm a great catch."

"Yes, you are, sweetheart," Samson told her. "I've never been this happy with anyone."

They dropped Hazel off at her house before heading over to his place.

"Meagan, would you mind making one stop?"

"No, where do you want to go?"

"To my uncle's grave. I haven't been out there since we buried him. It's time I went to visit. I know he's not there really, but I just need to do this."

"I understand," Meagan said.

Twenty minutes later, they were sitting down in front of the grave. Samson ran his fingers across the lettering etched in the granite. "Hey, Uncle."

He felt movement and asked Meagan, "What are you doing?"

"Pulling the weeds and arranging the flowers we purchased for your uncle."

Samson turned his attention back to the gravestone. "I know you're no longer in pain, but I want you to know that I really miss you. Auntie misses you terribly. She's not sleeping or anything. I wish there was something I could do to help her."

Samson paused for a moment as if to wait for his uncle's response.

"She loves you so much, Uncle. Oh, I have a little girl. Her name is Jamie and she's a beauty. Kenya and I have an agreement—we're working things out just like you wanted."

When he was done, he told Meagan, "I have one more stop."

"You want to visit with your parents," she said. "We have fresh flowers for them too."

"How did you know?"

"Samson, you love your family and I know how much you want to honor them. I knew that you wouldn't come all the way here and not pay them a visit. That's just not who you are."

EPILOGUE

One year later

"You all know what I've been through—the womanizing, the accident, and my blindness," Samson said as he stood up at the pulpit. "Your storms may not have been like mine, but storms are storms, right?"

A wave of murmurs moved around the sanctuary.

He allowed the murmurs to die down before continuing. "We're going to talk about tests and trials this morning. First, I want you to know that the trials we go through are God's means of transportation. Remember in Matthew chapter fourteen, the disciples were afraid of the sea, but God used it as a vehicle to reveal Himself to them. When did Jesus come to them?" Samson asked.

"The Bible tells us that Jesus came to them in the fourth watch. I really want you to catch this in your spirit. During the darkest hours of the night, Jesus came walking on the water. So you see, you may be walking in darkness right now and wondering where Jesus is. Even the darkest hours of life cannot hide you from the face of God. He is there even when you cannot see Him.

"Jesus sends the disciples away so he can be alone on the mountainside and pray. Even in his busy schedule, spending time with God is a priority for Jesus. There are several points I want you to remember. The disciples didn't recognize Jesus in the storm. Sometimes we don't recognize the Lord when he comes to us in the middle of our storms.

"Second, Peter doesn't begin to sink until he starts looking around at the wind and the waves. Taking our eyes off Jesus will cause us to get under our problems. But when we cry out to Jesus, he catches us by the hand and raises us above the seemingly impossible surroundings. Church, even though we may not walk on water, we will go through faith-testing storms."

Samson ended his sermon by saying, "I'm here to tell you that sometimes it's hard to see the blessings for the storm. Sometimes it is hard to imagine the Lord bringing any good out of what you are going through. I'm talking about what I know. I couldn't see any good coming out of my being blind. I don't know the nature of the storm you are facing in your lives right now, but I do know the One who still walks on the waves. I know that if you will bring your need to Him, He will carry you through."

Before he dismissed everyone, Samson said, "There is a special woman in my life and I'd like to bring her up here. Meagan, come up, please."

He couldn't see her, but he could imagine that she wore an expression of shock on her face right then. Samson hadn't told her what he'd planned to do. He hadn't even mentioned it to his aunt.

"Samson, what are you doing?" Meagan asked in a low voice when she joined him in the pulpit.

"Just trust me," he whispered. Taking her hand in his, he went on to announce, "This is Meagan Montgomery, the love of my life. I called her up here because I know without a doubt that this is the woman God created just for me. I wanted her up here with me so all of you can witness this testimony of my love for her." Samson cleared his throat, and then said, "Meagan, would you do me the honor of being my wife?"

She gasped in surprise. "Samson . . ."

"Sweetheart, will you marry me?" He could hear her crying softly. "I love you, Meagan, and I don't want to spend the rest of my life without you in it."

"I love you too, Samson," she said finally. "Yes, I'll marry you."

Applause and cheers erupted all throughout the sanctuary.

After the service, Hazel was one of the first to congratulate Samson. "Hon, I'm sincerely happy for you. Meagan is a lovely young woman and she's perfect for you, thank the Lord."

Samson laughed. "Auntie, I'm so glad you approve."

"I've only wanted the best for you," Hazel responded. "And Meagan's it. I only wish my Zachariah were here to see you settle down once and for all."

"Me too. I made some terrible mistakes and I really wanted to make him proud of me before he stepped out of time into eternity."

"You did," Hazel reassured him. "Your uncle was very proud of you. You could do no wrong in his eyes."

"I hate that it took losing my eyesight to finally see what God called me to be. I was blind, but now I see . . . that's my testimony."

Meagan joined them. "Your sermon was great," she said. "Samson, I really think you outdid yourself this time."

He laughed. "I think you just might be a little bit biased."

"Maybe just a little."

"You were fantastic," Aunt Hazel chimed in. "Meagan, I'm so happy for you two. If you need any help in planning the wedding, I'd be thrilled to assist in any way I can."

"Miss Hazel, I'll need all the help I can get."

Hazel hugged Samson. "I'm so glad you're walking in your calling. You allowed God to continue to use you even during what you considered your weakness."

"I would never choose this for myself, but I finally accept what has happened to me. This is my life now. It is a new beginning. I have a wonderful woman who is going to be my wife, and a beautiful daughter. I'm the pastor of a Holy Ghost–filled church. This is my life and I accept it."

Readers Group Guide for

SAMSON
Jacquelin Thomas

INTRODUCTION

In this modern-day adaptation of the Bible story of Samson and Delilah, Samson Taylor, the charismatic associate pastor of Hillside Baptist Church, marries Savannah Ramsey, a beautiful young Buddhist, despite their different religious faiths. Over time, their union unravels: Samson discovers that Savannah has betrayed him with his best friend, Trey, and he insists on a divorce. Hungry for revenge, Samson seduces Savannah's younger sister, Kenya. When Kenya reveals that she is carrying his child, Samson reluctantly agrees to marry her to protect his professional reputation as pastor, but this second marriage also dissolves.

Samson loves God and wants to do right, but his lust for beautiful women cannot be stopped. When he becomes romantically entangled with Delinda Lewis-Hatcher, the wife of an NBA superstar, her cuckolded husband responds with violence, injuring Samson in a vicious fight that results in Samson's blindness.

Eventually, Samson's faith, his love for family, and his path to recovery bring him to a new place in his walk with God, one that transforms his life.

QUESTIONS AND TOPICS
FOR DISCUSSION

1. "'I am still a man . . . there's no denying that I love women, and that won't ever end, but I'm not going to do anything that will taint my ministry or put a dark stain on my uncle's sterling reputation.'" How would you characterize Samson's call to the ministry? What role does his family's history as religious leaders in Hillside Baptist Church play in Samson's decision to become a pastor? What does his resolve against yielding to sexual temptation suggest about his awareness of his own weaknesses?

2. How does Samson's initial encounter with Savannah Ramsey foreshadow the nature of their relationship as husband and wife? Why isn't Samson more forthcoming with Trey about his true feelings for Savannah? How does his dishonesty jeopardize their friendship?

3. "'Samson, I know that you love this girl, but you are a man of God,' his uncle said. 'What do you think the members will say when they find out you're married

to an unbeliever?'" Why doesn't Samson listen to his family's concerns about Savannah's Buddhist faith? To what extent is it problematic for a Christian religious leader to marry someone who doesn't worship the same God? Why is Samson eager to marry Savannah despite their different religious beliefs?

4. How does Trey's conversion to Buddhism impact his relationship with Savannah? Given Trey and Samson's shared attitude about never letting women come between them, why would both men risk their friendship for Savannah's affection? What aspects of Savannah's character make her so compelling to both Trey and Samson?

5. To what extent is Samson's behavior toward Kenya in the aftermath of his divorce from Savannah in keeping with the moral standards of a Baptist pastor? Why does he treat her as he does? What does Kenya's decision to sever ties with Samson and refuse him access to their child suggest about the impact of his behavior on her?

6. "Samson vowed to be a better man now that he had been given a second chance. He . . . was going to do his uncle proud. He was not going to make the same mistakes as before." How do Aunt Hazel and Uncle Zachariah together function as Samson's moral compass? In what ways do Hazel and Zachariah embody traditional Christian values in their lives? How do those values help them accept and love Samson, despite his personal failures?

7. How does the author's decision to set the story of Samson in the context of a religious institution—a pastor of a Baptist Church who engages in extramarital sexual activity—impact your appreciation of the

personal tragedy that befalls Samson? How would a secular setting—a law firm or a bank, for example—alter your sense of Samson's true character, and the physical, professional, and spiritual risks implicit in his behavior?

8. "'I can't go with you. Samson, I've already told you that what we had is over. I'm not going to leave Bobby.'" How would you characterize Delinda Lewis-Hatcher's feelings for Samson, and his for her? Given her suspicions that Bobby has been unfaithful and was having her followed, what accounts for Delinda's refusal to end her marriage? Are Delinda and Samson's affections grounded entirely in physical lust, or is there something larger that connects them?

9. Why do you think the author gave Delinda a name so closely associated with that of Delilah in the Bible story of Samson and Delilah? To what extent do Savannah, Kenya, Teà, and Delinda all serve as symbols of Delilah—the feminine temptress who causes an inherently good man to stray? Is Delinda the worst of these temptresses, or just another in a series of women who cause Samson to depart from his spiritual obligations? How responsible is Samson for his own downfall, and to what extent is he the victim of these beautiful women?

10. "'This is my life and I accept it.'" What role does Meagan play in Samson's transition from life as a sighted person to life as a blind person? How does Kenya's willingness to include Samson in Jamie's life affect him? What does Samson's adjustment to his new reality reveal about his character and his faith in God?

TIPS TO ENHANCE YOUR BOOK CLUB

1. Are you interested in learning more about Jacquelin Thomas's creative process in writing the novel *Samson*? To read little-known biographical details about the author and to learn about her many other works of fiction, visit her official website: http://www.jacquelinthomas.com.

2. Jacquelin Thomas may be available to participate in your next book club meeting, either in person or by telephone. Visit http://www.jacquelinthomas.com/bookclubs.htm to set up a meeting!

3. The Biblical story of Samson and Delilah is one that has undergone many contemporary retellings. Your book club may enjoy viewing the 1949 film *Samson and Delilah,* starring Hedy Lamarr as Delilah and directed by the famed Cecil B. DeMille. After your club views the film, discuss as a group how Jacquelin Thomas's modern story of the aftermath of a passionate affair compares to the relationship portrayed in the movie.

4. Savannah Ramsey is a committed Buddhist who adheres to her faith in spite of pressure from her husband, Samson, to convert to his Christian faith. How familiar is your book club with either religious tradition? To learn more about what Christians, Buddhists, and other people of faith believe, visit the Big Religion Chart chart at http://www.religionfacts.com, a comparative religion site that analyzes different faiths and examines their underlying beliefs. Your book club may want to examine what Buddhists and Christians have in common, and where they differ in terms of their religious tenets.